PRAISE FOR BRANDILYN COLLINS' KANNER LAKE SERIES

"... fast-paced ... interesting details of police procedure and crime scene investigation ... beautifully developed [characters] ..."

— *Publishers Weekly* for *Violet Dawn*

"... a magnificent storyteller. Ms. Collins has written another fantastic mystery and *Violet Dawn* is a great beginning to a new series."

— FreshFiction.com

"Collins' ability to bring characters to life rivals that of Barbara Kingsolver [*The Poisonwood Bible*]. If you're afraid of the dark, live in a house that squeaks, or are terrified by things that go bump in the night, try reading *Coral Moon* in broad daylight."

— TitleTrakk.com

CRIMSON EVE

Brandilyn Collins

Seatbelt Suspense™

Other Books by Brandilyn Collins

Kanner Lake Series

1 | *Violet Dawn*

2 | *Coral Moon*

3 | *Crimson Eve*

Hidden Faces Series

1 | *Brink of Death*

2 | *Stain of Guilt*

3 | *Dead of Night*

4 | *Web of Lies*

Bradleyville Series

1 | *Cast a Road Before Me*

2 | *Color the Sidewalk for Me*

3 | *Capture the Wind for Me*

Chelsea Adams Series

1 | *Eyes of Elisha*

2 | *Dread Champion*

BRANDILYN COLLINS

KANNER LAKE SERIES

CRIMSON EVE

BOOK 3

ZONDERVAN.com/
AUTHORTRACKER
follow your favorite authors

Crimson Eve
Copyright © 2007 by Brandilyn Collins

This title is also available as a Zondervan audio product.
Visit www.zondervan.com/audiopages for more information.

Requests for information should be addressed to:

Zondervan, *Grand Rapids, Michigan 49530*

Library of Congress Cataloging-in-Publication Data

Collins, Brandilyn.
Crimson eve / Brandilyn Collins.
p. cm.—(Kanner Lake series ; bk. 3)
ISBN-10: 0-310-25225-3
ISBN-13: 978-0-310-25225-2
1. Women real estate agents—Fiction. 2. Resorts—Fiction. 3. Idaho—Fiction.
I. Title.
PS3553.O4747815C75 2007
813'.6—dc22

2007012727

Interior design by Beth Shagene

Printed in the United States of America

07 08 09 10 11 12 13 14 15 • 18 17 16 15 14 13 12 11 10 9 8 7 6 5 4 3 2 1

Want to Discuss Crimson Eve *with Your Book Club?*

Insightful questions about the story and how it applies to your life can be found at *www.kannerlake.com/discussions*

For Sister #3,
Sandy Sheppard,
a.k.a. "Perfect Sister."
Because you are.
(It helps that you
prayed for me to be born.)

"Shall we never, never get rid of this Past?" cried he....
"It lies upon the Present like a giant's dead body."

Nathaniel Hawthorne,
The House of Seven Gables

What is past is prologue.

William Shakespeare, *The Tempest*

Whatever is has already been, and what will be has been before;
and God will call the past to account.

Ecclesiastes 3:15

INTRODUCTION

Dear Reader,

Back for more, are you?

In *Coral Moon* (second in the Kanner Lake series), I warned you that the wheels of the roller coaster on which you were about to embark just might leave earth. For *Crimson Eve,* I issue a warning of another kind. This roller coaster stays on the track, all right. But it is frighteningly long, its cars stretching so far that the front one catches up to the back. Or is it that the back circles around to meet the front?

Imagine being on a ride in which you do not know the start or the end. Which car is pushing, which is pulling? Which one drives the rickety climb to the top, the stomachless plunge to the bottom? Which one determines when you stop? Whether or not you've made it to safety?

If you find your way off this thing, you might look about you, check your possessions. Not everyone who boards leaves with all that was brought. I'll let you decide if that is a good thing.

And now—you know the drill. Keep your hands inside the car, strap yourself in tight, and don't forget to *b r e a t h e*...

CRIMSON EVE

Tuesday, September 25, 2007 **Wednesday, September 26, 2007** Thursday, Sept

PART ONE
Exposed

ONE

"Really, is a heinous murder any reason to devalue such a glorious piece of real estate?"

The words rolled off the man's tongue in a luscious British accent and with a hint of tease, lending him a cocky James Bond air. He was dashingly handsome (a good British description, what?). Dark hair, rich brown eyes, a jaw cut just so—not too square, but firm. Carla Radling glanced at his left hand. No ring. But then he'd already intimated he was single. A real-estate developer, he'd said over the phone yesterday. And apparently rich, although no proper English gentleman would say so. He was "seeking a beautiful and private piece of property near water as a second home," and the half-page ad in *Dream Houses* had caught his eye. If he liked the place, he'd pay cash.

To think she'd complained about the high cost of the ad.

Behind them, the heavy wrought-iron gates of the estate that once belonged to the late actress Edna San closed with a muted clang. Carla steered her white Toyota Camry down the impressive driveway curving through forest. Her client, David Thornby—although James Bond fit so much better—dignified her front seat. His legs, in impeccable beige trousers, were confidently apart, his left arm draped over the console, fingers casually drumming. His navy sport jacket boasted a thousand-dollar weave.

Carla laughed at Thornby's "heinous murder" remark. "No devaluing here. But often that's what happens to the homes of celebrities caught in a scandal—or murder. Gives potential buyers the willies to picture the crime occurring in their living room."

"Technically, it didn't occur here, correct? Edna San was taken out of the home, with no one being sure exactly where she was killed."

That accent was just to die for. "Right. The news was where they found her, not where she was killed."

But enough of this morbid topic.

"The property has only been for sale a little over a year," Carla said. "That's not a long time given its price for this area. I told Edna's heirs I fully expected that someone out of the area would buy it."

Carla rounded a curve in the wide driveway, and the actress's magnificent two-story home of wood and stone swept into view. A front porch with thick round pillars ran its entire length, the arched and mullioned windows giving it a castlelike quality. Surrounded by twenty acres of forest, it included a smaller home on the property for a full-time caretaker or perhaps a gardener, whatever a well-bred English gentleman might prefer.

Thornby drew in a breath. "It's stunning. And look at that view."

Kanner Lake sparkled some three hundred feet beyond the backyard of the main house, its waters tinged crimson in the sunset. Carla caught a glimpse of it through the side yard as she pulled up to the front of the house.

"Yeah, isn't it great? Like the ad said, a large dock and two hundred feet of sandy beach. Plus, with the forest all around you, it's completely private. And you'll see plenty of wildlife. Deer, with their new spotted fawns each year, wild turkeys." No need to mention the skunks, coons, and occasional bear.

Carla slid another look at Thornby. He leaned forward, anticipation on his face. The man liked what he saw.

A vague warning twinged in her stomach. Such obvious excitement didn't fit the demeanor of a suave British gentleman, did it?

Carla pushed the thought away. Pure stereotype.

She stopped close to the wide porch steps and cut the engine. "Wait till you see the inside."

He smiled at her, and his eyes twinkled. *Twinkled.* Carla hadn't known a pair of eyes could do that—outside the romance novels she used to read as a teenager.

How old was this guy? Maybe forty? Not so much older than her thirty-two years.

Please, oh, please, buy this house, you handsome thing. Then marry me quick.

"Thanks for letting me leave my car outside the gate," he said. "This was a treat, being free to ogle while you drove in."

"We aim to please."

They mounted the three curved flagstone steps side by side, Thornby a good eight inches taller than her five-six frame. Power and control emanated from him, his back straight, chin high, and eyes alert. He ran his knuckles down the huge carved door as Carla, trying her best to appear unaffected by his charm, slid her key into the lockbox. She removed the lock, pushed back the door, and waved him inside. "After you."

He stepped over the threshold onto gleaming tile floor, Carla following. Thornby's head tipped back to admire the grand curving staircase to their left.

"Truly stunning."

Carla hung back, giving him time to admire the sights—a formal living room on the right, furnished in leather couches and Persian rugs, rich wood wainscoting on the walls.

"Of course if you don't like Edna San's taste in furniture, you could always—"

"I do like it, very much. Makes it easier to buy a second home when it's turnkey."

"Well, that's good." Carla dropped her keys into her purse. "Since Edna's son and daughter didn't seem to care a whit about taking anything. Other than the crystal and china, that is, and the photos of Edna with Bette Davis and other movie cohorts."

"I thought Edna San hated Bette Davis." Thornby stepped into the living room and leaned down to inspect the fifteen-thousand-dollar rug.

Carla shrugged. "Didn't all the legendary female movie stars hate each other? It's a cat thing."

"Cat?"

"Yeah, you know how women can fight over ..." Carla eased up beside him, and he looked at her with those incredible eyes. Carla pressed her lips together. "Never mind."

He flashed another smile, sending a tingle down Carla's spine.

"So." She pointed toward the entryway. "How about if I show you the kitchen and dining room?"

"Yes, certainly."

In the large kitchen Carla pointed out the amenities. Thornby stood back while she opened cabinets, the refrigerator.

Odd. Prospective buyers typically inspected every nook and cranny.

Must be a man thing. The guy probably didn't even cook.

He glanced at his Rolex watch more than once.

Carla tilted her head. "Are you in a hurry?"

"No, no, sorry. Just the habit of a businessman."

Down a short, wide hall off the kitchen they stepped into the formal dining room. A highly polished cherrywood table lay beneath a sparkling crystal chandelier, the matching hutch elegant despite its emptiness after Edna San's children had claimed its dishes and goblets. On the hardwood floor spread another luxurious Persian rug. Carla walked around to the other side of the table, gesturing toward the large back windows. "Great view of the lake."

Thornby put his hands on his hips. "Splendid." He gazed at her, mouth curving. "And so are you."

Carla blinked. Was he talking about her skills as a realtor?

Huh-uh—the look on his face said something far different.

He sighed. "It's such a shame."

Carla was half tongue-tied. This man was so ... mesmerizing. "What is?"

He spread his hands. "You. This place. That I can have neither beauty."

Whoa, where had *that* come from? She searched in vain for one of her typical witty comebacks. "You can't?"

"No. You see, unfortunately things aren't quite as I represented."

It took her a second to realize the glorious accent had vanished. The guy now sounded as American as her coffee-guzzling pals down at Java Joint.

Carla stared at him. What was going on? She thought of the things she'd chosen to ignore—his request to leave his car outside the gate, his obvious anticipation of ... something, the refusal to touch anything, the glances at his watch. Her spine tingled, but this time it didn't feel so exciting.

"You're not British." She would not let her voice tremble, even though the ten-minute drive to town suddenly seemed like a trip to the moon. What was she thinking, coming out here alone near dusk? After all the trauma Kanner Lake had seen in the past year.

But good grief, he'd sounded so *normal.* Not to mention anxious to buy.

His lips spread in a slow smile. "No."

Fear flushed through Carla—and that ticked her off. She raised her chin. "Well, how about that. So tell me how much you told me *is* true. Are you a real-estate developer?"

He shrugged. "It seemed like such a respectable line of work at the time."

"At what time?"

"When I called you."

She stuck her tongue between her lip and top teeth. "Okay, let's cut the games. Just what *are* you?"

His graceful right hand slid into his coat pocket. "To use the vernacular, vulgar though it is"—his voice carried a light, engaging tone—"I'm a hit man."

He pulled out a handgun and aimed it at her heart.

TWO

As the last of a glowing sun dipped below the horizon, forty-seven-year-old Tanya Evans drove through the small town of Terrin, Washington, contemplating death.

Not physical death—in her former career she'd seen enough of that, and at very early ages. Spiritual/emotional death was another matter.

Tanya Evans had died at thirty-one.

She turned onto the road leading to her five-acre property, barely noticing the wooded, semirural scenery for which Terrin was known. The sun spilled a bucket of blood red in her rearview mirror, making her squint. The color plunged that bucket deep into her memory well, refilling it with the dark, roiling waters of remorse.

She knocked the mirror askew.

What else could you have done? The ancient question, asked for the millionth time. Followed by the same convenient answers.

Rationalization was a lovely thing, as long as one sank bulldog teeth into it and never let go. Hard to do day in and day out. Muscles cramped, energy waned. And guilt had a way of loosening the most stubborn of jaws.

For sanity's sake, Tanya hung on. Yes, what could she have done? At thirty-one she'd been a single mom, newly divorced, struggling to balance work with raising a rowdy seven-year-old boy. The money had been much needed; look at the neighborhood its careful investment had bought. She'd been able to give her son, Curt, a decent life. Put aside for his college. Scraped together the money to go back to school herself and earn an MBA, after which she'd landed a stable job at a health insurance company.

And the money had allowed her to support charities and volunteer through the years—oh, how she'd volunteered! Rocking babies in church nurseries, cooing to them in a free medical clinic, helping young unwed mothers find natal care.

If only these things had eased her conscience.

Tanya turned into her long driveway, passing the fenced pastures where her two horses had once run. Tired of caring for them alone after Curt went off to college, she'd sold them four years ago. At the end of the drive sat her red brick house, its three-columned porch and flower-lined walk beckoning after a long day of work in downtown Seattle. Her refuge from the world.

But there was no refuge from oneself.

At every birthday for Curt, she'd put candles on a cake and thought of another child.

What we think, or what we know, or what we believe, is, in the end, of little consequence. The only consequence is what we do. The first time Tanya had heard the quote from late author John Ruskin at some book club discussion, the words had pierced her soul. She'd fled home, claiming a headache.

What we do. The choice she'd made may have seemed inescapable. But every day since then she'd made another choice, and another. She'd remained silent. Watched others' lives unfold as a result of her action, some rising in glory, some falling to dust. And never confessed her wrong.

Stop it now, Tanya, stop thinking!

She pushed the garage door button. All right, so her life was difficult. She wasn't the only one with problems. What to do but pick yourself up and go on.

And hope the sin was never exposed.

Tanya had managed until now, treading water with the muscled strength of long years' practice. Then three days ago a new current had swept in. She'd received a visitor. Someone who'd splashed into the threatening waters of those bygone years by accident—and now demanded answers. Answers that if given, could finally, if not completely, assuage her conscience. But at cost of all else.

Tanya smiled grimly. Such irony, worthy of the fine literature she so craved. Sometimes she wondered why she was drawn to such books, bleak as they were. But of course, therein lay her answer. The pain and tears rang true to her soul, reminding her she was not alone.

But there was a difference. The books ended, however darkly. Her life dragged on.

Tanya slipped into the garage, shut off the car engine, and closed the door. She faced another evening alone. How she missed her son. But he was twenty-three now, out of college and married, a baby of his own on the way.

Tanya ached to hold that baby. As dedicated as she'd been as a mother, she would double it as a grandmother. Curt had deserved no less, and neither would her grandchild.

All babies deserved to live and grow and be loved.

Tanya slid out of her car, purse in hand. Her weary steps echoed through the garage as she headed for the side door leading into her home. In the familiar stone silence of the house, she flicked on the hallway light and dragged herself over the faded carpet. Past kitchen on the right, front door and hall on the left, opening into the family room.

From that dim room, peripheral movement caught her eye. Something on the couch near the front window. She swiveled, saw a figure—and gasped. Her eyes locked on a familiar face.

The intruder rose from her couch. "Ms. Evans." The voice was low, weighted with menace that need never yell. "I've been doing a little checking up on you."

THREE

A hit man? What was this, some Edna San film noir?

Carla stared at the gun and David Thornby—or whatever his name was. Her mind split in two, one side pleading this was some sick joke, the other screaming it was all too real. Her throat ran dry, air backing up in her lungs. She licked her lips.

"Sorry I'm so slow, but—are you saying you're here to *kill* me?"

"I'm afraid so."

Such nonchalance. "*Why*?"

"I never asked."

Okay. Now was the time for him to put the gun away, tell her it was fake. Admit her favorite person to argue with, crusty old Wilbur Hucks down at Java Joint, had sent Thornby to pull the biggest stunt on her Wilbur had ever pulled …

The man before her did none of these things.

Carla's brain couldn't process. What exactly was the social protocol when a gun was pointed at you? As real as the weapon looked, hope still flew its flag—*It* is *a joke; he's going to crack up any minute.* "You're telling me you staged all this to get me out here and kill me, and you don't know why?"

He shrugged. "A half-million dollars silences the most curious of questions."

"A *half-million dollars*?"

One of his eyebrows rose. "Apparently you've angered the wrong person quite thoroughly."

"Would you cut the British phraseology already? We're kind of past that."

"Sorry. I rather enjoyed the part."

Carla gripped her purse, thoughts whirling. "Did Edna San's son and daughter send you? If I'm not selling the house fast enough, there are easier ways to fix the problem. I can give you names of plenty other realtors. Tell you what, take the whole Rolodex."

"I doubt that's the reason."

What then? Some hangover from the murders six months ago? But that case had been solved. Memories of the craziness of that time, the unsettled days and frightening nights, flashed through Carla. Even with the confessed killer in jail, it had taken her three months to feel safe in her own home at night.

So *why* on earth had she fallen for this man's spiel?

In her peripheral vision, Carla caught the fading glitter red of the setting sun upon Kanner Lake. A crimson eve, she thought. How dramatically apropos. Maybe this was an Edna San movie after all.

"Please. You've got the wrong person. There's no reason for someone to want me dead. I don't have any enemies."

"Then you'd best rethink your friends."

"But there's ... Look, let's just call the whole thing off, like the song says. I'll go my way, and you go yours. Cross my heart I won't say a word to anybody."

Remorse flicked across his face. "I hate this part. Really I do. Especially with someone as gorgeous as you. The two of us should be at a romantic dinner, with pale moonlight and a sonorous ocean as our backdrop."

Sonorous?

Carla's nerves prickled. The guy said he was here to kill her—and now he was *flirting*? And using poetic words to boot. All hope of jokes melted away. This man was crazy.

Carla surveyed her chances. She wore heels, but she could ditch them in a hurry. The pepper spray was in the right corner of her tote-style purse—had been ever since Vesta Johnson's murder six months ago. It had an eleven-gram stream that would shoot up to ten feet and contained five one-second bursts. Plenty enough to stop the guy in his tracks while she knocked away the gun …

"Yeah, right, a romantic dinner. In your dreams, pal."

The man shrugged. "Your loss, Miss Wit." His eyes flattened to cold calculation. "Now. We're going to take a little walk. Come around the table, and head toward the front door."

Uh-uh. No way was she letting him get behind her. Carla imagined the bullet searing through her back into her heart. Besides, he might as well kill her right here. What was he going to do, shoot her on the beach and weight-sink her body into the water? Kanner Lake had been there, done that.

Her heart knocked against her chest. "Guess what, I've changed my mind. That ocean-side date sounds just spiffy."

He sneered. "Thanks, but I'm happily married. Get moving."

Carla moved, her muscles trembling with a panic she would not show. She'd lived through enough, hadn't she, to be strong now? Endured pain in her teenage years—more than anyone should have to face. She'd learned a few things since then. Made her way in life alone. Gotten bolder, cockier. She needed to hold on to that cockiness now, squeeze every last drop out of it. Because she was not going down without one massive fight.

She skirted around the end of the table. Carla clutched her handbag at her waist as she headed out of the room. No need to look to know that he followed. She could *feel* the glacier at her back.

"Wait. Put your purse on the table."

"No way, I paid a lot for this thing. It's going down with the ship."

"Put it *on the table.*"

That did it; the time was now or never. *Note to all hit men: never separate a female from her designer purse.*

Carla slid her left hand into the bag, curled her fingers around the pepper spray, and pushed off the safety top. "Okay, okay." She turned toward the table, right hand holding up the purse, her left down by her side. "Satisfied?" She reached toward the table with the bag, watching his eyes as they followed her movement.

The second her purse met the table, Carla whipped up her left hand, feinted to one side, and jammed her index finger on the canister's release. A stream hit David Thornby in the face.

"Ahh!" Both eyes screwed shut. His hand jerked up. *Bap, bap.* Two bullets whizzed by Carla's head.

She screamed. Pumped the pepper spray twice more.

The man wheezed and staggered back. Dropped the gun. His hands flew to his face and clawed.

Some force outside Carla took over. She lunged for the weapon. Her foot kicked it, sending it sliding across the rug. She chased it and snatched it up. Turned to yank her purse from the table. The man coughed and cursed mere feet away, face scrunched and eyes cinched shut. One arm swung blindly, groping for her. Carla jumped out of his reach, threw both gun and pepper spray into her bag. Swiveled toward the hall.

She'd gone only two steps before her left high heel caught the edge of the Persian rug. Her ankle turned. Pain shot up her leg.

Carla stumbled and crashed to the floor. All breath knocked from her lungs.

No, no, move!

She scrabbled to her knees. The floor turned to lake waves beneath her. She kicked off both shoes, tried to push herself upright, ignoring the throb of her ankle.

Behind her, David Thornby growled like a wild animal. Strong fingers closed around her calf and pulled. She smashed to the ground a second time, her head hitting hardwood floor. She lay there, dazed.

The hand around her leg tightened, the man spewing curses.

How determined *was* this guy? She'd hit him with enough pepper spray to stop a horse.

His fingers bit into her skin. "I ... will ... kill you ... slowly ... for this."

Carla's world blurred.

FOUR

Shock tore through Tanya's body, and every limb went weak. Her purse slipped from her fingers, hit the carpet with a soft *thump*. Futile shouts for help stuck in her throat. "How did you get in here?"

"I'll ask the questions." The figure stood mostly in shadow, illumination from the hall light touching one nostril, one eye, distorting the face. The invader's body, though not large, loomed huge in threat, as if in one move it could fly at her and devour. For a surreal moment Tanya flashed on every vampire movie she'd ever watched as a teenager.

One arm raised toward the couch. "Would you prefer to sit, Ms. Evans?"

Tanya could only stare.

A shrug. "As you like."

Outside the window, dusk spread dark wings over the front yard, tainting the family room in shades of gray. The intruder drew closer to Tanya. "Since we last talked, I've learned a little more about that 'discussion' of yours."

"I told you that wasn't my idea!" Her words sounded breathless. "I was completely surprised. And I didn't say *anything*. I pretended not to know."

"You must not have pretended very well."

Tanya swallowed. "I did the best I could. What was I supposed to say?"

"That the questions are more than ridiculous. That you are *absolutely convinced* the truth is what it's always seemed."

"But the proof shows otherwise!"

"Proof is all in perception, Ms. Evans." The voice hardened. "It's in what we choose to believe. You should have reinforced those beliefs. You could have put the fears to rest quietly, quickly. Instead I hear you hemmed and hawed, and ended up raising more questions than you answered."

A large crow landed on a thin branch just beyond the window, swaying the limb and sending shivers through the leaves. Tanya trembled in rhythm.

"I'm sorry. Next time I'll do better. Believe me, I just want to be left alone. I don't like the questions any more than you do."

"Believe *me*—there won't be a next time."

The crow emitted a raucous *caw,* as if nature itself reinforced the intruder's dire meaning. Prickles danced down Tanya's back. All the *years* she'd kept quiet. Suddenly they loomed so fruitless. How could she have believed the truth would remain hidden forever?

The intruder sneered at Tanya—and a thread within her snapped. Just enough to fray the edge of her years-worn complicity. Indignation stirred in her bones. "If you have the situation under control, why bother to come here and threaten me?"

"I don't recall saying a single word of threat."

"You broke into my house. I'd say that's threat enough."

"Let's call it a gentle reminder. You wouldn't *have* this house were it not for certain generosity."

But I might have a life.

"Agreed, Ms. Evans?"

The snapped thread frayed a little more. Tanya's fingers curled toward her palms. "Yes. Agreed."

"Good."

They regarded each other, Tanya fighting to hide her growing defensiveness. The stare that met her eyes was hard, laser-like. Under its heat, Tanya's rebelliousness wavered, then melted away. She lowered her gaze.

Her visitor made a throaty sound of approval. Then pulled out a cell phone, hit one button. "Come pick me up." The cell phone snapped shut.

The words, so casual. A sign to Tanya of power, of the planned staging of this moment, the fear it was intended to instill. Her indignation returned. "Leaving so soon?"

The intruder moved with the swiftness of an animal pursuing its prey. The gap between them closed, leaving them nose to nose. "Have you forgotten who I *am*? What I can do? With one word, *one word*, I can make you disappear. I've worked too hard, waited too many years to get where I am today. Tomorrow promises even better things. And *nothing* is going to take tomorrow away from me."

The words dropped like molten lead, sizzling Tanya's skin. In that instant she saw the full truth. This heartless person despised her knowledge. Saw her as a bomb that could explode any minute. As long as she lived she would be viewed as a fizzling fuse needing to be doused. The wrong word, one sideways glance might be all it took.

Could she live like that? On top of the constant remorse—could she survive, always waiting for the other shoe to drop?

And if she didn't survive—the knowledge would die with her.

The crow cawed again. Tanya jumped.

Her intruder stepped back, smirking.

The sound of a car engine filtered from outside. Through the corner window Tanya spied a dark sedan with tinted glass pull into the circular drive out front.

Her visitor shot a final glare at Tanya, then strode to the front door and pulled it open. Turned back. "Remember. *One* word."

The door closed firmly. Tanya stood unmoving as the hated figure slid into the sedan's backseat, and the car drove off.

Only then did she begin to shake.

FIVE

Carla blinked rapidly, the brown fuzz of hardwood floor swimming before her eyes. Her head pounded, her left ankle throbbed, and viselike fingers wrapped around her lower calf.

Where was she?

Grunts and coughs erupted behind her. Clarity flooded Carla's brain. Her purse. The gun and canister. Had they fallen out?

Carla slapped both palms against the floor, pushed herself up. She shook her head, trying to clear her vision.

The man yanked at her leg. She kicked with the other and connected with something hard. His head? He groaned, and she kicked again.

She swept her half-focused gaze left and right, searching for her purse. There, near the door. She stretched out a hand, missing the bag by two feet. Terror and rage shot through her veins.

"Oh, no, you won't!" Thornby's words ground like mixing gravel.

Carla clenched her teeth and thrashed, inching across the floor toward her purse. The man's fingers loosened but didn't let go. She kicked with both legs, pummeling hard with her free limb until she felt the man's fingers fall away. With a cry she shot forward and grabbed her purse, fingers scrambling for the gun or spray. She felt the small container, yanked it out, bent her body at the waist back toward the man, and hit the button. The stream hit his chin, drops bouncing into his eyes.

He gagged and curled into a heap, hands slapped to his face.

Carla pushed to her feet and stumbled toward the doorway. Pain knifed her ankle so swiftly it rolled nausea through her stomach. She hissed and squeezed her eyes shut, then forced herself forward, limping, hopping, clutching her purse. Through the dining room threshold, out to the hall, into the entry. The door seemed miles away.

Go, girl, go!

She hit the front door and bounced off, hand scrabbling for the knob. She found it, threw the door open, and heaved herself outside. Tears blurred her vision as she grunted her way down the three porch steps, fumbled around to the driver's side of her car, and threw herself inside.

The key, where's the key?

Carla plunged her fingers into her purse, searching. She felt wallet, checkbook, makeup kit, paper, pen, cell phone. No gun, no pepper spray. What had she done with the canister? And *where* was the key? Her hand flew left and right, turning items over, feeling the bottom of the bag. Precious seconds ticked by. Had it fallen out of her purse?

In her side vision, she saw a shadow in the yawning front door. Carla jerked her head around. The man staggered in the doorway, breath heaving, face purpled with rage.

"No, God, *please*." She dumped her purse on her lap, raked through the contents. No key.

Her attacker stumbled down the porch steps. Carla smacked the button to lock her car doors.

Thornby barreled into the passenger door, fought to open it.

Did he have the gun? Maybe his blurred eyes hadn't seen ...

Her cell phone. What had happened to it? Carla found it on her lap, snatched it up.

At that moment her eyes fell on the car key—stuck in the ignition, where she'd left it.

Carla threw down the phone, turned the key hard, and roared the car to life. Smacked the gear in drive and squealed off. Thornby hung onto her car door for a terrorizing second, then fell away. Carla surged around the circular portion of the driveway and up toward the front gate. She flicked a glance in the rearview mirror but didn't see him.

At the white caution line before the gate, she skidded to a stop.

The gate was automatically tripped from this side. Slowly, it unlatched, swinging open toward her. Thornby's rented black Durango sat on the other side, a little off to the right. Maybe she could drive around it.

"Come on, gate, come *on*."

Her foot shoved against the brake, her arms shaking. She threw another look in the rearview mirror and saw the man stagger-running up the road with teeth-gritted, superhuman strength. How could anyone get hit that many times with pepper spray and still be standing? He plunged a hand in his pocket. Up came the gun.

The gate was three-quarters open.

Thornby slowed, took wavering aim.

"Go, gate, *move*!"

Carla hit the accelerator, fishtailed her Toyota partly off the driveway and around the gate. On the other side, she jerked the steering wheel left, plowing off the drive once more and around the rental car, barely missing two huge fir trees.

Ping. A bullet hit metal. The gate? She didn't stop to look back.

At the end of the drive, she skidded left onto Lakeshore and toward town.

It took a minute for her brain to catch up with her body.

She'd *made* it.

He couldn't catch her now. Carla knew that, but her fingers still froze to the wheel. She forced her trembling right hand to seek her cell phone on the passenger seat. She had to call the police immediately; every second counted. If they could just get here in time to catch her attacker before he ran, leaving what would surely be a trail of false identification. How could she ever feel safe again if he was on the loose?

How much time before he could see well enough to drive?

Her fingers found the phone. As she picked it up, it rang. Carla jumped and nearly dropped the thing. Then, with a surge of hope, she flipped the phone open. "This is Carla! Whoever this is, call the—"

"Shut up and listen to me."

All sound withered in Carla's throat. She sank back against her seat.

"Now you've made this messy." The guttural, hate-filled words chewed into her ear. "Bad mistake. And you'll pay." The voice squeezed off, coughed once.

"You can die alone, Carla Radling, or you can take people with you. Vince Edwards is your chief of police. His wife is Nancy. He has a daughter, Heather, a little granddaughter, Christy. You call *any* law enforcement, one of them dies. Got that?"

Carla couldn't respond.

"And by the way, you won't know what law enforcement to trust, because some of them just might be working for me."

A long pause as the words sank in. Carla's blood pounded in her ears.

"Or maybe I won't go after Edwards's family at all. Maybe I'll kill your friend Bailey, or someone at work. Or Wilbur, how about that? Maybe even his wife, Trudy, too. In their bed at night. They'll never know what hit them. Get it? It'll be my little surprise. As for calling friends—don't even think about it. *Any* friend who helps you is dead. You hear, Miss Wit?"

Carla's mouth hung open, but still no words came.

"*Do* you?"

"I ... Y–yes."

"Good. And don't bother running. I'll have people looking for you everywhere. No matter where you go, I'll find you. Within twenty-four hours—you are *dead*."

SIX

Carla drove into town, following the winding Lakeshore Road. Forest and fields whizzed by on her right, the lake on her left. She barely noticed. Her limbs were wooden, her brain hardly able to function.

She had to call the police.

She couldn't call the police.

Of course she could. Wouldn't they respond to the Edna San estate before David Thornby, or whatever his real name was, could get away? All they had to do was catch him and she'd be safe. Vince's family would be safe.

But what if they didn't arrive in time? What if Thornby was able to drive away? Or if he fled on foot, with darkness now falling? Once he was loose—with who knew how many identities and accents to assume—there could be no stopping him.

Carla shuddered. What could she do now? Where could she go? Certainly not home. If Thornby knew so much about people in Kanner Lake, he certainly knew where she lived. Neither could she go to a friend's house. Anybody she turned to would be placed in danger.

Carla gripped the steering wheel as she rounded a bend on Lakeshore Road. Darkness was descending fast. A few more miles, and she'd enter town.

She checked every few seconds in the rearview mirror but saw no one. Surely the man couldn't drive yet. Could he?

Who had sent this man to kill her? Why?

Was her life even worth a half-million dollars?

She'd been a realtor in Kanner Lake since moving to town six years ago. Before that she'd lived in Spokane for ten years, working for the last eight as an administrative assistant in a real estate development company. She hadn't wronged anyone, hadn't fought with neighbors. Hadn't faced any major trauma since her teenage years in Terrin, Washington. But that was half a lifetime ago. She'd long since stuffed those memories deep inside her. And she'd never spoken of what happened to anyone.

Carla passed the sign at the city limits to Kanner Lake.

Fear willed her arms to steer toward the police station on Main. Vince would call other law enforcement for help. He'd tell her she'd done the right thing.

Or would he? The man would also be forced to place his wife, daughter, and granddaughter in hiding until David Thornby was caught. Vince, who'd already lost a son to the Iraq war just a little over two years ago. Who'd done so much to help this town through the previous tragedies.

She couldn't do it.

Carla headed straight, bypassing Main. Up a half mile until she reached Claremont, then turned left. Her beloved two-bedroom house sat two blocks up on the left. Blue wood with white trim, tall front windows and four square pillars across the recessed front porch. The house she'd bought four years ago and so proudly decorated.

She turned into the driveway at the right side, where the garage protruded an additional ten feet. Hit the remote button on her visor, casting feverish glances right and left as the door rose. She drove inside. Smacked the remote to close the door.

Twenty minutes max to gather some critical items and flee town. She'd hide out in some hotel until she figured out what to do next.

And when she found a place to hide, she'd wrap her ankle and put it up. The throbbing wouldn't stop.

Carla left the key in the ignition and hobbled to the door that opened into her front hall. Every step made her wince. She pulled open the door and jumped up the one step on her good leg.

The house was dim, but she was afraid to turn on the light.

She veered right, limped through her living room. At the threshold to her bedroom, she pulled up short.

Someone had been here.

A pillow lay askew on the bed, one drawer of her dresser slightly open. Nothing that would be obvious to anyone else, but she was particular about her house's neatness and knew how she'd left things.

Violation surged through her. How *dare* someone go through her house? How would she ever feel safe here again? Carla gripped the doorway, legs trembling. Willing the emotions to settle enough so her mind could sort out what to do.

Okay, Carla, think!

She'd been in her office before meeting Thornby at the San estate. He must have been watching her, knew he could come here and search the place. Had he picked the lock to the back door? She hadn't noticed any broken windows.

What was he looking for?

The answer to that question might lead to whoever had hired him.

Carla rattled in a deep breath, glanced at her watch. She could cuss and scream later. Right now she had to *move.* If she wanted to save her own skin, she needed to be out of here in under fifteen minutes.

Teeth gritted against the pain, she stumbled through the bedroom—*her* bedroom, even now tainted by the lingering sense of an intruder's presence. She could almost smell him—and it was no longer the smell of expensive cologne. Carla pulled a small red suitcase from the floor of her closet, threw it on her bed. In went her laptop in its case, the charger to her cell phone. She grabbed toiletries in the bathroom, some jeans and tops, a jacket, a pair of slip-on flat shoes, which she put on. With every second that ticked by, her fear ratcheted higher until she could hardly breathe. As she pulled out drawers, yanked items from her closet, her eyes flicked right and left, up and down, cataloging. Was anything missing?

Come on, get out of here!

Her hands shook as she fought to zip the suitcase closed. Placing the bag upright on the floor to pull, she turned from the bed—and her eyes landed on the shoebox in the right corner of her closet shelf. Its top was ajar. Carla froze, staring at the box.

Sudden realization pierced her brain.

No. It couldn't be that.

She hobbled to the shelf. Pulled down the box and threw off its top. Rifled through its contents. Recent photos, scrapbook memory stuff—ticket stubs, newspaper clippings of her first sales—all were still there.

But no photos of her at sixteen. With *him.*

Carla dropped the box. Slapped both hands to her face.

Could this be true? *He* wanted her dead? Why, after all these years? She'd fled that life, hadn't said a thing about him to anyone. His secrets were *safe* with her, didn't he realize that by now?

Dizziness washed over her. Carla sucked air in, blew it out.

If this man from her past had come back to harm her, she might as well give up. He was too powerful and loved. He could destroy her with lies, hire to kill—and who would believe the truth?

Oh, God, help me.

Outside her window, a tomcat yowled. Carla jumped. The sound thrust her into desperate action. She grabbed her suitcase and stumbled back to the garage to her car. As she was about to slide inside, a thought sped through her brain.

The diary!

Had they found it too?

Dwindling time yanked at her to *go*. Carla hesitated a split second, then turned back, returning to her bedroom closet. With trembling fingers she snatched a hatbox off the shelf, flipped aside the lid. Inside were a dozen stacked baseball caps. A green one sat on top. She lifted them out, removed the top five, six, seven—and exhaled in relief. There, hidden between number seven and eight, sat the small yellow-flowered diary. She picked it up. Those pictures her attacker had taken meant so little. They weren't even intimate photos, nothing that could have given away the truth. But *this*.

For a split second, she considered leaving it. If something happened to her, police would go through her place, looking for clues. Vividly she pictured flashes of scenes—her body lying crumpled and dirty in a forest, undiscovered. Police searching through her house for clues to her disappearance. Frank West, Kanner Lake's youngest officer, finding the diary, flipping through it. His eyes going wide ...

The diary might lead them to her killer. But it would also spill her heinous secrets. Even in death, she couldn't bear it.

Carla put all the caps back as she'd found them and slid the box onto her closet shelf.

Clutching the diary to her chest, she hobbled back to her car. Behind the wheel, Carla threw it under her seat.

Breathing a prayer, she smacked the garage door button, half expecting to see her killer's black Durango on the other side.

No one was there. But he could be mere minutes away.

Carla screeched in reverse onto the driveway, closed the garage door, and fled into the night.

SEVEN

Man, would the cell phone in his pocket *ever* stop ringing?

Tony Derrat wasn't about to answer. The ring tone told him it was his boss. Tony just wanted to smash the phone on the late Edna San's long driveway. His eyes still stung and his throat burned like fire. Rage alone kept his feet moving toward his rental car outside the gate.

How *dare* some smart-mouthed realtor think she could outwit him. No way was he going to lose that half-million dollars.

Tony hadn't climbed into his job; he'd fallen into it. Down and drunk ten years ago, living on the streets—and out of the blue, a proposition from a woman he barely knew. Five thousand bucks for getting rid of her abusive husband.

Five thousand dollars. All he had to do was pop off some lowlife who knocked his wife around.

The job had gone down like smooth vodka—and Tony's new habit was born. The next two years brought a dozen more hits. Meanwhile he cleaned himself up good. Landed a pretty wife. Learned new skills and made some key friends. He studied accents, how to dress. How to look educated around hoity-toity people.

Four years ago he'd hit the big time, working behind the scenes for one very powerful person. Was paid more than ever and hadn't even had to kill anybody. Until now.

Tony stumbled and nearly went sprawling. He spit out a curse, caught himself with both hands. Rough asphalt scraped his palms. Gritting his teeth, he pushed himself back up, dragging searing air in, out, in, out.

He *had* to get off this property.

Tony's eyes wouldn't focus on his watch. How long had he laid on the ground after Carla Radling screeched away?

She could be headed any direction by now.

His cell phone went off again, different tone. Queen's "Crazy Little Thing Called Love." Great, the home ring. Tony told himself he'd call his wife back later, but the next thing he knew, he was pulling the phone out of his pocket. Robyn would worry if he didn't answer. He tried to make his voice sound normal. "Hello."

"Hi, Daddy!"

Timmy, his three-year-old. Tony's heart surged. Timmy was the one person who made this gopher job worth it. "Hey, Boo. What's up?"

"Mommy said I could talk to you before I went to bed."

"Yeah, great." Tony turned his head and coughed hard.

"You sick, Daddy?"

"No," he wheezed. "I'm fine."

"Then whatcha doin'?"

"Just got out of a dinner meeting."

"Whatdja eat?"

Eat, what did he eat? Tony's mind went blank. "Uh, hamburger. And fries. And a chocolate shake."

"Wow! Yummm. I wanna go with you next time."

A click in Tony's ear. Had to be his boss calling on the other line. He made a face. "Hey, Boo, gotta go, another call's coming in. I'll talk to you tomorrow, okay?"

" 'Kay, Daddy. Love you."

"Love you too, big guy."

Violent coughing seized him as he closed the phone. A fireball from his chest rose up his throat.

The phone rang his boss's tone. Spitting curses, Tony snapped the thing open. "Yeah." The word sounded like a sick bark.

"What kind of a way is that to answer a phone?"

Hello to you too. Tony bit back a retort. This voice covered his bills—and then some. This voice had agreed to pay him a half million to take out Carla Radling. What he could buy his family with that money.

"Sorry, I was coughing."

"Well, cough on your own time. Is it done?"

"Not yet."

"Why?"

"She didn't show for our appointment."

A long breath seeped over the line. "Think she's onto you?"

"No way. She just got held up at her office. We'll probably meet tomorrow morning."

"*Tomorrow?* This was supposed to be done tonight, Tony. I was all set for a peaceful night's sleep."

"Don't worry, I'm working on it."

"What is this, a crocheted sweater? I didn't agree to pay you a fortune so you could 'work on it.' "

Tony's jaw clenched. Someday he was going to pop some teeth right down that pompous throat. "I *am* taking care of it. You know these things don't always go as scheduled. If Plan A doesn't work, I'll get her in Plan B. I'm always prepared."

"I *do not* want this left hanging until tomorrow. Put a bullet in her head while she's sleeping tonight."

"You wanted her to disappear, remember? Pretty risky getting a body out of a house on a residential street. Better to have her meet me at the estate as planned."

The caller grunted. Tony wondered if his lie had been believed.

He wiped his eyes with the back of his hand. "I went through her house. Took some photos I found. Nothing personal, though."

"Sure you got them all? Could make a real mess, leaving something behind."

Yeah, no kidding. Despite what he'd told Carla Radling, after finding those photos Tony could make a pretty good guess why he'd been sent here. Wouldn't be the first time something like this had happened in America. Sometimes powerful people were powerfully stupid. "I *told* you I'll take care of everything."

"Watch your tone; who do you think you are?" The voice hardened to stone. "*Nothing* you have ever done is as important as this job, Tony. So let me make this clear to you, in case you're not getting it. This doesn't go down as planned, you're as good as dead. *After* I get through with your son. Do you understand?"

Tony's blood turned to water. His mouth hung open, fingers crushed against the cell phone. Knowing this person the way he did, the driving ambition involved, he didn't dare doubt the threat.

"Derrat?"

"I hear you."

"Good." Breathing sounded in Tony's ear. "Tell you what, now that we've had our heart-to-heart, I'm feeling especially generous. I think you're right about the hit at night. I'll give you until ... three o'clock tomorrow afternoon. That's more than enough time."

Three o'clock. Timmy would be at preschool. Robyn would pick him up at five. Nobody would bother his son at school. Right?

"No problem; I'll call you by then."

"Be assured if you don't, I'll be calling *you.*" A pause, followed by a satisfied sigh. "Beautiful sunset over here. Hope yours is equally pretty."

The line clicked in Tony's ear.

Slowly, he lowered the phone and slid it into his pocket.

More coughing shook him. Tony hacked and spat, his brain already spinning desperate plans.

When the coughing ceased, he forced his feet toward the rental car. No matter that he could hardly see.

Nineteen hours. No matter what it took, Carla Radling would be dead in nineteen hours.

EIGHT

In Tanya's house, every light burned. In all bedrooms, all baths, the dining and living and family rooms, even the garage. Outside every porch light beamed, plus the powerful front and back spots at the house's four corners.

All doors were locked and bolted. All windows shut and double-checked.

Tanya felt anything but safe.

The violation of her home stretched from room to room. Every corner she turned, every door she passed threatened to yield another unwanted intruder.

With one word, I can make you disappear . . .

Tanya perched on the edge of her office chair, focusing on her computer screen. On her right sat a cup of tea, still steaming. To her left, beige blinds on the large windows were closed tight. Her desk was neat, every pen in place, the phone angled just so.

The feigned orderliness of her life.

Tomorrow loomed unyielding and unsure. But tonight while she had the chance, Tanya would follow the clarion of her conscience. It had begun to blow the minute the hated intruder disappeared out her door. After all these years of complacence, Tanya now felt driven to find the name that had so haunted her: *Carla Radling.*

She went to *Google.com*, typed in her search. Up popped dozens of hits. Tanya sucked in a breath. Could it be this easy?

She started down the list.

Apparently, more than one Carla Radling existed. Tanya read the 2003 obituary of ninety-six-year-old Carol Whitamah in Atlanta, Georgia, survived by numerous children, one of them a Carla Radling in Westchester, Tennessee. *Mother who was ninety-six.* The ages didn't fit.

A Carla Radling in Little Rock, Arkansas, currently played in her high school's marching band. A third in Wheaton, Illinois, age fifty-six, had been elected to city council. This one offered the most hits—Web site after Web site. Tanya skipped over all similar links, praying to find the Carla she sought.

There—a fourth. Carla Radling, realtor in Kanner Lake, Idaho.

The town name alone was enough to steal Tanya's breath. *The* Kanner Lake, where the famous Edna San had lived and been murdered. Where just six months ago, other fearsome killings had occurred, spinning the town onto TV screens and newspaper pages for a second time. Over a year ago, Tanya had never heard of Kanner Lake. Now, who in the United Stated *hadn't* heard of it?

According to this Carla's Web site, she was the realtor who'd listed Edna San's estate.

Tanya stared at the photo.

Same glossy black hair, same dark eyes, same lovely face. The eyes that had cried so hard, the face that gazed at her with a trust that shattered Tanya's heart into pieces.

Her throat tightened.

She eased back in her chair, unable to rip her gaze from the picture. Pressed her palms to her mouth. The computer blurred, tears falling on her cheeks. She didn't bother to wipe them away.

When she could move again, she pulled pen and paper close and wrote down Carla's office number. No cell number. Strange. Didn't most realtors live on their cell phones?

Tanya's tea grew cold as she read every Web site that pertained to Kanner Lake realtor Carla Radling. One was a blog at *www.kannerlake.blogspot.com* called Scenes and Beans. "Life in Kanner Lake, Idaho, brought to you by Java Joint coffee shop on Main." *Java Joint.* Tanya remembered the name. It too had made the news last spring after the town's murders. Carla was listed as one of the blog's contributing posters.

For the next two hours, Tanya read the posts from Scenes and Beans.

Carla rotated with the other bloggers, appearing about every two weeks. Tanya both laughed and cried as she read Carla's posts. She could see the feistiness she once saw in the teenage girl. At least Carla hadn't lost that. What Tanya didn't see, as opposed to most of the other bloggers, was anything about Carla's past. No mention of childhood, of her teenage years, of anything but the present. No mention, either, of a husband or boyfriend.

Had the events of years ago cost Carla that?

Fresh guilt pierced Tanya. What had she done to that young girl?

She finished reading. For a long time she sat staring at the blue water background of the Scenes and Beans blog. And Carla's name as contributor—"realtor at your service."

With one word ...

No matter. It was too late to turn back now. She'd known that the moment she saw Carla's picture. Maybe even before, when those threatening words had wound the noose around her neck, poised a foot to kick away the flimsy stool upon which she'd stood for all these years.

Tanya erased the Internet history, then shut down her computer.

Tonight she would sleep with her bedroom door locked and one of her son's old baseball bats on the bed beside her. If she lived to see tomorrow, she would set out to do what should have been done years ago. Who knew if she would survive after she'd accomplished her task?

Even so, for the first time in years, Tanya Evans's conscience felt a hint of peace.

PART TWO

Driven

NINE

Eight-thirty. Less than nineteen hours.

Tony Derrat's eyes and throat still burned, and his face was beet red. But he had work to do.

He parked the Durango a block away and headed for Carla's house, keeping his head down. He'd stopped at a gas station and changed his clothes in the men's room. Jeans, a navy button-down shirt, running shoes. His silk pants and expensive sport coat looked like they'd been dragged through the mud. It would be a miracle if they ever came clean.

Tony didn't expect to find Carla at home. No doubt she'd run off by now. But she'd probably stopped to pick up some things. Women were so predictable. About to die, and they'd want a makeup kit.

He needed to know what she'd taken. Just might tell him which direction she'd headed.

Tony reached the house. Nice-looking place. Green lawn and flowers. He walked up the driveway as if he belonged there, around the side and to the back. He put gloves on, then pulled a small flashlight from his pocket and aimed it at the kitchen door lock. With practiced ease, he jimmied the lock for a second time that day and slipped inside. He closed the door without a sound.

Tony moved through the dark kitchen, senses prickling. He could tell things about a person from her house. This one had a feeling of order and coolness. Everything in its place, no clutter. In the living room sat a light blue sofa—in the daylight he'd seen its color. Matching chairs grouped around a white-tiled fireplace, magazines stacked on a glass-topped coffee table. Knickknacks and books on built-in shelves. No photos. Art prints on the walls. Nothing commemorating Carla Radling's life.

Who *was* this woman?

His own house was homey. Timmy's shoes on the kitchen floor, toys in front of the TV. The smells of cookies and peanut butter.

Timmy.

Tony slipped into Carla's bedroom.

He aimed the flashlight down, avoiding windows. Feeble light from a streetlamp puddled on the dresser. Open drawers. The shoebox of pictures was dumped on the bed. In the closet clothes were pushed to one side.

She'd been through here in a hurry, all right.

In Tony's head, a clock loudly ticked. But he forced himself to check every inch of the room. A small red suitcase was missing from the closet. Tony could barely make out its wheel tracks on the carpet. Also gone were a laptop and case that had sat on the desk.

He should have been more careful this afternoon. But he was in a hurry to meet Carla at the estate. Then, it hadn't mattered. He'd figured he could return here if necessary after he'd dumped her body where it wouldn't be found. In that case he'd have known exactly what he was looking for and where it was. He hadn't planned on killing Miss Wit until he'd forced every piece of pertinent information from her.

Tony panned the flashlight beam over the closet again. Something wasn't right.

The hatbox on the closet shelf.

The top was crooked, and it wasn't where he'd put it. He'd replaced it close to the shoebox, just as he'd found it. Now the thing lay some four inches away from where the shoebox would have been, and it stuck out beyond the edge of the shelf.

Tony's heart fell to his toes.

He pictured a frantic Carla, stumbling through the room. Yanking clothes off hangers and out of drawers was one thing. But out of a hatbox? Especially when it sat right next to the shoebox of pictures ...

But he'd looked through that hatbox. Nothing but baseball caps in there.

With his gloved hands, Tony lifted down the hatbox and set it on the bed. Holding the flashlight in one hand, he rifled through its contents.

Baseball caps, just like before.

He unstacked them, examined each inside and out. A green one sat on top, yellow next, followed by others of red, blue, and black. He reached the bottom one—white—and turned it over. Again nothing.

With all caps out, the hatbox was empty.

Why had Carla Radling, running for her life, stopped to look through this stack of caps? And then taken the time to replace it on the shelf?

He stared at the box, his blood running cold. He'd missed something. More pictures? Letters? Something important, tying back to the past.

Something that could get his *son killed.*

A minute ticked by. Tony's fear melted away. In its place, a dead, iron-willed calm.

When he slipped out the back door, he relocked it, leaving no trace of his presence.

He hurried to his rental and drove to an unlit back corner of a grocery store parking lot. From there he would throw out the net to catch his target. People thought they could hide, just up and leave no trace. Didn't work that way. There were *always* traces.

Throw out the net, reel it in. Throw it out, reel it in. Keep doing that, and he'd catch Carla Radling.

First, some calls, using the second cell phone he'd bought for this job.

The people he called knew him as "Barry." They weren't surprised at his new cell phone number; his numbers were always new. Some had never seen him. They figured he was CIA, a private detective, whatever soothed their consciences. They never asked why he told them to do certain things. Barry wanted information, they gave it to him, he paid them—that's all they cared about.

Within fifteen minutes he had people watching the roads leading north, south, east, and west. They knew the make of the car, color, license number.

Next he talked to a man in Spokane. The man agreed to take up his assigned post in Kanner Lake by six a.m. He would report to "Barry" the minute he heard anything useful.

Finally, a small surveillance matter Tony took care of himself. Nothing to it, with his experience. When you're paid to dig up dirt on people, you learn a lot of tricks, and you always come prepared to play them.

That job done, he drove through the night streets, looking for Carla's car. He knew where some of her friends lived. Maybe she'd been stupid enough to run to one of them, not believing his threats. *Hope so.* Tony smirked. The way he felt tonight, he'd shoot through a whole household of people just to get to Carla Radling.

The clocked ticked toward his deadline, but Tony had no fear. He knew he would win. He always won. Good thing his orders were for the target's body never to be found. He would so enjoy getting rid of Miss Wit.

One piece at a time.

TEN

Carla hunched behind her steering wheel, back muscles tight, fingers cramped. Her left ankle ached. She'd give anything to put it up. With all the swelling, she'd kicked off her shoes long ago.

It felt like she'd been driving for hours.

At the edge of Kanner Lake, she'd nearly had a meltdown from the mere decision of which way to turn. West toward Spokane? North toward Canada? Nope—no passport. East to Montana? South toward Boise?

After a moment of paralysis, she headed toward Highway 41 and turned south. She hit Interstate 90, veered east for a few miles, then exited onto south 95 toward Moscow—a university town. Carla knew the road would be lonely and dark—the very thought made her sweat—but that also meant fewer cars. If Thornby had people watching for her Toyota, they'd more likely be on the freeway.

I hope.

Eight miles out of Coeur d'Alene, passing the Kidd Island Bay turnoff, Carla started watching the rearview mirror. Her head pounded and her imagination ran wild. Every car behind her held an insane Thornby, ready to shoot at her out the window. Or she'd be forced off the road and strangled. Tomorrow morning someone would find her purple-faced body, ripped of clothes and dignity. Within a day her friends at Java Joint would be mourning her death over their lattes and mochas. Maybe even Wilbur would shed a tear or two.

Bailey would make a small fortune on all the lattes.

Dark forested hills alternated with open fields—usually beautiful country. Now the fields rolled sullen and cold, the trees gnarled and monstrous.

Carla passed the turnoff to Windy Bay on Lake Coeur d'Alene, followed by a sign that read "Moscow, 76 miles." The road narrowed into one lane each direction. The Indian casino loomed ahead, the block-lettered sign flashing in garish yellow. Inside people drank and laughed, slot machines *chink-chinked.* A normal night—while she ran for her life.

Why was this happening now? She hadn't done *anything.*

Maybe the fact that she lived was enough. Imagine what could happen if she ever talked. And now that her enemy was rising to the greatest power he'd ever known ...

He had a lot to lose, all right.

Carla swallowed hard. Even after all the years, the thought of him brought familiar pain. She'd been so young, so naïve. He'd played her like a fiddle. She should hate him. She *did* hate him.

Most of the time.

Carla slowed through the tiny towns of Worley and Plummer. As she sped up again, bright headlights shone in her rearview mirror. A large car—maybe an SUV—loomed close behind. Was it black? Was it him? How could she know in this darkness?

Just drive.

She passed a lumber company, logs stacked like gaunt corpses against the night sky. The forest closed in, trees crowding the road. Carla gulped in air until the trees shrank back, replaced with open fields.

Another tiny town—Tensed. Weird name. A sign read "Moscow, 37 miles."

Her headlights bore into the night. Bugs hit her windshield with wet smacks.

Carla's neck felt like iron. How long could she drive like this? And to where? Her brain was a battery-drained engine, chugging ... chugging. Carla shook her head, blinked hard. She had to *think*.

Thornby knew the make of her car. Probably knew her license plate number too. What if he did have "people looking for her everywhere," as he'd threatened? What if they were watching the roads in all directions? She'd chosen the most obvious southern route.

The hair on her arms rose.

She should get off the road—as soon as possible. Hole up for the night. In the morning she'd ditch her car for a rental. That was the most important thing—getting out of this car. More important than driving all night, putting miles between herself and Kanner Lake. Tomorrow in the rental she'd drive as far as she could.

But she'd have to show her driver's license to rent a car. And use a credit card. She'd leave a trail.

And where would she go?

Carla's eyes burned. She didn't cry often—enough tears had fallen years ago to last a lifetime. But she'd never felt this alone and desperate. Not even then.

You're doing this to me, aren't You, God.

After Vesta Johnson's death, Carla had gone to Pastor Hank's church a few times. One Sunday he talked about how God could "use our past to change our present." That a person first had to ask God to forgive the past, then "walk with Him in victory over it." Sounded good, but it wasn't for her. One, her past was unforgivable. Two, God seemed to only want to punish her for it.

Haven't I been punished enough?

At ten o'clock Carla entered Moscow.

Highway 95 ran through the town. Carla glanced right and left. She had to find a motel off the highway—with a place close by where she could hide her car. She didn't dare leave it in some lit parking lot.

She passed a hardware store, a Rosauers grocery store, the Hillcrest Motel Inn, and the Mark IV Motor Inn. Highway 95 curved to the right. Carla checked cross streets. Which one to take? On impulse she turned right on Third Street and found herself on Highway 8, headed west toward Pullman, just across the Washington border. She checked her rearview mirror. Was anybody following her? Thornby might have friends in Moscow ...

Fresh fear washed over Carla. Every minute could count. She *had* to get off the streets.

Businesses grouped on her right—a Jack-in-the-Box, a car dealership, a Wendy's. Ahead she saw the sign for a Super 8 Motel, and her heart lurched. Carla veered right onto a street running by the motel, turned left into the parking lot. She cruised the lot, hoping to see that it circled the building.

It didn't.

Now what? The minutes closed in, Carla's pulse hammering. She was no longer on dark roads. These were well-lit town streets, her white car screaming to be spotted.

She continued west on Highway 8, passing up the Palouse Inn, a McDonald's, a Shucks Auto Supply. Frustration nearly closed her throat. Carla pressed a fist against the steering wheel. How much farther before she hit the west side of town? The last thing she wanted to do was turn around.

There—past the 76 gas station, across a side street from a long strip mall. A sign for University Inn, a Best Western.

Carla swerved right, then left into the motel parking lot. It was a long squat brown building, two floors. No walk-out sliding doors on the first-floor rooms—only windows. Good. She couldn't take stairs with her ankle, and a sliding ground-floor door in her room would be terrifying.

She rolled through the lot. It encircled the building, but even at the rear, she would feel too exposed to leave her car. She hesitated, then pulled back onto the side road, turning left, then left again on a dark road that ran behind the motel. She hit a cross street and found herself facing the strip mall. She checked both directions. Turn left, and in one block she'd be back on Highway 8. She turned right, then spotted a turn on her left, leading to a long delivery area running along the back of the strip mall. The area was dark and narrow, dumpsters hulking at its sides. She saw one large light pole, but no light coming from it.

Carla turned into the area.

There—on her right. Some small white building. Housing a generator of some sort? Carla headed toward it and saw she could drive all the way around it. Behind that building, on unlit asphalt with no person in sight, she found the hiding place for her car.

It would be a long, lonely walk to the lobby of the motel. With her throbbing ankle, Carla wondered if she could make it at all.

Wait. She should make sure the motel had a vacancy first. Put her suitcase in the room, then hide her car.

As the digital clock in her car flicked to 10:28, Carla pulled up in front of the Best Western. Gathering her nerve to step into light, hoping no friend of David Thornby watched her every move, she opened her car door and began her limp into the lobby.

ELEVEN

Ten-thirty. Tony had sixteen and a half hours.

He'd checked the houses of Carla's friends and found nothing. Then he began a patrol of every street, like a grid search at a crime scene. If Carla's car was parked anywhere in Kanner Lake, he'd find it.

As he turned a corner, his cell phone for "Barry" went off. He snatched it off the passenger seat. "Yeah."

"Roy here. I spotted her car."

Roy was an Idaho state trooper, working the night shift.

Tony's mouth curled. His net was working already. "Where?"

"Heading south on Highway 95, just north of Moscow."

"Just now?"

"About twenty minutes ago."

"Twenty—! What took you so long to phone?"

"I got pulled off on a call. I *am* on duty, you know."

Tony gritted his teeth. Twenty minutes—*wasted.* "Any idea where she went from there?"

"No. She could have pulled off in Moscow, headed west from there over to Pullman, or continued south on 95. But give me credit for telling you this much. Beats looking for her all over Canada."

Tony grunted.

"I expect my money."

Yeah, yeah. "You'll get it. Just keep looking."

"Count on it."

"Can you search the hotel parking lots in Moscow?"

"For awhile. The town's not my jurisdiction, so I can't be obvious about patrolling the streets. And I'm off at eleven. Have to get home after that. My wife's nine months pregnant, and she'll have a fit if I don't show up on time."

"Okay, okay, do what you can. I'm on my way." Tony pulled a one-handed U-turn in the middle of the street. "How long will it take me to get there from Kanner Lake?"

"Two hours plus—if you really hoof it."

Two hours. *Please, Miss Wit, stop in Moscow.*

"Okay. I'm on my way. How do I get there?"

Roy gave him directions.

Hope surged. Tony flipped the phone closed and dropped it on the passenger seat. He drove to the nearest intersection, then turned right, pulled toward the south as surely as metal to magnet.

TWELVE

Behind the Best Western counter a young girl with long blonde hair and flawless skin gazed at Carla as she approached. She wore a pin with her first name—*Chrissy.* Prickles danced up Carla's spine. She imagined some friend of Thornby showing Chrissy her photo—"Have you seen this woman?"

"Looks like you really hurt your foot." Chrissy gestured toward Carla's ankle.

Carla managed a shrug. "I twisted it. Just need to get off it as soon as possible."

"I'm so sorry. Let's get you checked in right away."

Carla held onto the counter, weight on her right foot as Chrissy accepted her credit card for processing. Too late Carla remembered she should have hit an ATM for cash. Already she was leaving a trail. What if Thornby could watch her bank accounts? Maybe she should just leave right now—

Stop it. The transaction wouldn't go through until tomorrow. By that time she'd be long gone.

Chrissy looked up. "I assume you'd like a first-floor room."

"Please."

"Queen bed all right?"

Anything, just hurry! "Yes. Great."

"Nonsmoking?"

Carla's fingers pressed harder against the smooth counter. "Yes."

Chrissy nodded and checked her computer. Carla struggled to stay calm. The world beyond the entrance was a looming monster at her back. She couldn't help throwing glances over her shoulder.

"You worried about your car out there?" Chrissy asked.

"Oh. I just ... didn't want it to be in anyone's way."

"No problem, there's plenty of room for someone to drive around it."

Carla nodded.

Chrissy slipped a key card into the machine for programming, then handed it to Carla with a smile. "There you go. Probably easier to drive to the next outside door and park." She pointed in the general direction. "Inside the building, turn right, and your room's three doors down."

Carla managed a tight smile. "Thank you."

"Just a sec, I'll get the door for you." Chrissy came around the counter and pushed open the glass door, stepping aside so Carla could hobble through. Carla repressed a cringe. She'd wanted to check the area before exiting.

"Okay. Thanks."

She stepped outside, muscles rigid, eyes darting right and left. She saw no one.

Carla slipped into her car and drove down to the next entrance. There she parked, heart hammering. She slid the diary from under the seat and stuck it in her purse before getting out. Then lifted her red suitcase from the passenger seat and pulled it across the pavement and into the building. At her room she shoved the suitcase and her purse inside, leaving only her car keys and the key card in her hand. How she longed to collapse on the bed, leave her car where it sat. But she didn't dare.

Back down the corridor she limped. Stepped outside after checking in all directions and slid into her car.

She drove back to the small white building and parked. Turned off the Toyota's engine and lights.

The world fell into a darkness that would swallow her whole. Carla could hear her own hitched breathing—a sound of nerve-wracking fear.

Her hand slid to the door.

She couldn't open it.

A dozen new imaginings snarled all threads of logic in Carla's brain. Hands reaching for her the minute she got out, the growl of an attack dog, a gunshot piercing her chest. David Thornby was *here*. He'd been near the whole time, smirking as she placed herself where no one would witness her death.

Carla's chest tightened, the air in the car thickening. She longed to open the window, feel freshness on her cheeks—but her killer waited out there ...

Girl, get a grip. You want to sleep here all night?

She took a deep breath and pushed the door open. Coolness rushed at her as she pushed to her feet, weight on the right leg. With a shaking finger she hit the button to lock her car doors. Painfully, wishing she could run, she began making her way back toward the motel. Around to the front of the white building, down the rear delivery road for the strip mall. Every shuffled footstep echoed like calls in a canyon: *Here I am—come kill me!* Carla crossed the street. She reached the road running behind the Best Western, a tiny, lone figure in the looming night. The pain in her ankle grew. If only she had a pair of crutches, even one. Carla slowed, feeling sweat pop out on her forehead. For a crazy moment she considered giving up. Just lying down right there on the dirty, dark road.

Sure, babe, with the motel and shelter in sight.

Determination urged her on. She clutched her car keys harder until the metal bit into her palm, her key card in her other hand. Tears burned her eyes at each step, the motel so close, yet so far away.

An eternity passed before she reached the outside door to the motel, drew it back, and stumbled inside. Then down the corridor, and finally, weak-limbed and shaking, across the threshold into her room.

She closed the door and slumped against it, flooded with an almost sickening relief.

Carla picked up her purse and pulled her suitcase farther into the room. Leaving the bag standing upright, she tossed her purse onto the bed, then sank down beside it. Turned lengthwise and hoisted her legs up. She didn't dare examine her throbbing ankle. Seeing the amount of swelling would only make the pain seem worse. She knew she should ice it, but she hadn't seen an ice machine on the way to her room and couldn't bear to get up again.

Tonight, tomorrow, if she came face-to-face with Thornby and needed to run—she'd never make it.

Carla melted into the bed, time sliding by in a hazy blur. At some point she pulled over her purse and slid out her cell phone. Held it in her hand. How she wanted to call someone for help, ask for advice. But her attacker's words pounded in her head. *Any friend who helps you is dead.*

She tossed the cell to the foot of the bed.

Carla rolled to one side, burying her face in the bedcovers. For a long time she struggled to untangle her thoughts. What was she going to do tomorrow? Rent a car, yes ... but then?

She moaned. If only she knew why this was happening now. If she knew *why*, maybe she could do something to save her life. Say the right words, pledge some action ...

She dragged in a breath and rolled to her back. Her gaze landed on the diary sticking out of her purse. Carla stared at it dully. Thornby had come looking for anything linking to her past—she knew that because of the photos he'd taken. He probably thought he'd found everything. He couldn't know about the diary. She'd never mentioned it to a soul.

Carla gazed at the small journal, remembering the pain and suffering those pages held. She hadn't been able to even look at it in years. Maybe some entry contained the information she needed. Had she made some threat years ago they now had to silence? Done something that suddenly unnerved them?

Carla's shoulders drooped. Didn't they think she'd lost enough?

With a sigh, she pulled the diary from her purse. For all the emotional weight of it, she was amazed at its lightness. She gazed at the now faded yellow daisies on its cover, remembering. Inside that cover years ago she'd drawn a heart containing the words "Carla Radling loves Scott Cambry."

Scott. Even now her heart panged at the mere thought of his name.

She turned the diary over, rubbing a thumb against the fabric. The words inside contained the culmination of her life as a teenager—her dreams, her soaring hopes. Her crushed spirit. Everything she was today—and was not—had been forged within the glowing heat of its pages. The thought of reliving those terrible moments now, tonight, after all she'd already been through, filled her with dread.

Yeah, well. Watching TV isn't exactly a picker upper either.

She laid the diary on the nightstand.

Carla sat up and arranged the two pillows against the headboard. Then peeled down the bedspread, slipping it beneath her body, and balled it up as elevation for her left foot. She leaned back against the pillows, doing her best to find a comfortable position. Then with a deep breath, she picked up the diary and opened her soul to the summer when it all began. When she was sixteen—and met *him* for the first time.

THIRTEEN

Can you believe it—I got a job for the summer! And *what* a job! I'll be working as a clerk/assistant for Bryson Hanley! Yes, *the* Bryson Hanley!

Mom tried to bring me down as usual. Said who was I, getting so uppity that I should think I can keep a job in a state senator's office. Said I'd type letters full of mistakes and file documents that would never be found. Isn't she just the Carla cheerleading squad. Got herself new pom-poms and everything.

Just because I don't want to spend my life waitressing in some dirt-crusted, smoky little diner.

Anyway, the job. I don't know much about politics, but I learned a lot just this afternoon from Paul Jilke, this serious-looking, long-faced guy who runs Senator Hanley's campaign office. (He reminds me of a Muppet. Jilke, I mean.) Senator Hanley is a Democrat, "representing Washington District #1," Jilke told me (I'd better not call him that to his face), and the state legislature has finished meeting for the year. So now Senator Hanley's back from Olympia, working at his real estate development stuff in Terrin. But what he's really focusing on is his 1992 run for the US Senate. And that's where I come in—as an "aide" for his campaign. Is that cool or what! I'll be doing mailings and general office work. I really impressed Jilke because I can type ninety words a minute. (Who'd have guessed old Mrs. Delligouser's typing class would actually amount to something?)

First thing I did when I heard I got the job was run all the way to Mary Kay's house to tell her. She jumped up and down with me. Mary Kay knows how much I need the money. For once I'll be able to buy some decent clothes. Act like somebody. I'm tired of looking like the old worn country girl with an emphysemic mother and no dad. Not that my real friends care, but it would be nice to show the Snooty High Societies a thing or two in my junior year.

I spent an hour telling Mary Kay about the office and Jilke and my own little desk in the corner. I swear I sat in that chair and felt so grown-up. Kind of like the first time I held my driver's license in my hand. Suddenly I'd jumped into another era. Sixteen going on twenty-five. Out in the world, with nobody to tell me what to do. And a real *job*.

Jilke and I share a space that's just next door to Senator Hanley's own huge private suite. We don't even have to walk down the hall to see him—there's a door that leads straight from his office into ours.

I told Mary Kay about meeting Senator Hanley. But I couldn't bring myself to tell her everything. And that was strange, holding something back from her. I had to work hard not to show it on my face. But ...

How many times have I seen Bryson Hanley's picture in the paper and around town? Not to mention his name on the local news. Terrin's own "Golden Boy." Mr. Destined for Greatness. Not to mention a rich businessman. And really good-looking, for an old guy. (That's me talking, not the papers.) He'll put this Seattle suburb on the map, they say. "Charismatic," that's what they call him. And he's always looked it too. Even on TV, you can tell how he charms people.

Let me tell you something. "Charismatic" doesn't *begin* to do the real man justice.

After interviewing me for over an hour, Jilke told me to wait by his desk. He knocked on the door leading to Senator Hanley's office, then went inside. I got all nervous, hoping, *hoping* I'd land the job. After a couple minutes Jilke stuck his head out the door and waved me into Senator Hanley's office. I nearly fainted. I hadn't expected to meet him so soon.

I stood up, legs shaking, and smoothed my skirt. Suddenly wishing I'd had money for a new dress. And did my hair look okay? Next thing I knew, I was standing before Senator Hanley's desk and Jilke was introducing us. Senator Hanley stretched out his arm, and I managed to stick out mine—and we shook hands.

I swear there was heat in those fingers.

Senator Hanley's probably about six feet—six inches taller than I am. But he looked like a tower. And his shoulders aren't real broad, either, but he still made me think of a linebacker in full gear. There's just something about him. This *power.* It *surges* from him. And those eyes. They're milk chocolate brown and so very deep. You could swim in those eyes. When he looked at me and smiled, I felt like I was the most important person in the world.

Now I know what they're talking about when they say Bryson Hanley is destined for greatness. The man could charm a snake. If a politician's career is all about getting people to like you and vote for you—this guy's got it made. One look at him, and forget voting—I'd go to the moon for him.

This is what I couldn't tell Mary Kay. I mean, the guy's over forty. I have never looked at somebody that old and thought a thing about him. But Bryson Hanley just makes you feel special.

"Carla Radling, is it?" Senator Hanley said as our fingers still touched.

I managed a yes, then clamped my mouth shut. Last thing I needed was to fall into my smart-alecky routine to hide my nervousness.

He took back his hand. "Welcome. Paul tells me you interviewed very well. I'll be glad to have you around for the summer."

He has this crease on the right side of his face when he smiles. Sort of a half dimple. And his smile is almost playful – like he knows a secret about you but promises not to tell.

I'll be glad to have you. Not *we'll* be glad.

"Thank you."

We talked for a few minutes. He asked me about my parents (I tried to make Mom sound decent, but I don't think I fooled him) and my school. If I knew what college I wanted to go to, what I wanted to study. I answered pretty well, if I do say so myself. In fact, I kinda gained my ground as we went along. Funny, but I think he sensed that. Don't ask me how I know. It was just this feeling between us.

Scott's real happy for me. He and I have been going out for three months now, and it's the first time he's seen me with a job. He took me out for pizza tonight, then we hung around his house until eleven o'clock. His parents were out, and his sister was staying with a friend for the night. Perfect time for us to be alone.

Now I need to go to bed so I'm fresh for the morning. Already got my clothes laid out. Can't wait to start.

Something tells me this job is going to change my life.

FOURTEEN

Twelve-thirty. Less than fifteen hours.

Tony rolled through Moscow, narrowed eyes flicking from the Durango's navigation system to the quiet streets. Thanks to the pepper spray his face was still red, and now his nose ran like crazy. He'd made a pit stop to buy two boxes of tissues. On the passenger seat sat the first open box and a plastic grocery bag now filling with used wads.

The annoying symptoms only made him madder. He couldn't wait to find Carla Radling.

A state trooper stationed twenty miles south on Highway 95 had informed Tony that Miss Wit had not been spotted. Which meant she'd likely either stopped in Moscow for the night or she'd headed west on Highway 8.

Tony had programmed the GPS to flag all hotels in the area. One by one, if it took all night, he would cruise their parking lots, looking for a white Toyota.

Three times Tony had snatched up his phone to call Miss Wit. How he'd love to hear the panic in her voice. But each time he'd put the cell back down. Better not let on just how close he was.

He'd started at the Hillcrest Motel on 95, then on to the Mark IV Motor Inn and down the highway. At the numbered streets downtown he had to make a decision. Sixth Street would take him into the university. No use going there. Looked like the lower numbers would be his best bet.

As he drove through motel parking lots he imagined Timmy at home, sleeping in his small bed with the Superman sheets and spread. He'd be wearing his red soft jammies, hugging Tito the Bear. Robyn, who believed Tony was working on a case for his CIA job—which he could never talk about—would be in their room curled up on her side of the bed, one hand reaching toward his empty half.

Then he pictured gut-wrenching scenes of his family if he didn't find his target.

Tony's fingers curled into the wheel.

The net, man. Just pull in your net.

He turned onto Third Street—Highway 8. Passed various businesses on the right until he came to a Super 8 Motel. He pulled into the lot, rolling past the cars. At each white sedan he shone his flashlight beam on the license plate.

Every time he was disappointed, his anger at Carla Radling simmered a little higher.

The Super 8 parking lot was small. He pulled out of it and headed west on the highway.

Tony was used to killing quickly. Get in, do the job, get out. Not this time. Carla Radling deserved to suffer for putting his family in danger. Tony wiped his runny nose and dreamed of taking her apart limb by limb.

Next on his right—the Palouse Inn. He cruised its lot but saw no white Toyota. Breathing a curse he turned back to the highway, headed for the next motel. Soon he saw the sign for University Inn.

FIFTEEN

At one o'clock, Carla was still reading.

The going was slow. There were a lot of entries—she'd written in the diary practically every day. But certain entries were so wrenching, she had to stop and settle her emotions. Wipe away tears. And every little sound outside the room scared her. What if Thornby showed up at her door? Twice she started to get up and flee the motel. But then what? Spend the night by herself on some dark road until she could change cars? At least here she was locked in the room, close to other people. Close to a landline phone.

As for the diary, it was a wonder she still had it at all. In the past sixteen years she'd come close to burning it at least a dozen times. But for some crazy reason she'd never been able to let it go. The pages held memories too painful to read, but they were her *life*. They made her what she was today. Sometimes she'd thought, *This is all I'll ever have.*

Carla sighed. *This* is why she had lived her life so close to people, yet so far. Making friends—to a point. Laughing, teasing. But nothing closer, no real intimacy.

She hadn't shed a tear at her mother's funeral ten years ago. Okay, maybe two. Not because she would miss the unloving woman who smoked herself right into the grave. Because she missed the mother she never had.

As for men, forget it.

Sure, she'd had a few relationships. Burt when she was twenty-five. He'd lasted almost a year before moving across the country to a new job. Convenient, since she was losing interest. He was too charming—like the man of her memories. You couldn't rely on those charming types.

If she hadn't learned that sixteen years ago, she'd certainly learned it tonight.

Then Alex came along when she was twenty-eight. She'd moved to Kanner Lake by then. He lived in Spokane. She couldn't trust him either. That's when she realized the sad truth. She couldn't really believe in *any* man.

Or was it herself she couldn't trust?

Carla gazed at the diary. Hard to believe such a little thing could bring down one of the most powerful men in the country. Soon to be *the* most powerful man. Washington's "Golden Boy," their US state senator Bryson Hanley. The man who, most pundits declared and polls showed, was destined to win the 2008 presidential election. His nomination to the Democratic ticket was almost a certainty.

Golden Boy. Yeah, right. The man who oozed empathy for the American people. Who would lead this country in the dark age of terrorists and who fought for the common man. Who stood for children's welfare and women's rights, who supported education and pledged medical care for all.

The family man, handsome, smiling, with his beautiful wife, daughter, and son by his side. Each time Carla saw Bryson Hanley's picture—and it was everywhere—the painful memories stabbed. "Our lives are an open book," he was fond of saying on talk shows. "I've been in politics all my life. You know what you're getting when you vote for me."

Yes, Carla knew the man the nation would be getting.

She tapped a finger against the diary. So far she'd found no clue as to why her death was suddenly so important. Maybe it was just ... overdue. The man whose life was an open book had decided there were a few pages best ripped out.

But, Bryson, don't you see? I would never tell. Think how it would hurt others. Think what it would do to my own life.

Fourteen months ago she'd seen it happen to Paige Williams, a newcomer to Kanner Lake. Paige had fled a haunting past only to find herself the fascination of the entire country. How much more attention would Carla face herself as the woman who brought down Washington's Golden Boy?

No way. Even now, with her life on the line, *no one* would ever see this diary. She couldn't bear for anyone to know its secrets. Not for herself, and not for Scott, wherever he was today. He never deserved to be hurt. How cruel it would be, sixteen years later, to see him thrust into a salacious limelight—and through no fault of his own. Carla felt sick at the thought. Maybe he had a family, children. Think how they would feel.

And think of Bryson's kids—Brittany and Benson. How awful it would be for them to hear the truth about their father. Brittany was now almost sixteen, the very age Carla had been when she'd poured out her heart on these pages. She couldn't bear to see another teenager hurt as she had been.

Carla shifted her left leg. It throbbed a little less. She laid the open diary on the bed and raised up to peer at her ankle. Still swollen. Man. She dreaded walking on it tomorrow.

She fell back against the pillows and picked up the diary. A strand of hair fell across her eyes, and she nudged it away. Muscles still tense, ears cocked for any noise outside, Carla turned a page—and read on.

SIXTEEN

I've been at my job over a week now. Today Mr. Hanley's wife came in.

She's pretty. Dark hair – not black like mine, but a deep brown. A little shorter than me. Walks like a princess.

Jilke introduced us, and for a second she just stared. Was my nose on crooked? Too much mascara? What?

"Nice to meet you." She smiled tightly and lifted her chin.

Yeah, right.

"How long have you been working for my husband?"

My husband. Okay, now I was getting her.

"Just a week." I kept my voice light. "I feel more like I'm working for Mr. Jilke, though. I don't work directly with Senator Hanley all that often."

Hey, I need this job. No harm in smoothing over Mrs. "My-Husband." All the same, I swear I came close to calling Senator Hanley by his first name, just to needle her.

She gave me another fake smile, then went into Senator Hanley's office. Didn't come out for half an hour. I was addressing invitations to a fund-raising dinner, but I kept listening for her. I wouldn't feel right until she was gone. Why were they talking so long? Didn't they see each other at night?

Last week I studied old newspapers at the library. I found out Senator Hanley is forty-two. His wife is thirty-six. They don't have kids. Don't know why. Maybe they're just too busy. Maybe she's too uptight.

The Hanley campaign is going well. Jilke says next year's election for US senator is "in the bag." So why does Jilke run himself like a chicken with its head cut off? He works twelve hours a day. Never takes a break. Eats lunch at his desk and drinks coffee all day. He's always on the phone. Sometimes I think I'm gonna go crazy with all his yakking. The man's got no life, that's for sure. Bryson Hanley *is* his life. Jilke isn't married. I think he's around thirty-five because he told me what year he graduated from high school. He's been the Hanley campaign manager for eight years. Helped Bryson Hanley earn his state senate seat. Next it's the US Senate—which means Washington, DC. All the bigwigs. Then, if things go like he says, some day it will be the White House. If you ask me, Jilke wants to run a presidential campaign more than anything in the world.

What I told Mrs. My-Husband is true. I don't see Bryson Hanley nearly enough. To keep this job, it's Jilke I need to satisfy.

So I keep my head down and work hard. Use my best handwriting, type letters carefully, make sure the documents I copy aren't missing any pages. And remember to call the man *Mr.* Jilke to his face. He tells me I'm doing good. But he says it almost reluctantly, like he'd love to catch me in something. Don't know why. He reminds me of Mom—not believing I can do anything I set my mind to, that I can *be* somebody.

Catherine's her first name. Mrs. My-Husband, I mean. When she came out of Senator Hanley's office, she didn't look at me. Her lips were pressed, and she clutched her white leather purse like it was trying to escape. Jilke stared at her like he was trying to figure if she'd upset his man Bryson. Mrs. My-Husband left, and Senator Hanley came out of his office a minute later. Gave Jilke a worn look. Then he turned to me—and smiled. A smile that said: *She's a pain sometimes, but I feel better just seeing you work so hard for me.*

I swear that's what it said. I think Jilke saw it too, 'cause he gave me the eye after Senator Hanley went back in his office.

I worked even harder the rest of the day.

SEVENTEEN

Tony wiped his nose as he turned into the Best Western, heading to the back of the hotel. Not many cars. The parking lot lights shone on a few here and there, pulled into spaces lining the building. No lights on in any rooms.

No white Toyota.

He drove around to the front. More cars here, but still not many. He passed a shiny new black Ford pickup, a red Honda, an Explorer, two Jeeps—all clustered around the entrances to the long building.

Dim light glowed through the window of a downstairs room.

Tony slowed, staring at the closed curtains. His eyes flicked to the nearest cars, some distance away. None was parked at the entrance closest to this room.

Strange.

He tapped his thumb against the steering wheel.

The customer could have parked at the back of the building and entered from that side. Tony tried to remember the closest entrance in the rear. Had a car been parked near it?

He leaned his elbow on the console and considered the building. Beginning closest to the lobby, he counted windows. The lit room was number ten.

Tony drove around to the back of the motel again and counted off ten rooms. The nearest entrance was three windows down, after room thirteen.

Two cars—a Camaro and a Suburban—were parked on either side of the door.

He spat out a curse. How he'd hoped to find nothing. How he wanted reason to believe Miss Wit was in that room …

Tony's nose dripped more snot. He yanked out a tissue and swiped at it.

Turning the wheel hard, he scratched off a U-turn and headed out of the parking lot. His thoughts flashed to Carla Radling's bedroom. The photos he'd found, the hatbox out of place …

What had she taken? And just as important—had she given it to someone else?

Back on Highway 8, Tony picked up his "Barry" cell phone. Time to call for reinforcements. He *would* find Carla Radling—if not tonight, tomorrow morning at the latest.

And that's a promise, Miss Wit.

EIGHTEEN

The night wore on, and still Carla read. Sometime during the early morning hours she laid the diary down, her head and heart too full to go on. For a long time she stared at the wall, thinking ... remembering.

The things she had done. The choices she'd made. As terrible as her current situation was, a part of her whispered that she deserved it. That, in fact, she should be glad she'd managed to survive, unexposed, for this long. Now she'd been driven out of her home, the life she'd built—and where could she possibly go that would be safe?

She'd been driven then too—by desire and the desperate need to *be* somebody.

But you didn't have to give in.

True. She *had* been manipulated. But in the end, the choices were hers. And for the worst decision of all, she had no one but herself to blame.

Sick with grief but knowing she should continue, Carla picked up the diary and read on. Slowly. One page, some parts even one line at a time.

Remembering.

Reliving.

She finished shortly before five a.m., the diary like a dead weight in her hands.

Exhausted, her gut twisting and unshed tears burning her eyes, Carla laid the diary on her chest. Her brain could not take one more thought, one more emotion. She stared ahead, unseeing, her eyes growing heavy . . . and finally sank into a sleep filled with dreams from the diary.

NINETEEN

Two weeks. I've only been working for Bryson Hanley for two weeks, but it feels like forever. What did I do before I got this job?

I love what I'm doing. Well, I don't like Jilke very much – in fact, he almost scares me. He's so protective and all of Senator Hanley. But I love learning how to do all the stuff in the office. And I really like talking to Senator Hanley whenever I can. He makes me feel good about me.

Not that I get to talk to him very much. Jilke watches me like a hawk.

Today I took my camera to work, hoping to get a picture with Senator Hanley. Wouldn't you know, people were in and out all morning. One meeting after another. Then he went out with two men and their wives for lunch. I think they were rich and give him campaign money or something. The women just had that look about them. I can always spot a rich woman. It's not that they're all cold and huffy like Mrs. My-Husband. Some are pretty nice. I can tell they have money by their good haircuts and their clothes and makeup. They just look classy.

I want to be like that some day.

Anyway, the pictures. After lunch Senator Hanley was finally alone, and his door was open. I sneaked the camera from my purse and hurried toward his office. Jilke's head jerked around.

"What are you doing?"

I raised the camera, talking loud enough so Senator Hanley would hear. "Just wanted to take a picture for my scrapbook."

Jilke gave me one of his looks. "Senator Hanley's had a busy day; I don't want you—"

"Come on, Paul, give her a break." Senator Hanley's voice sounded from around the corner. "I can take one minute."

I heard his desk chair squeak, then his footsteps across the carpet. I stood frozen, watching Jilke and trying not to smirk. Senator Hanley stuck his head around the door. "Come on in, Carla. Paul, come take our picture."

Okay, I smirked then for sure. I turned away so Jilke wouldn't see, but I think Senator Hanley did. He gave me this knowing little smile.

Jilke heaved a sigh and pushed to his feet like he'd just been told to walk barefoot over nails. Without a word he headed over to me and held out his hand for the camera. I kept my voice real light while I told him what button to press and how the flash worked.

We ended up taking six pictures. Three of them were of Senator Hanley and me. We stood in front of his desk, and he put his arm around my shoulders. He smiled and I smiled. Jilke didn't smile, but he did push the camera button. That hand around my shoulder only lasted a minute, but it just ... felt right being there. That's the best way I can put it. It felt right.

Then Senator Hanley let me take a few shots of him at his desk. Jilke huffed back to his own chair. Senator Hanley pretended like he was reading a file or writing something. Like those pictures you'd see in the newspaper—but these are *mine.* Between the pictures, though, he'd raise his eyes and look at me. And one side of his mouth would curve, like he was giving me this private communication. I got bold and gave him one of my "well-ain't-life-something" grins. He laughed, then tilted his head in Jilke's direction like he was saying, *What's the matter with that guy, anyway?*

When we were through, he winked at me. "Carla, I like the way you take on the world."

And I thought—*I like the way you make my world feel.*

TWENTY

"Where *is* Carla? I swear, I'm gonna strangle that kid." Wilbur Hucks drummed his gnarled fingers on the Java Joint counter, his wizened mouth pulled in and a deep frown on his face. Jake Tremaine hunched on his usual stool beside Wilbur nodding with animation, the ever-present red baseball cap shoved low on his head. "Ya just can't depend on people anymore, I'm telling ya." Wilbur aimed these words in Jake's direction. "She *promised* she'd be here to help me!"

Bailey Truitt took the tirade in stride. She'd been hearing it for an hour now. And she did hope Carla showed up soon. What could be taking her so long? It wasn't like her to be late. Bailey had enough to do behind the counter and was very happy to let Carla type Wilbur's blog post while he dictated. They tended to argue the entire way through a post—brassy Carla never did let Wilbur give her any flak without returning it doubled—but at least it got Wilbur off Bailey's back.

Turning toward the espresso machine to make a nonfat latte, Bailey spoke in the old curmudgeon's direction. "She'll be here, Wilbur, and I'm sure with a very good reason for being late. Maybe that client she took to Edna San's mansion yesterday wants to buy it. Wouldn't *that* be something. She'd get the whole six percent commission after trying for over a year to sell that place."

Wilbur grunted. "Well, I've lived here my whole life. I don't cotton to some rich smart aleck coming along and thinking he's more important than me."

Boy, he *was* grumpy this morning. Maybe a free pastry would sweeten him up a little.

"How do you know what he thinks?" Jake elbowed Wilbur. "Just 'cause he's rich don't make him smart-alecky."

"What do *you* know about bein' rich?"

"Nothing myself, but my cousin's swimming in money, and he's decent enough."

"Then why don't you get *him* to come buy Edna San's house? Cash down. So Carla can stop fretting about that place and start paying attention to the more important things in life. Like typing my blog post."

Bailey refilled Wilbur's coffee cup. No "fancy milk drinks" for him—just straight, strong coffee. Black. "Give her a few more minutes, okay? If she doesn't show up soon, I'll call her. In the meantime keep gabbing with Jake. That'll keep you occupied."

"Whatdya think I've been doing all this time, woman! I've been gabbing enough to talk Jake's huge ears off."

Jake sniffed. "Yeah, but all you been talking about is Carla." He slid a hand up the side of his head. "And for your information, I've seen ears a lot bigger than mine."

"Where, on a sow?"

"Wilbur." Bailey frowned. "Now you're just being mean."

"Aw, I'm used to it." Jake's buggy eyes glanced toward the ceiling. His left hand explored the girth of his ear.

Bailey turned from the espresso machine and poured the latte into a middler cup. "Bev, your drink's done."

Across the café, Bev Trexel rose from her and Angie Brendt's usual table. Bev looked particularly stern this morning, aiming one of her disapproving stares at Wilbur's back as she approached. Both retired schoolteachers, Bev and Angie were best friends but couldn't have been more different. Bev's genuine concern for others was blanketed by a Miss Manners sense of protocol—a standard that Wilbur Hucks *never* met—while Angie tended to laugh things off. Giggle was more like it.

"Thank you, Bailey." Bev accepted her drink with her chin held extra high—a message to Wilbur that he'd managed to grate her nerves more than usual this morning.

Wilbur slid a sideways look in her direction but otherwise ignored her until she was on the way back to her table. Then he rocked his head side to side, flapping his mouth in a mocking silent harangue. Bev, all too used to his gyrations, didn't even need to turn around. "I know what you're doing, Wilbur Hucks."

He folded his arms in a huff.

For a moment it was silent in the café, save for the quiet tap of S-Man's computer keys. Ted Dawson, affectionately known as S-Man, hunched over his laptop, intense concentration knitting his dark eyebrows as he edited his science fiction manuscript, *Starfire*. After five months of rejections from agents, he was close to landing one—if he could fix a few "weaknesses" in the story.

Wilbur checked the round-faced clock on the wall and sighed. "After nine-thirty. She's over an *hour* late. I came here all fired up to write my post. It was going to be a zinger too. Now my creativity's draining away by the second."

"Why don't you ask Bev to type for you?" Bailey offered Wilbur a teasing smile. "I'm sure she'd just love to."

Jake snorted. "That'll be the day."

"Will you call Carla now, Bailey?" Wilbur sounded petulant. "I've waited long enough."

Bailey *was* getting a little worried. Carla would usually call if she was going to be late for an appointment—even just a blog-typing commitment to Wilbur. She had a strong responsibility ethic. "All right, I'll call."

She turned toward the phone, near the wall at the end of the L-shaped counter. First she dialed Carla's office at the realty company, only to hear that Carla hadn't come in yet. Next she dialed Carla's home. No answer.

Maybe Carla was in her car somewhere. Bailey would have to check the Rolodex back in her office for Carla's cell phone number. She headed around the long counter. "Wilbur, I'm going to—"

The phone rang, and Bailey turned back to answer it. "Maybe that's her now." She picked up the receiver. "Good morning, Java Joint."

"Hello. Would this be ... is this Bailey?" Not Carla. A woman's voice. Low and breathless.

"Yes."

"I'm sorry to bother you, but I need to get hold of Carla Radling."

Get in line. "I haven't seen her this morning. Do you have her office number? I don't think she's there yet, but you could leave a message for her."

"I've called there. But I need to talk to her *now.* Could you possibly give me her home number?"

Bailey hesitated. "I'm sorry. Who am I speaking with?"

A pause. "Ellie."

Bailey waited for the last name. None was given. And something told her to doubt the first. Pinpricks danced up Bailey's back. Carla not showing up—now this. Something didn't feel right.

"*Ellie,*" Bailey emphasized the name, "I'm very sorry, but I'm not able to give out someone's home phone."

"How about a cell number?"

Unlike most realtors, who advertised their cell as well as office numbers, Carla had always chosen not to give hers out to just anybody. She was a private person. Bailey and all who knew her had simply accepted that. "I don't—"

"Look, I *have* to talk to her as soon as possible. It's *important*."

The edge in the woman's tone only increased Bailey's tension. She worked to keep her voice even. "Carla will probably be here soon; we were expecting her quite a while ago. Would you like to leave a message?"

"You mean you don't know where she *is*?"

Real fear hitched the words. Bailey's thoughts spun. "I'm sure she's fine. I just—"

The woman gasped. "I have to go." Her words spilled over each other. "Tell Carla someone she knew years ago has to talk to her. I'll call back."

The line clicked.

Bailey pulled the receiver away from her ear and stared at it. Trying to tell herself this was some crazy coincidence, and Carla was all right. But Bailey couldn't forget the phone call six months ago that had changed her world—Kanner Lake's world—with word of a terrible tragedy. She'd stood in this very place, staring at the same wall ...

Slowly, she hung up the phone.

"Somebody else looking for Carla?" Wilbur's irritated voice cut through Bailey's thoughts. "They can just wait. I get her first."

Bailey pasted a smile on her face before turning around. No need to get Wilbur any more riled. "You two hold the fort down, okay?" She tapped her palm on the Formica, then headed toward the opening of the counter. "I'm going to look up Carla's cell phone in my office."

"Tell her she owes me a week's worth of coffee," Wilbur growled. "And when you come back you can fetch me one of those cinnamon rolls, heated. Put that on her tab too."

No need. Bailey would gladly give him the pastry free. She just wanted to hear Carla's voice—safe and sound.

Oh, Lord, please watch over her, wherever she is.

TWENTY-ONE

Carla woke with a start.

Her bleary gaze landed on a blanket in filtered daylight ... her left arm ... the diary. It was lying facedown on her chest, her fingers spread over it as if in protection.

Had she heard something?

Carla's heart drummed. She raised her head from the pillow, cocked it. A rush of awareness flooded her body with heat. What had she done, wasting the whole night so close to Kanner Lake? Thornby could have found her car hours ago. Why hadn't she driven across two states while she had the chance?

A knock at the door.

Carla sprang off the bed. Intense pain shot up her left ankle. She cried out, listed to one side, and crashed to the floor.

A harder knock. "Housekeeping!"

The rattle of the door.

Carla sat up. Her head fell back and she dragged in air. She slumped against the bed, one hand against her roiling stomach. For a moment her throat refused to form words.

Behind her, the door opened. How in the *world* had she forgotten to put on the chain lock?

She twisted to look over her shoulder toward the entryway. "Hello, I'm still here! Be checked out in an hour or so."

A short, red-cheeked woman leaned in, staring at Carla across the bed as if she'd never seen anyone sit on the floor before. "You okay, miss?"

"Yes. Fine." Carla managed a sickly smile.

The housekeeper held her gaze a moment longer, clearly unconvinced. Then she drew a deep breath, making her nostrils flare. "Sorry to bother you."

She backed up and pulled the door shut.

Carla exhaled and closed her eyes. Rested her head against the side of the bed. Her ankle throbbed and hunger pricked at her. She'd had nothing to eat since lunch yesterday.

She checked the clock radio on the nightstand: 9:54. Carla gasped. Almost ten o'clock! She had to get *out* of here. Rent a car and drive ... somewhere.

Hopelessness washed over her. She was so tired, physically and emotionally. Too much pain from reliving her past last night. All the manipulation, the lies. The wrong choices. Reading her teenage thoughts now, with the wisdom of an adult, she was amazed at what she'd survived. As the story played out, she'd watched the confident, brassy girl she'd once been reduced to a mere shell. Broken, no friends, no one to turn to.

And still the scenes haunted her. Even in the terror of running for her life, Carla knew those vivid pages from her past would flash through her mind all day. One word, a phrase, some object would be all it would take to set the scenes rolling. Worse, the terrible mistakes she'd made all those years ago would now affect innocent people. She knew her friends would be worried about her.

Bryson Hanley. How could such a brilliant politician, a man with the world ahead of him, take such risks?

No wonder she was in danger. Reading that journal had made her realize what a miracle it was they'd left her alone this long. If they'd known about the diary, she'd have been dead long ago. It was proof of all that happened.

Fear pushed Carla off the floor and onto her feet. She rested her weight on her right leg. No time to eat now. No time for a shower or makeup or change of clothes.

She limped into the bathroom, splashed her face, avoiding her reflection in the mirror. Pain still pounded her ankle, even though it had been elevated all night. How much worse would it be hours from now? She should get the thing wrapped.

Back near the bed, she snatched up the diary and stuffed it deep inside her purse. She flapped the blanket and sheets around, unballed the coverlet, seeking anything else she might have unpacked. What had she missed? Her brain wouldn't focus.

With each passing minute Carla's suspicion of the hotel housekeeper grew. And if not that woman, maybe the clerk at the desk last night, who'd seen Carla's name on her credit card. What if Thornby came around this morning? She'd left a trail, the last thing she should have done.

Carla's hands trembled.

Sudden memories flooded her. She held out her shaking left hand, picturing a delicate ruby heart ring upon her finger ...

Stop it!

She swallowed hard, tossed down the bedcover. She *had* to focus. Did she have everything? She dared not leave any item behind that could lead to her.

Carla scanned the room. Saw nothing.

Okay, you're fine—just go.

She picked up her purse and began pulling her suitcase toward the door, trying not to wince.

Somewhere behind her, a cell phone rang.

TWENTY-TWO

I missed writing in this diary last night. I was too excited. Scott gave me a ring to celebrate four months together! It's beautiful—a gold band with a little ruby heart. It fits perfectly. I'll wear it forever. I know he makes good money on the construction crew, but still, it must have cost at least two weeks' pay.

We were in his car, parked in our favorite spot on that dirt road in the forest, outside town. Not exactly Paris, but it beats sitting in this house. He kissed me and whispered, "I love you." First time I've heard him say that.

"I love you too." I hugged him hard, never wanting to let go.

I could marry Scott. No one could ever treat me better. I love everything about him. The creases in the corners of his eyes when he smiles. The stupid jokes he tells to make me laugh—especially when I'm mad at Mom. The way he holds me, the way he kisses. His muscles. His smell. Mostly the way he lifts me up. "You're the most beautiful girl in this town," he says. "A thousand guys want you—and I'm the one who got you."

Okay, he's exaggerating a little. Maybe nine hundred and ninety-nine.

Then—today.

I was in the campaign office alone. Jilke was on some errand. Senator Hanley came in from a late lunch, looking for Jilke. "He not back yet?" He fiddled with his tie, like his mind was on a million important things. He'd had a haircut. It was a little shorter over his ears.

"He shouldn't be too much longer." I pushed back from my desk. "Can I do something for you?"

He stopped messing with his tie. Stood there looking down at me. For some reason I felt all hot. I started thinking crazy things. Scott, and his blue eyes, only Senator Hanley's are brown. Scott, and the way he stands with his feet apart, arms folded, only Bryson Hanley was now leaning with one hand on my desk. "Too bad you'll be going back to school in the fall, Carla. I could use someone like you full-time."

Where was my tongue? "I could still work for you after school. Besides, Mr. Jilke would fall apart without me."

Oh, great, a smart remark. Slipped out before I could stop it.

Bryson Hanley grinned. *Grinned.* Like I'd told the funniest joke. "And a sense of humor too." He shook his head, but his eyes never left mine.

I sat glued to my seat. I wasn't thinking about Scott anymore.

Senator Hanley straightened. I tilted my head up at him. "Have you ever taken dictation, Carla?"

Why did the sound of my name from his mouth give me such chills?

He smiled, like he knew his effect on me. And he didn't mind.

"No." I shrugged. "But I'm a fast learner. Start talking; I'll write."

He laughed. "Let's try it then. I have a letter I'd like to get done now. Besides, you're a lot prettier than Jilke."

Pretty. And he called the man Jilke. Just like I do. Like he knows.

I grabbed a pad of paper and pen. Tried not to show my legs were trembling as I sat down in his office, right across the desk from him. He dictated slowly enough for me to keep up. Leaning back in his chair, hands behind his head, watching me the whole time. Not that I had a chance to look up, but I could *feel* his eyes on me.

By the time I typed the letter, Jilke was back. I walked to Senator Hanley's office, ready to knock, so he could sign the letter.

"What are you doing?" Jilke demanded.

I waved the paper at him. "He dictated a letter. It needs to be signed."

Jilke was on his feet in a heartbeat. "I'll take it in."

I shrugged. "Whatever." I gave it to him and went back to my desk. Sat there kind of pouting, twisting my ruby ring, while he was with Senator Hanley.

An hour later Jilke was down the hall, and Senator Hanley came out of his office. "Carla, perfect job." He gave me one of his dazzling smiles.

"Thanks."

He leaned on my desk again – this time with both hands. I could smell his aftershave. "I'll have to put those skills of yours to use more often."

I twisted my ring. "Anytime."

TWENTY-THREE

Two steps from her room door, Carla froze. A silent second ticked by. Her cell phone rang again.

A vague memory surfaced of lying on the bed hours ago, tossing the phone down by her feet . . .

What if it was Thornby, taunting her? Telling her he was waiting for her outside?

Carla stumbled around her suitcase, looking for the phone. On the third ring she found it half under the bed. She snatched it up, checked the ID.

Java Joint.

She sucked in a breath. *Bailey.* How Carla wanted to answer. Just to hear Bailey's voice, to tell her she was in terrible trouble and needed her help—

Any friend who helps you is dead.

A fourth ring. One more, and it would go to voice mail. A friend so near and yet so far. Carla closed her fingers around the phone hard, as if to squeeze out an answer of what to do.

The fifth ring began—

Carla snapped the phone open. Then stared at it, wild-eyed. What had she done?

She steeled herself, willed her voice to sound normal. "Hello."

"Carla, it's Bailey! Are you all right?"

"Sure. Why?"

"Oh, I'm so glad. You really had me worried."

Carla sank down on the bed. The closed drapes cast a blue pallor on the room, turning her beige slacks a sickly gray. "Why would you be worried?"

"Well, you were supposed to meet Wilbur here a long time ago. He's fit to be tied. I called your office and home but couldn't find you. And then—"

"Oh, Wilbur. I forgot all about him. I just … I've had a busy morning." Despite her efforts, Carla's tone took on an edge. "Tell him I can't come today. I'll make it up to him."

"What's going on?" Bailey's voice tightened.

"What do you mean?"

"Carla, come on. You don't sound right. Plus it's not like you to just not show up somewhere when you've promised. And then this strange woman called you a little while ago."

Carla sat up straighter. "What woman?"

"She said her name's Ellie. No last name. Said she knew you years ago, and it's very important that she talks to you soon."

Ellie?

"Do you know who she is?"

Years ago. The timing couldn't be coincidental. Carla sorted through old friends' names. "I don't remember any Ellie."

"Frankly, I think she was lying. She hesitated to even give me a name at all. Why she'd lie, I don't know. And she sounded almost scared. Like she was in a big hurry. She cut off the conversation all of a sudden. Said she'd call you back."

Ellie … Think as Carla might, no one came to mind. Had her old friend Mary Kay called and given a false name? Could *she* know something?

But Carla had never told Mary Kay.

Who could know something about the past? Could this person tell her why her life was suddenly in danger?

"Carla, you there?"

"Yeah."

"What's going on? This is scaring me. After all that's happened here, it's easy to think the worst."

Carla squeezed her eyes shut. How she wanted to tell Bailey. *Call Chief Edwards—tell him someone's trying to kill me. Tell him to protect me; I'm coming home...*

"I'm fine, Bailey. Just fine."

Silence. Carla could practically hear Bailey thinking, *I don't believe you.*

"She wanted your cell phone number," Bailey finally said. "Do you want me to give it to her?"

What if this wasn't a friend at all? What if it was a ruse to find out where she was? Maybe this woman was working with Thornby.

"No."

But maybe she wasn't. Thornby already had her cell number. Maybe this Ellie really did have the information Carla so desperately sought.

"Yes." Carla's shoulders sagged. "I don't know."

"Carla." Bailey's voice fell to a near whisper. "*Tell* me what's going on. I want to help you."

Carla's throat tightened. "How did this Ellie know to call me at Java Joint?"

"Scenes and Beans, I guess. Anybody who reads our blog knows you're here every morning."

Oh. Right.

"So are you going to tell me?"

Carla rubbed her forehead. Maybe if she rubbed hard enough she'd wipe this nightmare right out of her mind. "I *can't*."

Silence again.

"I'll be praying for you, Carla. Hard. I suppose you know you're scaring me silly."

"I know." Carla could barely speak. "I'm scaring me too."

Her eyes fell on the clock. Almost ten thirty. Anxiety knocked through her veins. She should have been out of here long ago. She pushed to her feet.

"What do you want me to do about Ellie?" Bailey asked. "Give her your number or not?"

Scenes and Beans. A terrorizing thought pierced Carla. Bailey was right—hundreds of people across the country read the blog each weekday morning. If Ellie knew Carla's close ties to Java Joint, so did everyone else. Like Thornby. Come to think of it, when he'd first called about the Edna San estate, he'd mentioned the blog.

What if he had someone watching Carla's cell phone account to see if Java Joint called when she didn't show up? Was it possible to listen in on cell phone calls? Or what if they were watching Java Joint's phone?

"Bailey." Carla's voice sharpened, and she couldn't stop it. Not now, not after realizing just by answering her cell she may have placed Bailey in danger. "Just ignore that woman. She's some crackpot. And don't call me again, you hear? I *do not* want to talk to you! I don't want to talk to *anyone* at Java Joint. And in fact, *you* should mind your own business and quit talking on that phone so much."

Carla jerked the cell away from her ear and snapped it shut. With a heavy punch of a button, she turned it off.

She fell back onto the bed, dropped her head into her hands—and shook.

Ten minutes later, feeling lonelier than she ever had in her life, Carla checked out of the hotel and limped outside to the parking lot, pulling her suitcase. From the recesses of her mind rose the image of Bryson Hanley, smiling at her across a desk. The smile that had brought her to this day, this moment.

Weighted with memories and fear, Carla set out on what could be a death walk to her car.

TWENTY-FOUR

It happened today. The thing I've been dreaming of. And scared to death of.

Ever since that day two weeks ago, when Bryson Hanley leaned over my desk and smiled at me—hadn't I known deep in my heart I wanted it? Even though I tried to tell myself I was crazy.

Now I can hardly see straight. He's all I can think about.

Every time I was in his office the past two weeks, the air sort of tingled. Bryson would dictate letters or explain some project he wants me to do—no more going through Jilke. But no matter what he was talking about, he'd get this look in his eyes. The same look Scott gets. Only it's ... older. Wiser. Like he knows just what I need, and he's going to take care of me. Like he wants me so much, and the only thing holding him back is Jilke in the next room, and—oh, yeah, his wife.

Yesterday Bryson (I still have to call him Senator Hanley in front of anybody else) handed me some papers, and our hands touched. I swear I felt like I'd been plugged in. He felt it too. He stopped, those deep brown eyes of his just looking at me. His fingers slid over mine and pressed. Good thing the door was closed. Anybody seeing us could tell what we were thinking. Jilke would've had a heart attack. I think he's about to have one already. Every time I come out of a private meeting with Bryson, Jilke shoots me this hard look, like he's trying to see right through me. Like he knows.

I got all fluttery when Bryson held my hand. I started to breathe hard. His gaze dropped to my chest, then back up to my face. I couldn't think of one smart-alecky thing to say. We just stood there looking at each other. Then he let go of my hand.

After work that night I went out with Scott. We parked in our usual place in the forest. And every time he touched me, I thought of Bryson.

I love Scott. But Bryson's so much more. He's everything I ever needed. He makes me feel safe. I know he could sweep me away like a prince. Away from this run-down house and Mom's sarcastic mouth, and her cigarettes, and her hatred of life—which she always takes out on me.

But there's this thing about Bryson. He's strong and powerful, and everybody in the city loves him. But sometimes when he looks at me, I see his needs. Almost like he's lonely. Like I could make him happy, while he's stuck dealing with his jealous wife and doing everything the public wants him to do. He looks at me in a way that makes me think, *I'm the only one who knows your struggles. Who really understands you.*

Then—today.

Bryson asked me to come into his office. Jilke was out meeting with some campaign donors. I walked in with my pad of paper and pen, pretending to be all business, when deep down I *knew.* Bryson closed the door. He had his suit coat off and hung on a hook on his wall, as usual. I love to see him like that. The politician, taking off his jacket to get down to work. I sat in my usual chair. He walked over and stood looking down at me. My heart started beating so hard, I thought it would rip out of my chest. He gently took the paper and pen from my fingers, placed them on his desk. Then he held out his hand to me. I stared at it for a second, then took it. He pulled me to my feet.

Bryson ran a finger down my cheek. He had to feel me shaking, but he didn't let on. "You are the most beautiful girl I have ever seen." His voice sounded low and rough. "That black shiny hair, your dark eyes, your body. Everything."

He slid his hands to my shoulders. I could feel heat coming off him. It was sure coming off me. I knew if the next move happened we could never go back. I didn't care. I wanted it more than anything.

Washington State Senator Bryson Hanley—next year US senator—pulled me close and kissed me.

At first it was gentle. Like the first time Scott kissed me. Then a shuddering breath passed through him. He gripped me tighter, and my arms slipped around him. He started kissing me with a passion I've never felt before. Nobody has ever kissed me like that, not even Scott in his wildest moments. Bryson wasn't some guy my age kissing me; he was a *man.* Out of control and in control at the same time.

I don't know how long we kissed or what finally broke us apart. But it seemed like a long time. He held my face in his hands. "I think about you every waking moment. You make me feel so ..." He shook his head.

"I know."

What a dumb thing to say. Like I'm the one who had all the power over him. But I still just couldn't believe what was happening. That this man cared about me. *Me.*

He pushed back a strand of my hair. "You can't tell anyone, you know that, don't you? I'm risking so very much just being honest with you."

The words hung in the air. *Risking so very much.* I knew he was. And just to be with me. Bryson Hanley—Washington's favorite son. I have never felt so worthy, so special, in all my life.

"I won't tell anyone, ever. Promise. I would never hurt you."

He smiled and kissed me again, slow and easy. Like we had all the time in the world and we'd take every second of it. Suddenly I realized I wasn't shaking anymore.

Bryson pulled away. "Is there a way I can see you this weekend? Alone?"

Was he *kidding*? Name the hour. "Yeah, sure."

He closed his eyes, as if to say, *Yes, oh, thank you!*

"Tell you what, Carla." I tingled all over again at the sound of my name. Somehow now, coming from lips that had kissed me, it sounded different. "I have a cabin in the woods. It's my private place. No one goes there but me. I often visit it on weekends just to get away for a while. Can you meet me there tomorrow?"

I thought about it. What I'd tell my friends. How I'd get there. None of that mattered. I'd walk if I had to.

I looked into his dark eyes and nearly drowned in them. "Sure. Just tell me the time."

TWENTY-FIVE

Less than five hours.

Tony punched the steering wheel. He was parked outside a hotel on Highway 95 south of Moscow, feeling like a wreck. Ten minutes ago he'd gone in to use the bathroom and buy some coffee and a bagel. The food hadn't helped much. His face still looked like he'd spent two days in the sun. He was dog tired and madder than ever. And that was the good news.

All night and long after dawn he'd searched for Carla Radling—at every motel in Moscow, then Pullman. As much as he'd wanted to flash her picture to every clerk behind a counter, he'd resisted. He couldn't afford to have someone connect his face with hers once she was officially "missing."

Finally, after making a needed purchase, he'd headed back to Highway 95. The trooper patrolling twenty miles south hadn't seen Carla's Toyota. But according to the Durango's navigation system, there were quite a few motels along that twenty-mile strip. Tony should have checked them hours ago—but had no time until now. Even if Miss Wit had stayed in one, she was probably long gone.

No matter. If she was headed south, he'd hear about it.

Impatient as he felt, Tony knew he was closing in on her. Shouldn't be long now. He had new pairs of eyes watching the roads to the west and north, and in Moscow. And Andy, his buddy from Spokane, had called in early that morning when he'd taken up his post in Kanner Lake.

Tony didn't have all the resources he wished he had—not what would be available to him if he appealed to his boss. But that was out of the question. On the other hand, every person he brought in only increased his risk of getting caught.

Best-case scenario: you do a job yourself, no help. Which is exactly what would have happened at the Edna San estate. Now he'd had to bring in other people. When Miss Wit's picture started showing up on the news as a missing person, somebody just might remember a certain assignment—and wonder about the connection.

In the end, Tony counted on their own guilt to keep them silent. What state trooper would admit being paid to hunt down a woman?

Tony started the car. "I finish this job, I'm *out* of here." The minute he got paid, he'd move Robyn and Timmy as far away as he could get. Like to China.

The "Barry" cell phone rang. Tony snatched it from a cup holder on the console and flipped it open. "Yeah."

"Andy here. Got a couple of hits for you."

"Shoot."

Andy told him two pieces of information. The first was useless, except that it told him he'd succeeded in scaring Carla Radling away from her friends. He smiled at that. The second made no sense. Heat flushed through Tony. "That it? That's all you *got*?"

"Hey, man, I'm just the messenger."

He gritted his teeth. "Yeah, yeah. Thanks a bunch."

Tony slapped the phone closed, then on impulse flipped it open again. Time to rattle Miss Wit's cage. Make her pay for the night she'd cost him. He punched in her number, threats crowding his tongue.

The line clicked on to a recorded message.

Tony smacked his cell shut and threw it on the floor.

He pressed back in the seat, glaring out the windshield. In a field beyond the parking lot, tall green-yellow grasses rippled in a breeze. His mind flashed to a summer outing with Timmy, when they'd run through open land, trying to fly a new bird-shaped kite. Timmy had finally given up, sinking to his knees with the melodrama of a three-year-old. "I can't do it, Daddy," he sobbed. "I *can't*."

"Sure you can, Son." Tony plunked down beside him, pulling Timmy to his chest. "Sometimes the best things in life are hard to do. You just have to keep trying ..."

Tony shut his eyes and tried to push the memory away.

Four hours.

His thoughts returned to his target. How sweet the revenge would be when he found Carla Radling. The hunting knife he'd bought that morning in Moscow cried to be used. Over eight inches long, with a four-inch razor-sharp blade. Its outer layer was of 420 J2 stainless steel, covering an inside layer of VG–10 steel. The handle curved perfectly in his hand.

If Miss Wit had taken something important from her home and hid it somewhere, thinking to save her own skin, she was sorely misguided. His knife would soon prove that. And if she hadn't taken anything—too bad she'd aroused his suspicions. With such a fine instrument in his hand, he wouldn't be persuaded easily.

Tony opened gritty eyes and focused on the blowing grass. The alternating yellows and greens flashed his thoughts to the two baseball caps topping the stack in Carla Radling's hatbox. *Had* she taken something from there? Something from years ago?

Years ago ...

The words triggered a replay of his phone conversation with Andy. The man's second piece of information had included those two words. Tony honed in on them. What could they mean? Could be important. Made no sense to *him*, but it could mean a great deal to his boss.

Which meant he should report it. Besides, it could spell possible interference with his own plans.

But if he reported it, he'd have to say where the information came from. There'd be questions. Answering those questions would mean admitting he'd lost his target. Robyn and Timmy would be in instant danger.

Besides, it couldn't matter. He'd have his target within a few hours at most. Not enough time for some outsider to cause problems.

Tony thumped a fist against the steering wheel, weighing his options.

He had no choice, really. For his family's sake, he couldn't tell his boss.

His nose was running again. He wiped it with two tissues and tossed them in the plastic bag on the passenger seat. Time to get back to his search. Only a few more hotels between him and that twenty-mile mark. If those were all clear he'd return to Moscow, knowing he was that much closer to his *very* enjoyable meeting with Miss Wit.

Tony backed out of the parking space and headed toward Highway 95.

TWENTY-SIX

In her office with the door closed, Tanya Evans stared mindlessly at the document before her. She'd read the first two paragraphs three times, and still the words wouldn't register. Her concentration had been amorphous all morning, no logical thought patterns able to form. Whatever she looked at changed into the face of Carla Radling. Whatever voice she heard pulsed with the threat from last night: *With one word I can make you disappear . . .*

Tanya tapped her pen against the paper, reliving the call she'd placed that morning from a pay phone. She'd been too afraid to use her home phone or cell, or even a line at work. Who knew how she might be watched? A red SUV with tinted glass had cruised by while she was in the phone booth. The car slowed to a crawl, the driver rolling down his window and glaring at her. As if to say, *Watch yourself, Tanya, we know what you're up to.* She hung up in a hurry and ran to her car, heart beating in her throat.

During lunch hour she would dare to find another pay phone in downtown Seattle and call Java Joint again. She had to get a message to Carla, convince her to meet. Which might be difficult. Carla thought she was hiding secrets from the world—and she was. But Tanya knew more than she did.

Now that Tanya had made her decision, she couldn't find Carla fast enough. But she hadn't figured out the logistics. She couldn't imagine confessing over the phone, but neither could she just take off for Kanner Lake. If she was being watched—which now seemed highly likely—they'd know where she was headed. She'd never get there alive.

We were expecting Carla quite a while ago.

Bailey Truitt's voice repeated like a stuck record in Tanya's head. She so wanted to believe this was mere coincidence. Carla was running behind; she'd had a flat tire. There could be a dozen explanations for showing up late. But in light of her own terrifying visitor last night, Tanya couldn't help wondering if Carla had encountered one of her own.

Closing her eyes, Tanya prayed to a God she didn't know, hoping He would cease cosmic pursuits long enough to hear. If He'd whirled this earth into existence, shouldn't He care what happened on it?

Please, if You're listening, keep Carla safe. And let me find her in time.

991 Friday, July 26, 1991 **Saturday afternoon, July 27, 1991** Sunday, July , 2

TWENTY-SEVEN

It's time. I'm ready to go see Bryson.

Good thing Mom's working a double shift today. If she saw me taking so long with my makeup, she'd wonder.

Mary Kay said I could borrow her clunker car. I told her I needed to go to Seattle and buy some office supplies for Senator Hanley. She wanted to come with me. I said I needed the time alone. That Mom's really been on me lately—probably 'cause she's jealous of my job. Mom still can't figure out why her "stupid daughter" works for a senator while she's slinging burgers and fries.

If she only knew. I'm a whole lot better than she could ever imagine.

Mary Kay frowned. She got the mom part—she knows my mother—but I've never told my best friend I'd rather be alone than with her. "So let's talk about it while we're driving," she said.

I looked away. "I really just need to do this alone. Okay?"

She stared at me a long time. I don't think she believed me. Finally she shrugged. "Whatever."

So now I'm set to go—ten minutes early. I thought I'd write what I'm feeling so I can read it later. You know, a before and after. But it's hard to explain what I'm feeling. Part of me can't really believe that anything's going to happen. After all, Bryson's a *state senator*, and I'm just me. But then I think, well, Carla, that's just your mom talking. I *know* how Bryson feels about me. And he couldn't have asked me to his cabin so he could dictate a letter.

How will I be next time I write? Next time I hold this diary again? I think I will be very different.

Time to go. And yes, dear diary, thanks to your secrets, I'm hiding you like never before. A diary-sniffing hound wouldn't find you.

I can't wait to be with Bryson. I'm shaking, but I can't wait.

TWENTY-EIGHT

Carla hobbled toward the street running behind the Best Western, still shaking. Every step shot pain up her leg. Her eyes flicked left and right, looking for a black Durango or Thornby on foot. She'd decided to pull her suitcase rather than drive back to the room for it. Once she reached her car, she wanted *out* of there.

The weather was still unseasonably warm, the sky clear. But Thornby's presence hung over the asphalt like cold fog. Goosebumps popped out on Carla's arms. He'd been here in the night. She'd swear it. What if he was here right now, watching her stumble, with a grin on his face? Any minute now a bullet could slam her head . . .

Where would she go if she died today? Not something she'd had to think about before.

It wouldn't be heaven. God lived there—the God she'd hurled curses at years ago. The God who judged her for what she'd done.

Yeah, well, last time I checked, you deserve the judgment.

She reached the back road, turned toward the little white building behind the strip mall. It seemed a mile away. The sound of her suitcase wheels rolling over pavement grated the air. The parking lot smelled musty and wet, despite the September sun. Or was that her own sweaty clothes?

Interminable time passed before she reached the building. She drew to an abrupt halt. What if Thornby waited for her behind it? Gun aimed point-blank—*Get in your car.* What would she do? She couldn't run. No time to cry for help. The minute her mouth opened, he'd pull the trigger.

If only her ankle wasn't so sprained. She felt so *maddeningly* helpless.

She swallowed hard ... and forced her head slowly around the corner.

Sudden noise assaulted her ears.

Carla yanked backwards, nearly losing her balance. Fresh pain jolted her ankle. Her purse handle fell off her shoulder, crashing the bag against her thigh. Carla dropped the purse, both hands flying upward.

The sound came again.

On her left she saw it. A squirrel sitting on his haunches, chitting at her. The raucous noise took a razor blade to her ears.

A squirrel. That's all. Just a squirrel.

What was a squirrel doing in all this pavement? Almost as if nature had sent him as a warning ...

Carla hung there, shoulders hunched, feeling like an open target. A double wave of tiredness and hunger washed over her. A long moment passed before she gathered the strength to pick up her purse and venture around the building.

There sat her car, just as she'd left it.

She approached the Toyota with caution. Bent down to check underneath. What if he waited for her there, ready to grab her ankle as she neared the door?

Empty pavement.

Carla's eyes swept the length of her car and back. It looked fine.

She unlocked the driver's door with fumbling hands, tossed her suitcase and purse across the console onto the passenger seat. She slid behind the wheel, trying her best to place her left foot in a comfortable position. Fat chance. Carla punched the door lock button and started the car. Her heart fluttered as she pulled around to the front of the little building and onto the street.

A block down, she hit Highway 8 and turned west toward Pullman.

She could hardly believe it—she was on her way.

Now, her next moves. First up—get the rental car. After Bailey's call back in the hotel room, she'd gathered her wits enough to check for an agency in the Yellow Pages. Moscow didn't have any. But there were two at the Moscow-Pullman Airport—a Hertz and a Budget. She'd studied a map in one of the ads. The airport was just a few miles away—a right exit off Highway 8.

All she had to do was get there without being spotted. At the airport she'd leave her car among all those parked by airline passengers. Even if Thornby found the Toyota, he'd probably think she'd taken a flight somewhere. She'd throw him off track.

The long Palouse Mall stretched on Carla's right. She spotted a Starbucks and longed for a latte—the kind Bailey made for her every morning at Java Joint. She ached at the thought of her familiar counter stool and the smell of Bailey's coffee. Only two hours away from home—but it might as well be two million miles.

Past the Palouse Mall Carla saw an Office Depot, U-Haul, Staples, a Wal-Mart. An Applebee's, the Appaloosa Horse Club.

There you go—a horse. Thornby wouldn't be looking for that.

Somewhere along the way she crossed the state border, and Idaho's Highway 8 became Washington's 270, but she saw no sign. A few more miles until the turn to the airport. Carla's muscles tightened. *Hurry, hurry.* She'd feel so much safer out of her own car.

The town gave way to farmland, then rolling hills, a bike trail on the left now visible, now not. She saw an animal hospital ahead on her left—and in its parking lot, a Washington state trooper's car, facing the highway. She could see the trooper behind the wheel.

A voice shouted in her head: *Stop! Ask for help!*

No way. What if he was working for Thornby?

But what were the chances of that? Besides, if he wasn't he could immediately protect her. This nightmare would be *over.*

Slow down, Carla. Do it!

She lifted her foot off the accelerator—and Thornby's voice rang in her head. *Vince Edwards is your chief of police. His wife is Nancy. He has a daughter, Heather, and a little granddaughter, Christy. You call any law enforcement, one of them dies ...*

Carla pressed the gas pedal.

As she neared the state trooper's car, his head swiveled in her direction. In a drawn-out second, their eyes met. His intense gaze pierced through her.

The second stretched ... snapped by. Carla passed the trooper's car.

She cast a wild glance over her shoulder. He was still watching her, his face hard.

He pulled onto the road behind her.

Paranoia descended over Carla like a choking fog. She gripped the wheel, glancing nervously in the mirror. This was just coincidence, right? He couldn't be following her.

But the way he'd watched her drive by. The intensity in his eyes. As if he'd been *looking* for her ...

One long mile churned by. Still the patrolman trailed her.

Come on, Carla, he's just driving, that's all.

But with each second that passed, Carla's terror grew.

Maybe when she took the exit for the airport ...

There it was, ahead at the light! Airport Road.

Carla turned right.

The state trooper followed.

She gripped the wheel. Okay, so he was going to the airport. Lots of people went there.

Carla's back pulled away from the seat. She sat ramrod straight as she followed the curves of the two-lane road, acutely aware of its emptiness. Nobody ahead of her, nobody passing in the other direction. *This* was an airport road? Where were all the cars?

She checked the rearview mirror. The trooper was still behind her.

You won't know what law enforcement to trust, because some of them just might be working for me ...

She passed a lone building on the left. Its sign read "Bear Research."

Bear Research? Was she out in the middle of nowhere? And *where* was the airport?

After an eternity she saw the turn. Carla took it, and the trooper followed. She saw another sign: *Airport, Next Right.* Parallel runways appeared on her right. Soon she reached the airport and turned in. It was tiny—nothing like the Spokane airport. One little building, red brick at the bottom, large white squares at the top. A small parking lot with a few slots each marked off for Hertz and Budget rentals. That was it. No back lots where she could hide her car, no bustle of people.

Until then, Carla had clung to a strand of hope: maybe the state trooper's presence was just coincidence. Now, as she drove right by the airport building without stopping, turned left toward the road, then left again to head back to Highway 8—and he followed her every move—she knew. She glanced in her rearview mirror and saw him talking on a cell phone. Not a police radio. A cell phone. The thing he would use to call someone who'd hired him for a bit of extra duty ...

No denying it. Thornby had found her. She would not live through this day.

TWENTY-NINE

I can't believe I've lived through this day! A dozen times I thought happiness would plain burst me apart. I've finally calmed down enough to write.

I got to Bryson's cabin just before 1:00 this afternoon. The whole time I drove there I was planning what to say. Something very clever for sure. But the minute I saw him, every word fell out of my head.

He was wearing jeans and a blue cotton knit shirt. I've never seen him dressed like that. He looked so *good*. He came out, took my hand and pulled me from the car, then stood there looking deep into my eyes. We went into the cabin without a word.

It's a nice place. Better than this house any day. It has a den with a fireplace and two bedrooms – a master suite and a loft.

First we sat on the couch. He was drinking bourbon. He offered me some, and I put a little in my Coke, big drinker that I am. And we talked. He asked me about my friends. If I have a boyfriend. I felt weird talking about Scott. But I did tell him. After all, I know about Bryson's wife.

Didn't take me long to get comfortable. He's so good at making me feel that way. He put his arm around me, and I leaned on his shoulder. I got the nerve to ask him if he and his wife are going to have kids. I've been wondering about that. He said they wanted them more than anything and had been trying for ten years, but Catherine (I almost shuddered when he said her name) hadn't been able to get pregnant. He looked so sad when he told me. I hugged him and stroked his hair, like he was a little boy. Told him I was sorry. It felt amazing to be able to comfort him. At that moment he could have asked me for the sun, and I'd have run out to get it.

Then he started kissing me.

It went from there. I'd known it would, but a part of me still couldn't believe it. I couldn't help thinking how Mom would never guess how important I'd become.

The next thing I knew we were in the bedroom.

I felt really shy at first, taking off my clothes in the daylight. But Bryson kept telling me how beautiful I was. And so is he. I mean it. He's *incredible*.

"You've done this before, haven't you?" he asked.

What a question. I lowered my eyes. I didn't want to say anything for fear of spoiling the moment. Finally I shook my head. "No."

He smiled.

Bryson leaned over toward a table by the bed and opened its drawer. Pulled out a condom. For a minute I was embarrassed again. But then I told him about me. How I've been on birth control pills the last two months because of the horrible periods I was having. How the pills had really made things better.

"You telling me the truth?" He gave me a piercing look.

"Why would I lie? I can show them to you sometime if you want."

For a long minute he looked at me. Then he put the condom back in the drawer.

I could tell he tried to be gentle, since I'd told him it was my first time. And even though he's married and everything, he never made me feel dumb. "You are amazing," he whispered to me. "I've never been with anyone like you before."

I felt like I'd gone straight to heaven without even dying.

Afterwards, we lay there a long time until he said he had to go. I could have stayed forever.

I barely remember the drive home. It's amazing I didn't have a wreck. All I could do was relive those moments over and over again.

When I gave Mary Kay's car keys back to her, she looked at me real funny. I couldn't meet her eyes. The truth had to be all over my face.

"Tell me really, Carla, where'd you go?"

I shrugged. "What do you mean? I told you where."

She bit the inside of her cheek, hurt and anger flicking across her face. "Fine, then, if that's the way you want it."

I walked home feeling terrible and wonderful at the same time. Wonderful about Bryson—but Mary Kay ... I've never lied to her before. We've spent years telling each other everything. Suddenly I realized this is the way it would have to be. As long as I keep seeing Bryson—and of course I will—I won't be able to tell a soul.

That thought made me sad. And lonely.

When I got home I just lay on my bed, thinking of Bryson.

Tonight Scott and I were supposed to go out. The closer the time came, the worse I felt. How could I possibly face him? Finally I called and told him I was sick. He sounded so sweet and worried about me and offered to come over.

I felt so guilty! "No, no, it's okay. I just want to sleep."

So here I am at almost midnight—wide awake.

I don't know how I'm going to walk into the office Monday and act like nothing happened. Will Bryson be able to do that? Won't Jilke take one look at us and know?

And what am I going to do about Scott? I don't want to hurt him. But it's going to be so hard acting normal around him.

One thing's for sure—I'm not taking any more of Mom's mouth. I mean it, she starts talking me down, I'll walk away. I *am* somebody, no matter what she says. How I wish I could throw the truth in her face.

Today Bryson Hanley showed me how much of a Somebody I am.

THIRTY

Tony was headed toward Moscow on Highway 95 when his "Barry" cell phone rang. He checked the ID. *All right.* He snapped the phone open. "Tell me something good."

"I found her."

Bingo. "You sure?"

"Positive. Car and license are right, and I got a visual on her."

"Where is she?"

"Headed west on Highway 8 toward Pullman, not far from Moscow. I think she's on to me. I followed her at the turnoff for the Moscow-Pullman airport, right up to the building, but she passed it by. Went all the way back to 8 and kept going."

Not far from Moscow. Where on earth had she stayed?

Didn't matter now. Tony could already feel the knife in his hands.

"Hold on a minute." He punched buttons on the Durango's GPS. Eyes flicking between road and monitor, he studied the map. "Looks like in Pullman she can turn south on 27 or north on 195." Either way, didn't matter. Once he saw which direction she was going, he'd find a way to head her off. *Bad move, stopping for the night, Miss Wit. You could have been in Oregon by now.* "Can you keep on her?"

"As long as I don't get called off on something."

"Good. Let me know if she turns. I'm not that far away; I'll catch up soon. If you're called off I need to hear about it."

"Will do."

Tony dropped the phone on his lap and pushed his foot to the accelerator.

THIRTY-ONE

Bailey scrubbed Java Joint's long counter as if her life depended on it. Wilbur, Jake, Bev and Angie, and the rest of the morning crowd were gone. Only S-Man remained, typing away on his manuscript. In the silence—save for the *tap, tap* of computer keys—Bailey's imagination ran wild. She'd called Carla's realty office twice—only to be told Carla still had not shown. The second time the receptionist's voice bulged with impatience. "We don't know *where* she is. Now she's missed an appointment to show houses. If you hear from her, Bailey, *please* tell her to get in here."

Missed an appointment to show houses. That wasn't Carla. Absolutely not. Something was very wrong. But what could Bailey do? Carla had never talked to her in such anger. She was brassy, yes, but never mean. And even the sarcasm she was known for had never been aimed at Bailey. Wilbur was more her kind of target—but then, he purposely pushed her buttons.

Bailey rinsed out her cloth, sprayed unneeded cleaner on the cash register, and wiped it down too.

And that phone call this morning. Who was Ellie, and what did she want? Why was Carla so dead set against talking to her?

Questions, questions, and no answers. Just plenty of wild imaginings, all of them sending shivers down Bailey's back. She wanted to call her husband, John. Spill all her fears to him. But this was his naptime, and he'd had a difficult night. The latest medication he'd begun taking for his epilepsy was causing some bad side effects. She couldn't disturb his sleep now.

Bailey sighed.

The tapping stopped. S-Man looked up from his computer, and his dark gaze locked with hers. His bushy eyebrows slowly relaxed, the blank expression in his eyes clearing. She must have sighed more loudly than she'd realized to pull him out of his Saurian world.

He leaned back in his chair. Blinked twice. "What's up?"

Fondness and gratitude surged through Bailey. Ted, for all his odd creative spirit and seeming distance from reality, was in fact one of the smartest, most down-to-earth people she knew. Sometimes, because of his very creativity and constant thoughts of characterization, he picked up on things others couldn't see. Six months ago, the whole town had learned that surprising truth.

And six months ago, a few of the Java Joint crowd who'd bothered to notice had learned something more startling. At thirty-one, quiet, laconic science fiction writer Ted Dawson was in love with outgoing, ambitious Leslie Brymes, ten years his junior.

Now *that* would make an interesting couple.

Bailey dropped the cleaning cloth, wiped her hands on a towel. She stepped around the front counter and across the café, pulled out the chair opposite Ted, and sank into it. He watched her with mild patience.

Suddenly Bailey didn't quite know what to say.

S-Man folded his arms. "You're worried about Carla."

Bailey managed a little smile. She should have known, for all apparent focus on his writing, he'd sensed her nervousness. "I sure am." She started talking, and soon told him everything—the call from Ellie, how angry Carla had been, that she was still missing.

S-Man rubbed his forehead. "Doesn't sound good."

Bailey waited for more feedback, perhaps some thought she hadn't considered. But Ted merely refolded his arms. She suppressed another sigh. Sometimes his terseness left a few things to be desired. "So talk to me, Ted. What should I do?"

His gaze wandered over her shoulder toward the front windows. He drew a long breath, as if gathering his thoughts, his focus remaining in the distance. "When you write a scene where a character is, say, frightened, you're not supposed to just *tell* the reader she's scared. You're supposed to show it. And sometimes—actually many times—what a character *says* isn't really what she *means*. It's called subtexting. The meaning's underneath the words and actions." His eyes returned to Bailey. "You with me?"

Quite a long speech for Ted. "I think so."

He nodded slowly. "You said Carla sounded mad on the phone. Telling you not to call her again. Doesn't sound like her. Neither does missing appointments. My guess is, she wasn't really mad. She was scared."

She'd almost said as much. But of what? That was the question.

Bailey focused on S-Man's biggie cup, no doubt empty long ago. "Carla practically even accused me of gossiping too much, which she knows I don't do. She told me to quit spending so much time on the phone."

S-Man rubbed beneath his chin. His eyes pulled toward the phone sitting near the back of the counter. For a long moment he frowned at it. Then he pushed away from the table and stood. With the permanent limp that favored his once broken leg, he crossed toward the counter and reached for the wireless receiver. Examined it.

He looked toward Bailey. "Got a small screwdriver?"

She pushed to her feet, a dozen questions on the tip of her tongue. She bit them back. Ted would talk when he was ready.

"Yes, in the office." She hurried down the short rear hall and into her small office to fetch the tool. Back at the counter she handed it to Ted, then stood aside to watch, lacing and unlacing her fingers.

Ted inserted the end of the screwdriver between the outside plastic cover pieces of the receiver and lifted one off. Pulled out the set's small microphone and held it up. Turned it over.

His expression darkened. He gave his head a quick shake, as if surprised by what he'd found. Then laid the microphone on the counter, facedown, and pointed to it. "See this?"

Bailey's heart picked up speed. Already, she could guess. She drew near to look.

"It's not the microphone that came with this unit. This is an RF transmitter, a phone bug. Works when you're on the line. A low-end listening device. Easy and cheap to install, and easy enough to find, if you're looking for it. But hard to trace back to whoever put it here."

Bailey's eyes widened. She stared at the thing—small in size, huge in meaning—her mouth agape. This could not be happening. "But what . . . why?"

Ted considered the device, his wide lips pressed. "You let any customer who's a stranger use this phone lately?"

Bailey tried to think. "No."

He tapped his thumb against the Formica. His unassuming manner only frazzled Bailey all the more. This wasn't some *novel* he was writing—this was real life. *Her* life.

Ted pushed away from the counter. "Guess we'd better check the extension in your office."

A minute later, standing by her cluttered desk, Ted held another bug in his large fingers.

Two. This was too much. Bailey's mind reeled. Why her, why Java Joint? She leaned against the wall, a hand to her forehead. How long had these things been in her phone? Had someone been listening to every call? "I just don't ... I can't understand how they could have gotten here."

Ted pushed his bottom lip up, scrunching his chin. "Somebody must have broken in at night. Did a good job of it—without leaving a trace. This device"—he gestured toward the bug—"is simple enough for anyone to use. But getting in and out of here undetected—not so simple."

"But why would anyone want to tap my phone?"

"My guess?" Ted spread his hands. "Given the timing, it's about Carla. Someone is on to her about something—something big enough to make her disappear for awhile. That someone rightly guessed that she'd be talking to you by phone. Maybe a Scenes and Beans reader. Knows Carla's in here every day and would be missed." A flicker of new thought moved across his face. His gaze fell to a small pile of papers on Bailey's desk. "Which would mean maybe he—or she—did this last night."

Bailey blinked. This was too much to assimilate all at once. "How do you know about phone bugs?"

S-Man lifted a shoulder. "Used to read spy novels when I was a teenager."

Bailey gave a sage nod, as if this explanation and everything else that had happened today made ultimate sense. As if her life remained in perfect order. *Lord, please show me what to do. I'm drowning here.*

Ted closed his fingers over the bugging device. "You'll need to put the regular microphones in so you can use your phone. In the meantime you should call Chief Edwards on your cell. He may want to do a sweep of this whole place. Doubt he'll find anything else. But you never know."

The sound of footsteps filtered from the front of the café. Java Joint's lunch crowd was about to begin. "Hey, Bailey?" a male voice called. "Anybody home?"

Normal life summoned. No matter what had just happened, no matter the fear that beat through her veins, Bailey had to pull herself together. “Coming!”

She fetched her purse from beneath her desk and fished out her cell phone. Thrust it toward S-Man. “Here.” Her voice trembled. “Call the chief for me. Tell him what’s going on. I’ve got sandwiches to make.”

Not until Bailey was striding back toward the counter, a smile pinned on her face, did two realizations hit her. One, the call from “Ellie” had been tapped. And two, until those microphones were replaced, the woman wouldn’t be able to call back.

THIRTY-TWO

Carla could hardly think straight. All the way into Pullman, the trooper stayed behind her. She gripped the steering wheel, her muscles riveted into place. Her ankle throbbed, her head pounded, and her stomach writhed with dread. In the downtown area she had to decide which direction to go, north or south. Impulsively she turned right for Highway 195 going to Spokane. If she could lose the trooper somewhere along the way, she could go to the Spokane airport, get a rental car there.

The trooper turned with her.

Soon she was beyond Pullman. A sign read "Spokane, 73 miles." The terrain rolled into gentle hills, the road narrowing to one way each direction. With the trooper behind her, the miles seemed interminable. Carla's muscles hardened to stone. The world shrank—to her car and his, and the open, treacherous road. She couldn't outrun the trooper, didn't dare push the speed limit, or he'd pull her over. Couldn't stop and ask anyone for help.

She should have gone to Chief Edwards when she had the chance. He was one person in law enforcement she *knew* she could trust. Stupid, *stupid.*

Carla glanced in the rearview mirror. The trooper was on his cell phone again.

A tear of fright and rage dropped down her cheek. She pictured Bryson Hanley, victorious in the 2008 election, smiling wife and children at his side. The roaring crowds in the great hall, the confetti and music. She imagined him kissing his wife, hugging his son and daughter. His beautiful, young daughter—almost the very age Carla had been when he'd taken her to his cabin. Yes, she had been old enough to know better, but how much more was he to blame. All charm and suave he'd been to a girl looking to be Somebody. Look what he'd brought her to now.

Carla slowed for a twenty-five miles per hour speed limit and entered the town of Colfax. Population 2,880, according to the sign. Almost three thousand people. If only one could help her. The downtown area was small, with old, redbrick buildings. She passed a United Church of Christ—"Where God Still Speaks."

Deep longing rose in Carla. If only God would speak to her.

The town faded in her rearview mirror, the hated car still following. The next sign for Spokane read fifty-eight miles. Was the trooper going to follow her the whole way? She'd never last that long. Her body and brain would flat-out break down.

Flashing lights in the mirror wrenched Carla's eyes. She checked the trooper's car—and sucked in a breath. He was pulling her over.

THIRTY-THREE

I'm learning the meaning of *suave.* Two weeks ago, I hadn't even heard the word.

"Suave" is Bryson at the office, treating me all businesslike in front of everybody, never letting on what happens behind closed doors. "Suave" is Bryson when his wife came in today. Mrs. My-Husband in the flesh. Who's obviously not doing a very good job keeping her husband happy.

"Suave" is me talking to her all innocent, asking about her day. "Suave" is me with my friends, and with Scott. Acting normal, happy. It's become routine now. The more times Bryson and I manage to be together (we've found a spot I can walk to, and he picks me up to take me to his cabin—I just have to scrunch down in the seat until we get there), the bigger secret I have to keep. And the more times I'm with him, the more I love him. I tell him that, and he always smiles. I know he loves me too. I can tell by the way he treats me when we're together.

So here I am, living two lives. Especially when I'm with Scott. I tell Scott I love him, like always. And the thing is, I *do* love him. Really. It's just so hard to explain, caring for two totally different people at the same time. I don't even understand it myself. And then I go to work, and nobody would guess the words and the kisses that fly between Bryson and me the minute his office door is shut. True, that doesn't happen very often. But it's only because we have to be so careful. Bryson would have me in there all day if we had the chance.

I feel like I've been with Bryson forever. I want to stay with him forever. He's all I think about. Anything else just gets crowded out of my mind. Including Scott. Including all the bad things that could happen.

Problem is, Bryson has this wife and career. We talk about him being elected a US senator. How he wants to be president one day. That's always what he's wanted. I believe he'll get there.

I just wonder where I'll fit in.

He promises me I will. We can stay together; we just have to keep it a secret, he says. Yeah, no kidding. Almost as much for me now as for him. This town would hate me if they knew what I was doing. Mrs. My-Husband is very popular. She volunteers at schools and hospitals, and is always talking about "leading the cause for innocent and underprivileged children." Meantime, who am I? One of those underprivileged children she's talking about. Some high school girl who lives in a shack with no father and a mother who smokes too much. I'd get all the blame for sure.

And Mrs. My-Husband would kill me.

THIRTY-FOUR

Off the lobby of a downtown Seattle hotel, Tanya hunched at a pay phone, counting the rings at Java Joint. Voices filtered from around the corner, one woman's laugh raucous and unnerving. Smells of garlic and onions and grilled meat drifted from the busy restaurant catering to the business lunch crowd. Any other day Tanya may have been one of them. Now amid all the people she felt isolated, alone. Yet watched, as if the hallway were made of eyes.

The phone rang again. *Come on, come on.*

Tanya had done everything she could to lose someone who might be tailing her. She'd left her car in the garage. Walked to one hotel, watching over her shoulder the whole time, slipped out a back way, through an alley and into the side door of another. Still, she couldn't be sure. She was an amateur, up against people so much more powerful than she.

The sixth ring. A voice message clicked on for the third time in a row.

Tanya clattered down the receiver.

For a moment she hovered there, head tilted toward the floor, afraid to turn and face the world. Afraid that when she did, despite all her precautions, she would look into the same pair of eyes that had glared at her from the red SUV. Already, she knew, she had crossed the line.

With one word I can make you disappear . . .

Tanya stared at her shoes, brown against red carpet—and bloody memories from that day long ago screamed in her head.

Her eyes squeezed shut.

She pulled in long breaths until the emotions passed, then felt strangely empty for the lack of them.

Tanya put a hand to her forehead. She had to do something. She couldn't just return to her office, wait another day. Pretend that six hours' drive away, nothing was wrong in the little town of Kanner Lake, Idaho. Carla was still missing from her office; *no one* knew where she was. Now a coffee shop she frequented, one usually open all day, wasn't answering its phone.

Resisting the urge to check over her shoulder, Tanya dug into her purse and pulled out a small yellow sticky note containing a name and number she'd written down last night while on the computer. Using her calling card, she punched in the digits—and held her breath as she waited for the first ring.

THIRTY-FIVE

Carla's tires popped against gravel as she pulled off the road. The trooper's car rolled up behind her like a monster toying with its prey. She watched, heart kicking up her throat, as the man opened his car door and stepped out. Every move so casual and slow, as if he enjoyed making her sweat.

For a crazy moment Carla considered flooring it.

She tried to swallow, but her throat was too dry.

The trooper reached her back bumper. She hit the button to roll down her window.

He was tall. He pulled even with the driver's seat, bent down to look at her, the equipment on his uniform squeaking. The blue shine of his sunglasses hid his eyes, reflecting her own scared face. Carla saw lines around his mouth, parallel frown furrows above his nose. Hollowed cheeks, pocked with black stubble. A cold cynicism coiled around him, as if his job had long ago lost any satisfaction.

He stared at her. "License and registration, please." His voice was smoker's rough.

Carla's tongue wouldn't work. Shaking, she withdrew the envelope with registration and insurance papers from her glove box and handed it to him. Her purse sat on the red suitcase in her passenger seat. She pulled out her wallet. The trooper watched her, unmoving, as she jerked out her driver's license and gave it to him.

He straightened and backed up one step, taking his time with the documents. Carla couldn't see his face. She watched his thick fingers encircle the driver's license, pull the registration and insurance papers from the envelope. He seemed to read every line, turning the papers over to see their blank backs.

He's stalling.

Carla flashed on the image of the trooper talking into a cell phone a second time—and she knew.

She pressed back against the headrest, sudden, surprising anger washing through her. How *dare* he use his law enforcement job to do this to her. She drummed her fingertips hard against the steering wheel. "So what's the problem? I wasn't speeding. You were behind me for *miles*."

The fingers stopped moving. For a second the trooper froze, as if stunned she would dare speak. Then, slowly, radiating heat, the man bent down to look at her through his sunglasses. Carla had the wild thought that the eyes behind those lenses were demon red.

He raised an index finger and pointed it at her. "Sit here while I run your information."

He straightened and walked away, shoes crunching over pebbles. Carla watched him return to his car, reach in through the open window for his radio. She saw his mouth move but heard no words. Was it all faked?

Carla's mind went numb, the anger draining from her body as swiftly as it had come. Why bother being mad? No point in denying the truth—her time had run out. When Thornby showed up, she'd have nowhere to run.

Long minutes passed before the trooper returned. He thrust the license and envelope into her hand without bothering to lean down. She could see no higher than his chin.

"Drive safely."

He turned and walked away.

She stared. That was it? He was letting her *go*?

Carla checked the road behind her. No Thornby.

She jammed her license back into the wallet, threw the envelope in the glove box, and shoved the Toyota into drive. Put on her blinker, checked for traffic, and pulled out onto the highway, forcing herself not to scratch off.

The trooper made a U-turn and receded in her rearview mirror.

Carla almost dared to breathe.

A minute later she checked the rearview mirror again—and saw it. A car on the horizon, gaining fast. It didn't take long for Carla to recognize it. A black Durango.

THIRTY-SIX

Things haven't changed since I wrote two days ago. I knew I was late for a period then. Had known for awhile. I just didn't want to face it.

I can't deny the truth anymore.

Of course I know to the day. The birth control pills made me totally regular. About a day and a half after I took the last pill for a month, a period would come. Now – nothing.

How in the world could they work so well in stopping cramps, but not stop me from getting pregnant?

When the day came to start taking the next batch of pills – I didn't. Once I do, I for sure won't have a period. And I'd have to wait a whole other month to see if one starts on time.

I've been worrying so much, sometimes I think my head's going to burst. And I can't tell *anybody*. It hasn't helped that Bryson's been out of town a lot. He's traveling around the state, shaking hands and meeting people. I watch him on the news every night, and a knife goes through my heart. He's so charming and smooth. He talks about the things he'll do for the country as a US senator. How he's wanted to serve his country since he was a boy, and how his parents encouraged him. He talks about what a "team" he and Catherine are. How much she's behind him. I watched him give a speech about the importance of education and parenting and the "family unit."

Does he think of me here at home? Does he ever think how his speeches make me feel? Like dirt, that's how. Bryson is *so* far above me. I was lucky enough just to work for him. Bryson Hanley is "everybody's man," like Jilke says. Everybody loves Bryson.

Well, I love him too. But I'm left out of the picture.

Meanwhile I'm stuck in the office with Jilke, who gives me hard looks all the time, like he *knows.* Sometimes I wonder if Bryson has told him about us. I know he wouldn't, but ... Maybe we haven't been as great at keeping the truth off our faces as I thought.

But if that's true, who else might know?

Scott doesn't, at least. I've made sure of that. We park in the forest almost every night now – and I give him all the sex he wants. Not that I feel much of anything while we're doing it, but it keeps his mind off how down I've been lately.

I got Mary Kay to drive me to Seattle yesterday, supposedly to hang out. I went into a drugstore and bought a home pregnancy test kit and a bunch of makeup. Hid the kit at the bottom of the bag. That was less risky than buying one in town, where some cashier is bound to know me. Now the thing's stuffed under clothes in my dresser. I'm too afraid to take it. What if it's positive? What would I do? For now at least I have hope.

I don't want to lose hope.

THIRTY-SEVEN

"Jared, sure you don't want something?" Twenty-one-year-old Leslie Brymes pushed away from her desk in the cluttered *Kanner Lake Times* office and reached for her purse. Her crystal-studded watch read twelve-thirty—which meant one thing: it was past time for her second biggie latte of the day.

"No, thanks." Jared Moore, owner of the newspaper, waved a hand at her, eyes not rising from his computer. "Got to finish this story, then be going home for lunch soon anyway."

"Okay, your loss."

Leslie hustled across the dusty wood floor toward the front door, her mind flitting over various news items. Steel structures for the new hotel by the city beach two blocks away now jutted into the sky. Late that afternoon Leslie had an appointment with the developer for updates on the hotel's completion schedule. Some said next spring, some next fall. Leslie wanted the inside scoop. Completion in spring could make a lot of difference in next summer's tourism. Then in a couple weeks the suspect from the Kanner Lake murders last March was headed to trial—in Boise, thanks to a change of venue. Unfortunately Leslie would not be covering the trial. She'd be a *part* of it, called to the stand as one of the first prosecution witnesses. Of all the hard luck. Jared would get the byline on every article.

Yeah, well, don't be forgetting all you've learned. People dead, and you're thinking of a byline.

She pulled open the door and stepped out to a sunny afternoon, unusually warm for September. Once Labor Day passed, the Kanner Lake weather could turn on a dime. Warm one day, doggone frigid the next. She may have grown up in Idaho, but Leslie never could get used to the cold. She turned down Main Street, shielding her eyes from the sun. *Drat.* Her sunglasses still sat on her desk.

She turned back to fetch them. "Forgot something," she mumbled to Jared as she entered. He barely looked up.

As she neared her desk the phone rang. She picked up her sunglasses with one hand and the receiver in the other, noting the Seattle area code on the ID. "*Kanner Lake Times*, Leslie Brymes."

"Hello, I ... I'm ..." A woman's voice. Sounding downright scared. Just like Ali Frederick's voice last March. And that phone call had led to *terrible* things ...

Immediate memories rushed Leslie. Her mouth ran dry.

A crazy part of her wanted to bang down the phone. Whatever this was, she didn't need any more drama. Nobody in town did. But the reporter in her pushed her arm to grab a pen, sank her body into the desk chair. "Hi." She infused warmth into her voice. "How can I help you?"

"I ... need to talk to you about Carla Radling." The words now rushed. "I can't get hold of her, and the woman at Java Joint wouldn't give me her number, and that was hours ago, and now they're not even answering their phone. I must find Carla. I must talk to her—*soon*."

Leslie tried to make sense of the run-on. "Who am I speaking with, please?"

"Tanya Evans. That's my real name—so Carla will recognize it. I told the woman at Java Joint it was Ellie."

"Oh." Leslie frowned. "Why?"

"Because I was afraid. People are watching me. But now I'm afraid I'm running out of time." She drew a quick breath. "Have you seen Carla?"

"Not today." She'd never shown up at Java Joint. Leslie got an earful from Wilbur when she bought her latte that morning. "Have you tried her office?"

"She's not there. *Nobody* knows where she is."

Leslie stared at the worn wood on her desk. *Nobody* knew where Carla was?

"Please. You have to help me find her. I'm afraid she's in trouble."

"Why do you say that?"

"Someone broke into my home last night—to warn me not to talk about things of the past. Things that involve Carla."

Whoa. "What things?"

"I can't tell you. But I have a lot to tell her. Things she doesn't even know. I *have* to tell her in case ... in case I don't make it."

Leslie was already jotting notes. The scratch of pen against paper felt good, normal. She could almost convince herself this was an ordinary Kanner Lake call. Someone's dog had gotten lost, or somebody fell in an aisle of the IGA grocery store. Everyday inconveniences—not another trauma that could again spin lives in Kanner Lake out of control.

"Tell you what," Leslie said slowly. She wasn't about to give out Carla's number until she was sure who this woman was. "Let me give you my own cell number." She rattled off the digits, then repeated them. "I'll go look for Carla, and when I find her, I'll have her contact you. This number you called from. Is it your cell?"

"No, it's a pay phone."

"Oh. Well, I'll need a number for you."

"I can't give one to you. I'm afraid they may be watching my phones. Maybe not, but ... when someone breaks into your house, it's easy to get paranoid."

No kidding—*if* this woman was telling the truth.

But something in the woman's voice told Leslie she was.

"*Please* give me Carla's number." Tanya sounded desperate. "I'm running from one pay phone to the next. There's no safe way for her to call me, and I *have* to talk to her!"

Leslie closed her eyes. She shouldn't do it. Not a cautious move.

"Tanya, I promise I will hunt down Carla for you. But we need a way to reach you. Can you borrow somebody's cell?"

"I don't *know*. I just ..."

"All right then. Call me back on my cell as soon as you can give me a number. In the meantime I'll look for Carla. Promise."

"Okay." Defeat coated Tanya's voice.

Before Leslie could say anything more, the line went dead.

THIRTY-EIGHT

After work—another day with Bryson gone—I couldn't stand it anymore. I had to take the test. The stick turned pink.

Pregnant.

It's like I'm dead. I can't even feel. Can't even cry. I think about what I've done, and the lie I've been living, and want to wish that Bryson never happened. But I can't imagine him not happening. I can't imagine going back to the way life was, even after this. How *stupid* is that?

Scott knows something's wrong. I made an excuse not to see him again tonight—third time in a week. Probably thinks I'm about to break up with him. I'm not. I *need* Scott. He's so sweet to me. He doesn't deserve what I've done to him. Not at all.

Bryson comes back day after tomorrow. I've been counting the days. But I have no idea what I'm going to tell him. How can I possibly hide this from him? Still, I'm afraid if he knows, I'll lose him.

I should just get an abortion and be done with it. Except I don't have the money after spending my paychecks on clothes. Besides, look what happened to my friend Christine. She had one, then cried for two months. On the way out of the clinic we saw a picture of an aborted baby some protestor was carrying. Great help I was to Christine. I bawled almost worse than she did. The picture was awful. How can I do that to a little baby?

How *can't* I? No way can I stay pregnant.

Maybe Scott would help me pay for an abortion. Of course he'll believe the baby's his. Bryson would never need to know. But Scott's Catholic. What if he told me he expected me to have the baby? That he'd never forgive me for having an abortion. Then I'd *really* be stuck.

Or what if I told Bryson I'm pregnant with Scott's baby? Maybe he wouldn't be mad, and *he'd* pay for the abortion. I *so* need him to hold me and tell me everything's going to be okay. To help me figure this out. He's done so much for me already. He wouldn't abandon me now.

But what if he did get mad? The first time we were together, I told Bryson I'd never slept with Scott—and I've never said anything's changed. If he heard I was pregnant by someone else now, would he ever want to see me again?

I *can't* lose Bryson.

My thoughts go around and around, and I don't know what to do. Either way I'll be lying to somebody. How can I live with that for the rest of my life?

THIRTY-NINE

There she is.

Cold satisfaction surged through Tony. He pressed the gas pedal, eyes fixed on the white Toyota. At last. Just seeing the back of Miss Wit's head sent a zing through his veins. Never had closing in on a target felt so good.

He caught up to her car and slowed. Three car lengths away—that would do it. Far enough to react in case she hit her brakes. Close enough to keep another car from slipping between them.

Even though he itched to stop her now, he had to play this carefully. He couldn't just drive up beside Carla Radling and put a bullet in her head. He needed her alive, able to tell him what she'd taken from that hatbox. Where it was now. And who else knew about it.

Timmy's life depended on that information.

Tailing someone was tricky. Not like in the movies. Running a car off the road was a huge gamble. What if another driver came along and stopped to help? And what if that person noticed things—like white paint on the grille of his black vehicle. Traffic on this highway seemed to vary—some miles he'd seen no other cars, then three or four would appear. If he found a window of time, the right spot, he'd go for it. If not—Carla Radling had to stop somewhere, sometime. When she did, he'd be there.

For now, he could almost smell her fear. It made him smile.

His "Barry" cell phone rang. Tony flipped it open. "Yeah."

"Andy here. I think they found the bugs."

Tony blinked. "You're kidding."

"Nah. All's silent."

Not that it mattered, now that he had Miss Wit. Andy's hidden position in a van down the street from Java Joint, listening to phone calls, was no longer necessary. Still, what would have made an oblivious coffee shop owner search for bugs in her phone?

"Got any idea why?"

"Not a clue." Andy sniffed. "What do you want me to do now?"

"Get *out* of there, that's what."

"Hey, I'm long gone; they ain't gonna find me. Just wondered if you had a plan B."

Carla was watching him in her rearview mirror. Tony could tell by the slight movement of her head. His lip curled.

"Okay, Andy, here's what you do. Go home and eat some breakfast. Kiss your wife. Hide the tapes until I can stop by for the usual exchange—tapes for your money."

Always, phone call tapes before payment—that was non-negotiable. Tony never left evidence like that sitting around.

Andy grunted. "That one call I told you about—from Ellie. Anything useful come of that?"

The man was forgetting himself. First rule of the game—*don't* ask questions. Fortunately for him, Tony was now in a good mood.

"Nah, nothing. Now go home. Call you when I need you."

That could be next week, next month, next year. Tony snapped the phone shut and threw it on the seat. Right now he couldn't look past the next minute. Didn't want to.

He planned to enjoy every second of Miss Wit's terror.

FORTY

Leslie hurried out of the *Kanner Lake Times* office, turned to head down the street—and froze. Two police cars sat outside Java Joint.

Lunch break?

Maybe. But after Tanya's call, and Leslie's subsequent conversation with the receptionist at the realty company where Carla worked—who had absolutely *no idea* where Carla was and now sounded close to panic—Leslie doubted it. Plus, she'd called Carla's cell three times. It was turned off.

Wasn't like Carla to turn her phone off during a workday.

Leslie shoved her purse up on her shoulder and trotted down the street.

Through the coffee shop windows she spotted Chief Edwards and twenty-five-year-old Officer Frank West standing near the cash register, talking to Bailey. In spite of her worry, Leslie's heart performed a little tap dance at the sight of Frank. As usual, his dark hair was perfect, his jaw chiseled, and those shoulders just ached to be hugged. If only. Ted Dawson—S-Man—stood next to Chief Edwards, hands shoved in his pockets and thick brows together, looking perplexed.

No customers. Any lunch-timers must have gotten their sandwiches and run.

Leslie pushed through the door, and all four heads turned her direction. Chief Edwards looked grim. She huffed across to the counter. "What's going on?"

Frank and Chief Edwards exchanged a glance. Ted gave her one of those penetrating looks that went to her soul. She tingled with sudden awkwardness. Leslie knew how S-Man felt about her. The feeling had apparently grown ever since they'd been thrown together in a battle of life and death last March. Was she as transparent? Did he see her reaction in Frank's presence, even as something deep inside her, something inexplicable and not quite formed, tugged her eyes back toward Ted?

"Well, *what*?" Leslie tossed hair out of her eyes. "Does it have to do with Carla?"

Frank pulled back his head. "What do you know about Carla?"

"Not much except she's missing. She's not answering her cell; nobody at her work knows where she is. And some woman from 'her past' wants to get ahold of her like it's a matter of life and death."

Bailey drew in a breath. "Ellie? Did she call *you*?"

"Yes." Leslie slid her purse off her arm and clumped it on the counter. "Only her name's Tanya, not Ellie—she lied to you. And she says someone's after her, and they might be after Carla too, and meanwhile, you're not answering your phone, and Ted's frowning and all worried, and *you* two"—she wagged a finger from Chief Edwards to Frank—"are looking way too serious to be ordering roast beef on rye."

Chief Edwards drew a long breath, and Leslie saw a flash of his vulnerability. He'd lost a son in the Iraq war a little over two years ago—a son who would be her age. Chief had also lived through the events of Edna San's death, then the murders of last March. Vince Edwards was the last person who'd welcome any more tragedy to his town.

The chief put both hands on his hips. "Looks like we'd better compare notes."

Leslie told them of her conversation with Tanya Evans.

Chief frowned. "If she thinks she's in danger, has she gone to the police?"

"She didn't mention it. But I don't know why she wouldn't go to them."

When Chief Edwards told her of two bugged phones, Leslie's mouth dropped open.

He gestured with his chin. "The place is clear now. We called in some techs from the Sheriff's Department for a sweep, and they managed to get here in record time. The phones were also dusted for prints. Frankly, I'd be surprised to find any that can't be matched to Bailey or somebody. Whoever did this likely wore gloves."

Leslie worked to stay calm. *Think like a reporter, not a past victim. Not as Carla's friend.* Her eyes grazed S-Man's, then locked with the chief's. "What now?"

He straightened. "First, I suppose I don't have to tell you everything I just said is off the record." He gave Leslie a hard look.

She bit back her irritation. "You're right, you don't."

He nodded. "Second, I'm going to put out a missing person's bulletin on Carla. We'll start looking for her. Leslie, if you hear back from this Tanya, I need to know about it. I'll want to talk to her, see what she knows."

"Okay."

The two policemen took their leave, a nod passing between Ted and Frank. Leslie had no time to dwell on the meaning of that. Her thoughts were spinning.

If anybody found Carla, it would be her.

Forget being a reporter, Leslie was Carla's friend. Leslie didn't know her real well, she had to admit. Carla was over ten years older. But then—who did really know Carla? For all her teasing at the Java Joint counter, she'd always kept people at arm's length.

Leslie, Bailey, and Ted watched through the windows as the policemen slid into their cars and drove away. Before she knew it, Leslie's hand found Ted's arm. She squeezed, looking into his face. "I don't want anything to happen to her."

He nodded and slipped his hand over hers. "We'll find her."

We. Leslie managed a smile.

Bailey exhaled loudly. "Well." She wiped the palms of her hands together. "You want a latte, Leslie?"

Serving. Bailey's way of clinging to normalcy in the midst of this new unknown. Leslie shot Bailey an understanding—and grateful—look. "Please. To go. Then I'm out of here. I've got to find Carla."

As Bailey turned toward the espresso machine, Leslie's cell phone rang. She snatched it from her purse and checked the incoming number.

The Seattle pay phone.

FORTY-ONE

I told Bryson this afternoon at the cabin.

I wasn't going to. I'd decided to leave him out of it, just tell Scott. It was the right thing to do. Just let it be Scott and me, as it should be. Like before Bryson ever came along.

But in the end I couldn't do it.

We were lying on the bed, knowing we had to get up soon and get dressed. All of a sudden, Bryson said, "I'm not going to be able to see you as much, Carla. We've been taking too many chances, and as much as I want to be with you all the time, I just can't."

I panicked. Lying next to him, knowing I'm pregnant, I totally panicked. I know he's been taking a lot of chances. And suddenly, I could imagine him telling me we'd have to stop completely. Not because he'd want to, but because of his career and his wife. I couldn't let that happen. When it came right down to it, no matter what—I *couldn't* lose him.

The next thing I knew, I was blurting out, "I'm pregnant."

He pulled away from me, eyes bugging. His face went white. "You couldn't be that late; how do you know for sure?"

"I took a home pregnancy test."

He flexed his jaw. "I thought you said you were on the Pill."

"I did. I am. But it didn't work."

"*How* could it not *work*?"

"I don't know! I'm sorry. I never would've guessed—"

"Are you sure the baby's mine?"

The look on his face. He was scaring me. "Of course it's yours."

"Have you told anyone?"

"No way."

"You've told no one you're pregnant."

"No."

He rolled away, sat up, his back to me. I stared at the way his spine stuck through his skin. He put his head in his hands and stayed there for a long time.

I touched him on the shoulder. "I'm so sorry."

No reply.

Tears stung my eyes. I sat there looking at him, feeling very alone. Like a wall had gone up between us. He'd never been mad at me before. I couldn't stand it.

"I'll do whatever you want." My voice shook. "Just tell me, and I'll do it."

He pulled in a long breath. When he turned to me, he looked grim. "Do you love me, Carla?"

That hurt so much. "You know I do."

"I've trusted you. All my life I've worked my way up the political ladder. Even as a boy I knew what I wanted to do. I've laid it all on the line to be with you. Don't betray me."

"I *won't*." Tears fell down my cheeks.

He leaned over me, put his hands on my face. His eyes turned misty. "You want to be with me again, don't you?"

"Yes, *always*."

Bryson stroked my forehead. "I want to be with you too."

I was sobbing by then. "I'll have an abortion if you want. I just … I don't have the money to pay for it."

"I know."

"Is that what you want me to do?"

He gazed into my eyes. "Do you want an abortion?"

"Yes. No. I don't know. I think they're awful, but …"

He wiped my tears. "I couldn't make you do something you would regret."

"Then – "

"Shh." Bryson stroked my hair. "Look, let's not panic. Sometimes those home tests don't work so well. The first thing you need to do is go to a doctor for a test. I'll pay for it. You can go to the same one Catherine goes to – Dr. Hughes. He's the best doctor around. I've known him since I was a kid. Our families are very close, and he's almost like a father to me. He's also one of my biggest supporters. His practice is closed to new patients, but I'll get you in."

"Then won't he know – "

"You still have that boyfriend?"

I blinked. No way did I want to talk about Scott, especially not in the middle of this conversation. "Yes."

Suspicion crept across Bryson's face. "If you are pregnant, how do you know it's not his?"

"I *told* you the first time we were together that Scott and I hadn't done anything."

He studied my face. "But now you are. Aren't you. It's written all over you."

I wanted to run out of the cabin. Melt into the covers. How I wished I hadn't said anything to him. But now it was too late, and I wasn't going to lose him. I thought about telling him Scott and I hadn't slept together until *after* I'd been with him. But suddenly I didn't trust Bryson. What if he wouldn't listen? What if he insisted the baby was Scott's and walked away?

He leaned toward me, expression hardening. "*Aren't* you?"

"*No.* And you'd better believe that, Bryson Hanley. Scott's ... shy. This baby's *yours.*"

He pulled back, gaze holding mine. I refused to look away. A series of emotions flicked across his face. Doubt. Fear. And something else.

Triumph?

"All right, Carla. You said you'd do whatever I want."

No way could I lose him. My life would be over. I nodded.

"Start sleeping with your boyfriend. And do it often."

My eyes went wide. Numbness crept through my chest.

"I'll set you up with Dr. Hughes. I'll tell him you're afraid your boyfriend's got you pregnant, and I'm trying to help you out."

Well, what a twist. He wanted me to "start" what I was already doing. What I'd denied so hard. But how could Bryson *want* me to sleep with Scott? Wouldn't he feel jealous at all? And why did he think I needed to anyway? Why wasn't he willing to just lie to the doctor?

He ran a finger down my cheek. "Will you do it?"

I swallowed. Then nodded.

He smiled. "That's my girl."

I'm not stupid. I was just so distracted by the lies I'd told and Bryson's reaction to everything. By the time I got home I understood all too well. If anyone else found out I was pregnant, they had to have reason to believe it was Scott's. Including Scott himself.

How ironic—the trap I've gotten myself into. And how unfair that Scott will pay.

Tonight I went out with Scott. Parked with him in the forest as usual. We had sex. He told me he loved me, and I said I loved him. I started to cry and of course couldn't explain why. As sweet as he's been to me. As much as he loves me, and look what I'm doing to him. What I will do to him.

But there's no backing out now.

God will punish me for this.

FORTY-TWO

Every muscle in Carla's body shook. Her brain flip-flopped from numb to panic. She could smell her fear. She felt like a mouse running from a cat, knowing death was on her heels.

Thornby's black SUV kept a steady three car lengths behind her. Close enough for her to see the victorious expression on his face. The guy was practically salivating.

Carla stepped on the gas. Thornby sped up with her.

Cars from the opposite direction passed every minute or so. Apparently often enough to keep Thornby from doing anything wild. But that could change any moment. What she needed was a car *ahead* of her. Miles passed, but she saw none. Finally, as she rounded a curve, she spotted one about a half mile ahead.

She pushed the accelerator like some race car driver, fingers glued to the wheel. Thornby stayed with her. The Toyota's speedometer read seventy, eighty, eighty-five, ninety miles per hour. Golden hills whizzed by. Before long she'd closed the distance. Carla eased off the gas until her speed fell back to sixty, positioning herself three lengths behind the blue sedan.

Take that, Mr. Fake Englishman.

A speed-limit sign soon slowed the trio down. Carla swiped sweat from her forehead as they entered Steptoe, a tiny burg with a few houses and a church with a pretty white steeple. A Shell gas station with a Friendly Mart. All so quiet and normal. The few people on the street, the man coming out of the small store—they'd never guess the death dance between these three cars.

What if she swerved into the gas station and jumped from her car? Ran screaming into the mart—"He's trying to kill me!" Would Thornby follow? Would he shoot her and everyone else inside? Even so, maybe she'd have a chance ...

Whatever, Carla, just save yourself!

Her hands poised to turn the wheel—

A young mother with a baby in her arms stepped out of the Friendly Mart.

Carla's fingers jerked. The Toyota shot past the store.

Tears bit Carla's eyes. She slumped back against the seat, despair steamrolling her muscles.

Before she knew it, they'd passed the town.

The sedan in front of her gleamed in the sun, one remaining ray of hope. At least it hadn't turned into some driveway. Hills rolled by on either side, large silos jutting into blue sky.

A sign read "Spokane, 47 miles."

She'd never live that long.

For the hundredth time Carla glanced in the rearview mirror. Thornby's car was still three lengths behind her.

Cell phone. The sudden thought sprang to her mind.

Yes, cell phone! No point in keeping off it now that Thornby had caught her. In fact, the right call just might save her life. She could contact the Spokane police, then drive straight to their station.

Eyes on the road, Carla fumbled in her purse for the phone.

Call any law enforcement, someone in Vince Edwards's family dies.

Okay, call friends and acquaintances then. Lots of them. Thornby couldn't kill them all. Phone her work, and Java Joint, and Simple Pleasures, and ten other businesses in Kanner Lake. Tell everyone if something happened to her, they should look for a dark-haired man named David Thornby in a rented black Durango . . .

Right, Carla, like that's a valid ID. Your calls won't scare him off, 'cause he knows he won't be found.

No, huh-uh. She couldn't believe that. Carla's fingers scrambled. Where the heck was her phone? She felt wallet, checkbook, makeup bag—déjà vu of yesterday's frantic search for her car key. *There!* She yanked the cell out, snapped it open. Pushed the button to turn it on . . .

No service. And her battery was almost shot.

"No!" She shook it, turned it this way and that.

No bars.

Fear blew through her like a winter wind, and her bones rattled. Carla fought to keep calm. No time to wig out now; she had to *think*.

She threw the cell on top of the suitcase. Okay, okay. Cell service faded in and out. The minute she got a bar or two, she'd call.

Blue sedan, white Toyota, black Durango. The Highway 195 trio, locked in their dance, one partner not even knowing the part he played.

They passed a rest area on the left. Rest—what was that? Highway 271 south toward Rosalia exited on the right. Carla didn't dare swerve onto it. She needed to stay behind the sedan.

Spokane—thirty-two miles.

What would she do when she reached the city? Could she lose Thornby in traffic?

If so, what then?

The truth hit her like a rogue wave. Fact was, it didn't matter. Thornby would keep coming back. Again and again. And if she put him out of business—killed him, even—someone else would take his place. She wasn't dying for some 007 knock-off. She was dying for the empire of Bryson Hanley. Who would only become more powerful, and therefore more afraid of the damage she could do with each passing day.

There was only one last-ditch way to save her life. Expose Hanley. Give up the diary, tell the world what she knew.

Carla's throat crimped shut. She couldn't do it. Couldn't sacrifice herself to the gossip-hungry world. Couldn't expose other innocent people. Couldn't, *wouldn't* do it.

Her cell beeped twice. Was she in range now? Carla picked up the phone, feeling a stir of hope.

Still no service. She'd heard the low-battery warning.

Carla let out a long breath, her hope slipping away. No one to run to, no way to call anyone. She was safe in her car only as long as she drove, with other vehicles around.

Her gas gauge read less than a quarter tank.

She dropped the cell back into her purse. A few minutes later, with two final beeps, it turned itself off.

The trio of cars passed a tiny area called Spangle. A restaurant, houses, a few silos. Spokane was eighteen miles away.

If only she'd never told Bryson Hanley he was the father of her baby. If only she'd stayed with Scott. At least when the pregnancy was over and the world closed down around her, she could have clung to him.

How about it, Bryson? If it weren't for the pregnancy, would you let me live today?

Carla's mind dulled. She barely noticed the rolling hills giving way to flat land and forest, houses popping up. She snapped out of it when the highway divided into two lanes each direction.

They were nearing Spokane.

The blue sedan turned off, but it no longer mattered. More cars pulled onto the road from this or that entrance, traffic doubling, tripling. Carla saw more houses, stores. A sign reduced the speed limit to fifty-five. Then another sign: Interstate 90—one mile.

Interstate 90 dissected Spokane, running east and west. Her gas gauge was approaching an eighth of a tank.

Carla, babe, better figure out what you're going to do.

FORTY-THREE

I can't believe what Bryson wants me to do.

For the first time in three weeks, I got to be with him at the cabin. He's been out of town a lot. The closest I could get to him was watching him on the news, shaking hands and charming everybody as usual. But after the test at the doctor's office confirmed I'm pregnant and Bryson came back, he still kept telling me he couldn't get away. Didn't he want me anymore? I was crying every day. And I've been sick. Every morning. It's awful, throwing up when I'm trying to get ready for school. It usually passes after my first class. But I've been tired and *so* depressed, just waiting to see Bryson. Knowing I have to get money from him for an abortion.

Mary Kay knows I'm pregnant. I couldn't hide it from her anymore. Of course she thinks the baby is Scott's. What a two-faced—make that three-faced—game I'm playing. If anyone knew how complicated this whole thing really is.

This morning Mom attacked me. She's heard me throwing up so it's not like I could deny it. She stood there in her bathrobe, smoker-hacking as usual, black hair uncombed and all those lines on her hard face. She looks so much older than thirty-three. She slouched in my bedroom doorway and gave me one of her "you disgust me" looks.

"Don't even try tellin' me you're not pregnant."

I slumped on my bed, sweaty, with a sour taste in my mouth. Too sick to talk.

"Well?"

I raised my head and looked at her. Tears stung my eyes, but I blinked them back. I will not cry in front of my mother. "You shouldn't be surprised." My voice sounded dead. "You did the same thing at my age."

Anger screwed up her face. "Don't you talk to me like that!"

"Like *what*? I'm just telling the truth!"

Her eyes closed, as if she could hardly contain her disappointment. Breath sucked in and out of her mouth. "Whose is it?"

What, like she should think I've been sleeping with the world? "Whose do you think?"

"Does he know?"

"No."

"Good. Get yourself an abortion before he does and get rid of the thing. A good Catholic boy like him might give you a hard time about it."

The "good Catholic boy" dripped with sarcasm, but I hardly noticed. She'd called the baby a "thing." A *thing*. Suddenly it hit me. When she was my age, if she'd had an abortion, if she'd treated me like a "thing" to get rid of—I wouldn't *be* here.

"What makes you think I want an abortion?"

She stared at me. "What do you know about raising a baby?"

"What did *you* know?"

She drew back, eyes narrowing. Pointed a snaggy-nailed finger at me. "I do *not* want a baby in this house, is that clear? No way am I raisin' another squally kid. You were enough."

Heat flushed through my body. Did *no one* want me? Not Mom, not Bryson. It took everything I had not to cry. "You made that very clear long ago, *dear Mom*. So don't you worry. If I have this baby, I won't let you get *near* it."

"You can't have a baby, Carla! How are you going to finish school? You going to quit before your senior year? End up waitressing all your life like me? I want something better for you than that."

Really? Could have fooled me.

"Carla. Go. Get. An abortion."

"Maybe I don't have the money! You want to pay for it?"

She threw her hands in the air. "Don't look at *me*. It's all I can do to keep a roof over your head. You should have plenty money after working in that fancy office all summer. It's your fault if you've been spending it all on clothes and CDs."

We argued for another five minutes until Mom yelled, "Don't talk to me again until you get rid of it!" She slammed my bedroom door and stomped away so hard the walls rattled.

Such a fun morning.

But Bryson and I were meeting in the afternoon. Finally. I couldn't wait to see him, and I was also scared to death. Would he give me the money? Would he help me through this?

Did he still care for me?

Surprise—at the cabin we sat on the couch and talked. That's it. I didn't miss the sex at all. I just wanted to be close to him. To feel his arms around me and hear him say everything's going to be okay. I told him how much I'd missed him. Couldn't help crying. He said how sorry he was and held me tight. Said he'd been thinking of me all the time, trying to figure out what to do.

I studied his eyes. "Don't you want me to get an abortion?"

He got that look on his face that I've seen so many times on TV. That serious expression, like he's about to say something profound, something he absolutely believes is right, no matter who says otherwise. His eyes narrow a little, and his mouth firms, and he nods. And looking at him, you just know what a great man he is, and that you can believe every word he says.

"I've been thinking about this." He smoothed a strand of hair from my face. "I know the simple thing would be to just abort the pregnancy. But I'm going to tell you something about me that most people don't know. Something very ... hurtful. Can I trust you with it?"

"You know you can."

"Okay." He gave me a sad smile. "I've told you before that Catherine has been trying for years to get pregnant, and it's never worked. Her cycle is very irregular, often with months between periods. She's been going to Dr. Hughes. He's sent her to specialists. All the tests on both of us have indicated that we're fine as far as being able to produce children, if we can just time it right. But still, no pregnancy. Something had to be wrong with one of us. But who?" He took a long breath. "I thought I knew the answer to that, but still, in the back of my mind I wondered. When you became pregnant, I knew for sure."

I thought back to when I told him. That look of triumph on his face.

"Catherine and I have been thinking for some time about a private adoption. Carla, I *need* to have children. Not just because I want them badly, but because it's good for my career. People vote for a family man, someone who can show he's committed to his children. You understand that?"

My throat tightened. I did understand. I'd learned a lot about politics since I started working with Bryson. I heard the news enough to know that the *person* was every bit as important as the issues he stood for. I just hated to hear the term "family man" come out of Bryson's mouth. "Family" didn't include me.

"Yes."

"Good. And you know what an advocate I've been for giving children a stable, loving home."

I nodded.

Tenderness creased his face. He leaned down and kissed me gently. Like he loved me more than anyone else in the world.

He pulled away. "You once told me you thought abortion was 'awful.'"

I thought of my mom, how one visit to the doctor would have ended my life. Of the photo I'd seen of the dead baby. "I do, but—"

"Carla, I can make it so you don't have to have an abortion. So you won't carry that guilt in your conscience."

What did he know about "that guilt"? He was a staunch supporter of abortion.

"Here's what you do. Have the baby. Everyone will assume it's your boyfriend's. Let them. Catherine and I will sign an agreement with you and him for a private adoption. That means we'll pay for everything. You'll get the best of care from Dr. Hughes. Once the baby's born, you both can know he or she will be in a loving family. And *you*, alone, will know the baby's being raised by his own real father. You will be helping my career, as I know you want to do, because you love me. And more important, you'll be doing the best for the baby."

I stared at him, stunned. So many thoughts crowded my mind, I couldn't think what to say first. "Let me get this straight. You want me to tell Scott the baby is his, then turn around and ask him to sign it away. To you."

Pain flicked across Bryson's face, as if he couldn't believe I would think badly of him. "Scott is going to think the baby's his anyway. We have no other choice but to let people think that, do we?"

"Of course we have a 'choice' – not to let the pregnancy continue in the first place." My voice went flat. "In fact, isn't that your word for the whole abortion issue? Women should have a choice?"

"Carla." He shook his head. "You're going to be a great lawyer some day."

He smiled indulgently, but I couldn't smile back. He was asking me to stay pregnant. For *nine months*. To have the baby. True, I didn't like the idea of abortion, but to really think about staying pregnant. Being sick every morning. Getting fat. Going through labor.

"Look. Honey." He smoothed my hair. "Wouldn't it hurt you to know you got rid of a baby you and I created? When I wanted so badly to raise it?"

I looked down at my lap, feeling my cheeks burn. "But if I have the baby, aren't you afraid someone will find out about us?"

He nudged my chin up so he could look me in the eye. "*You* won't tell, will you? Knowing what it would do to me? Knowing what it would cost you and our baby?"

Our baby. The words knifed through me. How could I let Bryson think I wanted to harm the baby? "No, Bryson. I won't ever tell anyone."

"Neither will I. No one will know but the two of us. And Jilke. He'll help make sure everything goes smoothly."

My eyes widened. "*Jilke* knows?"

Bryson smiled again, like a father would smile at his child. "Carla, Jilke knows everything about me. He runs my career. He protects it. He's not going to let anything hurt me. So don't worry. He'll be kind to you and make sure you have everything you need."

"You make it sound like I'll never see you outside of work! That I can never really *be* with you again!"

"Carla, it's been too much of a risk all along. You know that. I'll still be here for you."

"But I can't lose you, Bryson!" Tears ran down my cheeks. "If having this baby means I'll never be with you again—I can't *do* it! I just want to *be* with you!"

"Carla, shhh." He pulled me close again, and I sobbed against his neck. "Don't. It's okay. Forget I ever said that. I *will* manage to see you. You know how much I want to."

I hiccupped. Wiped my eyes with the back of my hand. "You promise?"

"Of course I do. You won't lose me, Carla, you won't. And just think—even when we can't be together, we'll always be connected through the baby. Forever."

I pushed away and sat up. Feeling so very tired. "*Why* did I have to get pregnant? Why didn't the stupid Pill work? I just want it to go back to the way things used to be."

Yeah, and pigs want to fly.

If only I'd never told Bryson I'm pregnant. If only I could take it back. Maybe I could have borrowed the money for an abortion from friends. Scraped it together somehow. Maybe an abortion wouldn't be so bad. Maybe my conscience wouldn't hurt too much. Or at least I'd get over it. Someday.

Now I have to go to Scott and tell him he's going to be a father. Then convince him to give up his own baby. I'm already rehearsing the lines. "Are you ready to raise a baby? *I'm* not! This way, the baby can live, but we don't have to raise him. Or her. We can know she's in a good home ..."

I sound like a politician.

We will have to have meetings with Bryson and his wife to discuss the adoption, Bryson told me. We're doing what's called an "independent adoption." We'll have to go through the courts. Someone will be assigned to the case. That someone will meet with the Hanleys and make sure they'll be good parents. And also meet with me to make sure I want this. I'll get counseling. And I can change my mind. So can the Hanleys, but I can't imagine why they would.

When I think of Mrs. My-Husband raising my baby, part of me wants to throw up. But there's another part of me that thinks, *Now who's the better one, huh? Who gave Bryson something you couldn't?*

Bryson is right. No matter what happens, as long as he's raising my baby, we're connected. He *can't* forget me.

But when I look into Catherine Hanley's eyes, I wonder how I'm going to keep the smirk off my face.

FORTY-FOUR

"Tanya?"

Leslie Brymes's taut voice made Tanya shudder. Just fifteen minutes ago, Leslie had sounded totally calm. "Yes, it's me. Have you found Carla?"

"No. And her cell phone's turned off. But there's—"

"What am I going to *do*?" Tanya pressed a hand against her forehead. She'd been in this hotel far too long. Anyone she'd given the slip would've had more than enough time to find her. "I just don't—"

"*Listen* to me. Something has happened. That call you made to Java Joint this morning—it was tapped. You hear? Somebody out there knows you called."

Tanya felt the blood drain from her body. She slapped a hand against the wall, steadying herself. For a long, white moment, all thought fled.

"Tanya?"

"I . . . yes."

Somebody out there knows you called.

She had to get out of here. Out of Seattle. No way now could she return to work, her home tonight. The mere thought of pulling into her garage, walking into the darkened hallway made her shudder. She would be dead by morning.

Tanya straightened, feeling eyes at her back, but she was afraid to turn around. "I'll call you when I can," she whispered. Wondering if she'd ever have the chance.

"No, wait, Tanya, don't—"

Tanya banged down the receiver, then fled into the bathroom until she could think what to do.

She couldn't use her car. They would be looking for it. Maybe they even watched it now. Maybe, being on foot, she'd fooled them into thinking she was still at work.

She needed another car. And somebody's cell phone.

There was one friend who just might lend them to her.

Tanya checked down the hall both ways before leaving the women's room. She eased into the hotel's busy restaurant and out its side entrance. Scurried across the street and into another hotel. Two minutes later, out of breath and disheveled, she slipped out the building's back door—and hailed a cab to the outskirts of the city.

FORTY-FIVE

Interstate 90 rushed toward Carla. Should she turn west or east? West would take her toward the airport. Rental cars, flights. But what good were they with Thornby on her tail? East would take her through town, closer to Kanner Lake. But she couldn't go home, trailing death behind her. Besides, she only had an eighth of a tank of gas.

The decision moment arrived. Carla turned east.

Thornby followed. Close now, only a car length away. Too many cars rushed by in the four lanes. Carla knew he wouldn't allow someone to slip between them.

Her heart drummed. Where to go?

Carla chose the second lane from the right, close enough to exit if she chose, far enough away that maybe she could swerve last minute and leave Thornby on the freeway.

What now, Carla, what?

Rationality screamed it didn't matter. If she lost him now, he'd only find her again. But right now, thinking she could die any minute, she'd take any extra time she could get.

They passed Deaconess Hospital on the right—where Chief Edwards's wife worked. Nancy would be on shift now. Carla cried out to Nancy in her mind, feeling so near to help, and so very far. All the familiar sights of Spokane, a town she had lived in for ten years, now streamed by like dark passages pounded by a fugitive.

Carla passed the turnoff for the combined Highway 2/395, the freeway narrowing to three lanes. She found herself on the far right.

She threw a glance in the rearview mirror. Thornby drove with back straight, both hands on the wheel, his face like granite. For a split second their gaze met, and Carla saw herself through his eyes. She could almost feel his anticipation. His *hatred.*

I will kill you slowly for this.

Carla knew it was true.

She breathed deeply, trying to keep her head clear. Trent Avenue, exit 282, whipped by. How many more should she pass? Should she take one, try to lose Thornby on city streets? If she could jump from her car into the midst of people—surely he wouldn't kill her in front of a dozen witnesses.

They passed Altamont Avenue, then the Thor/Freya exit. A sign welcomed them to the city of Spokane Valley.

Carla checked the gas gauge. It was going down fast. It always did toward the end. She'd learned that the hard way the first month she owned the car. Ended up running out of gas on the way to Priest Lake to show some property.

Sprague Avenue approached. She knew it was a major thoroughfare, lots of businesses, many stoplights. Could she zoom through one, leave Thornby behind?

Her muscles tensed, waiting for the absolute last second she could swerve onto the exit. It spun at her, a fourth of a mile ... three hundred feet ... one hundred. The exit veered off. She continued straight, turning her head a little to check cars on her right. Anybody on the exit? Would she cause a major accident if she turned now?

The lane was clear. It was now or never.

Carla clenched her teeth and swerved.

Her tires squealed. Over the white line, across the no man's land, onto the exit toward Sprague. Somewhere close a car blew its horn, but she dared not take her eyes off the road.

Behind her, more screeching rubber.

Her shoulders jerked up, her body bracing for impact. The moment stretched out ... In the next second she found herself fully in the exit lane, still in one piece, knuckles white against the steering wheel. The squeal behind her faded. Carla flung a look at the rearview mirror.

Thornby was still on her tail. Lips drawn into a grimace that showed his teeth.

Carla hunched forward, raked her focus to the street ahead. She was on the far left side of Sprague, a large one-way street with multiple lanes. The car in front of her was some distance away.

Maybe she *should* cause an accident. Drive up on the curb and hit a light pole. People would stop to help, police would be called. But what if she hurt someone else? What if *she* got hurt? Stuck in some hospital bed sounded a lot like "sitting duck." It was bad enough that she couldn't run on her ankle.

A stoplight loomed ahead at Thierman. It was yellow.

Carla saw her chance.

She hit the accelerator. Closed in on the light, watching it stay yellow, knowing any second it would flash to red. "Stay ... stay ... stay," she whispered through clenched teeth. She could hear the roar of Thornby's engine behind her, knew he understood what she planned. Knew also that he would do everything in his power to follow her through the light, yellow or red.

Her car was thirty feet away from the light. She'd crossed the Rubicon—no time to stop when it changed now. No time at all.

Twenty feet. Ten.

The light blinked red.

She floored the gas pedal.

Horns blared as she hit the intersection. Tires screeched. She shot through toward the other side, a blue van hitting its brakes, squealing to a stop, barely missing her rear bumper. More screaming rubber. Carla glanced in her mirror and saw Thornby's Durango careening to the right. It skidded to a halt within inches of the van.

No impact. No shattering glass.

Just silence. Utter, vast silence. Then multiple horns, a man's curse, a slamming car door. The driver of the van stalked toward Thornby, fist raised, face red-purple. Carla caught the jerk of Thornby's left arm as he hit his door lock button.

Heart scudding, Carla headed on up Sprague. A small side street approached on the left. Elizabeth Street. Carla knew it would hook up one short block later with Sprague running the other direction. Off Elizabeth, she would only be able to turn left and follow the one-way street. Not good. Thornby would know which way she'd gone. On the other hand, following that route would soon take her back to the freeway. She could get on 90 headed either east or west, or go across it and lose herself on city streets on the other side.

She lurched her wheel to the left. Another fast check in the mirror showed Thornby in the intersection, trying to ease his SUV around the irate driver, who stood in front of him, shaking both fists.

Maybe Thornby was busy enough that he hadn't seen her turn.

Carla aimed for Sprague, vaguely noticing that she was passing a car dealership on her right. Then the realization pierced her thoughts. *Cars.* Lots and lots of cars.

Without second thought, she veered right into the dealership, forcing herself to slow as she hit the lot. For the first time she noticed the large sign—Spokane Chrysler. Near it, a shiny red PT Cruiser rose high on a lift. She drove up an aisle, new

Chryslers on her right and left, the showroom farther to her right. Carla prayed for a parking space in the midst of the new models. Like a miracle, one appeared four cars up. She pulled into it, hoping no car salesman would spot her and trot over, asking her to park in visitor spaces near the showroom. She found herself between two sedans. Perfect. Her car could not be seen from the side street.

In a flash she cut off the engine, yanked out the keys, and shoved them into her purse. She whipped her head around, looking for salesmen, looking for Thornby. No black Durango. Maybe he'd go straight once he pulled out of the intersection mess, passing Elizabeth. Or maybe he'd seen her turn and would follow. But then he would only have eyes for Sprague going the other direction.

Still, she couldn't be sure. What if he figured out her move, circled back?

Carla had mere minutes to get out of here.

She spotted the tall, slim frame of a young man halfway down the aisle of cars, his back to her. A salesman?

Grabbing her purse, she flung herself out of her Toyota. Pain sliced through her ankle. She bent over, hissing through her teeth. *This is it, girl, you'd better make it work.*

Carla forced herself upright, ran a hand through her hair, shoved her purse up her shoulder. Hoping to heaven she didn't look like some creature dragged in from the back swamp. She hobbled away from her car, not wanting to draw attention to where it was parked. When she was three vehicles away, she called out, "Excuse me!"

The young man turned. Raised one hand in a wave and started a graceful lope toward her.

A salesman for sure. And her salvation, if she played her cards right.

Carla limped to meet him, doing her best to wrench her grimace into a smile.

FORTY-SIX

I've been told my due date is April 19. Two weeks after my seventeenth birthday. Dr. Hughes calculated the date based on the day I told him I got pregnant.

April 19. That's it, girl, you'd better make it work.

Dr. Hughes is okay. He's nice and sort of quiet. Very confident. Makes me feel like he knows what he's doing, and I can tell he loves his job. Babies have been his life for a lot of years now. Still, I *hate* being examined. It's terrible to have to take off all your clothes and spread your legs on a table for some old man you don't even know—even if he is a doctor. Maybe it's stupid, 'cause I know he's done this forever and I suppose he's seen everything a billion times, but I'm not some other patient, I'm *me.* No matter how nice he is to me, when the whole thing's over I feel dirty. I'm just glad the nurse is in there with me.

Her name is Lisa, and she's wonderful. Heaven knows I need nice people in my life right now. She told me I can call her Lisa, even though she's older than my mother. Maybe she's this way with all the patients, but she seems to give extra care to me. Takes time to talk to me and asks how I'm doing—not physically, like Dr. Hughes does, but emotionally. She knows it's hard for me. I've told her I have all sorts of emotions about this whole thing. I told her all about Scott and how he agreed to the adoption because he couldn't stand the thought of abortion. And, of course, Lisa and Dr. Hughes both know the baby's going to Bryson. (I try not to think of

Mrs. My-Husband. The baby's going to *Bryson.*) Although nobody else knows about the adoption, they're not allowed to tell anyone. Lisa says I'm very brave to do this. She knows pregnancy is hard. But she says the time *will* pass (sometimes I wonder), and then I'll have a clear conscience, and the Hanleys will be happy with their baby.

If only she knew.

Sometimes I so want to tell her everything. Sometimes I think she's the only person I could tell, because she's a nurse and she's not supposed to talk about patients. But every time the story jumps on my tongue, I force it back. Problem is, the secret doesn't involve just me. It involves Bryson. And I promised him I'd never tell anyone.

Dr. Hughes says the baby looks very healthy. And a good size.

Mom is talking to me again. In grunts. What else can she do, when she got herself in the same fix at my age. At least I'm giving the baby up for adoption. At least my baby will be raised by a loving mother.

God, please let Mrs. My-Husband be loving, even if I hate her.

The court loves her, that's for sure. Mrs. Demarco, the woman who's visiting the Hanley home for all the legal stuff, has declared her and Bryson to be fit parents. Worthy of adopting my baby. Mrs. Demarco has also counseled with me to be sure I want this. I've told her I do.

Everybody at school knows I'm pregnant now. Once a few friends found out, the story went everywhere. I've told people the baby's being given up for adoption, but not to whom. I'm not allowed to talk about that to anyone but Scott. Not that I'd want to anyway. A lot of girls just say I'm crazy for not "getting rid of it." My mom says the same thing. Sometimes I wish I had. I'm still sick, and I'm tired all the time, and life just isn't fun. My body isn't mine. There's this thing growing in it, and it's making me fat. I can't fit into my clothes anymore. I'm really ugly!

Worst of all, I can't be with Bryson. I'm still working every day after school, and he whispers that we'll meet "soon," but it never happens. His senator stuff keeps him real busy, and when he's not doing that job, he's working on his national campaign. The polls show that if the election happened today, he'd win for sure. That makes him very happy. And he's thrilled thinking about the baby. I want to be happy for him. I *am*. I love him, how can I not be happy? But I'm beginning to feel like a cow. Just a big, old baby carrier. Like that's the only reason he cares for me anymore.

Meanwhile Scott is so sweet to me. Always asking how I feel. Half the time when I'm with him I cry. I just can hardly take how nice he's being. I don't deserve it. He talks about the baby and wonders if in the future we'll wish we had her or him ourselves. He's committed to the adoption, but sometimes he wants to take it all back. Says we could get married. He'd quit school and somehow we'd make it work. But deep down we both know how hard that would be. I hold him and tell him don't worry, we'll have other babies when we're ready. This is for the best. And I mean it when I tell him that. I love Scott, even if that love gets crowded out by my love for Bryson. Scott I can have for the rest of my life. Bryson I will never have. Not to live with. Not to be with forever. I know that now. How stupid I was to think otherwise.

How much I've learned in the past three months.

I wish I didn't have to learn any of it.

FORTY-SEVEN

The salesman looked young, midtwenties at the most. Blond hair, cut short. He was dressed in slacks, a light blue shirt, and striped tie. Sunglasses with small, bright blue lenses. Carla could see the smile on his full lips as he approached. His relaxed and friendly expression, the ease in his walk only frazzled her. She'd love to enjoy the same calm view of the world right now, but *couldn't he see she didn't have time!*

Not to mention her ankle was killing her.

She threw wild glances toward Elizabeth Street, out toward Sprague. She'd never seen Thornby drive by. Maybe he had gone straight up Sprague, not knowing she'd turned. If so, how long until he realized his mistake and came down Sprague in the other direction—right past the dealership?

As the salesman drew near, Carla could make out a few light freckles on his cheeks. He slid his sunglasses up until they stuck against his forehead, revealing light blue, almost translucent eyes. They met in front of a red PT Cruiser, the young man holding out his hand. "Hi, I'm Brandon. Welcome to Spokane Chrysler. And your name is?"

"Oh, um. Carla."

"Hi, Carla."

"Hi." *Girl, you'd better start talking—fast.*

Brandon frowned and gestured with his chin toward her ankle. "Wow, that doesn't look good. So swollen. Does it hurt? You should have it up."

Carla licked her lips. "Yeah, I just did it. Haven't had time to wrap it or anything. But anyway it doesn't matter; I need to test drive a car. *This* car. *Now.*" She slapped the hood of the red PT Cruiser.

Brandon blinked at her impatience, then grinned. "This one, huh. Right now."

"Yes!"

"Not a blue one or a green one. This one." He waved his hand at the Cruiser.

He was teasing her. Fine. He could play all he wanted once they got in the car. She hobbled up close to his face. "I. Want. This car. *Now.* Are you going to take me for a test drive—or do I need to find somebody else?"

He pulled his head back, mouth crimped in amusement, eyes mock widening. Not one bit rattled. He raised both hands, palms out. The third finger on his left hand curled inward as if stuck there. "Oookay. Let's do it." He reached for a key in his pocket, walked to a small box attached to the passenger side door and unlocked it, withdrawing the Cruiser's key. "Who's drivin', you or me?"

Carla twisted her head toward Elizabeth. Her hand slashed the air. "You."

Click. The locks popped open. Brandon moved to open the door for her, extending his hand in invitation. "Here you go."

Carla jumped inside, pulled her arms tight in her lap, and slid down in the seat. She flipped down the visor, peered in the mirror at Sprague Street. No black Durango.

Brandon slipped behind the wheel and eyed her curiously. "You comfortable sitting that low?"

"Yeah. Fine." Carla could feel beads of sweat on her forehead. *Go, just go!*

He surveyed her for a moment longer, biting the inside of his mouth, as if not quite sure what to make of this strange woman.

Brandon pulled his sunglasses down over his eyes and started the car. Backed smoothly from the parking space. Within thirty seconds, they'd turned left onto Sprague. Carla cast furtive looks all around, then pulled her head down between her shoulders, vulturelike.

He threw her a glance and cleared his throat. "So, Carla. Let me tell you about the Cruiser."

"Okay. Just ... keep driving while you do."

His mouth curved. "Don't have a lot of choice in this traffic."

She tipped her head—*guess not.*

"I call this the Swiss army knife of cars. There's so many different ways to configure the seats. The back seats fold flat, tumble, and pull out easily because they have rollers on them. The seat you're in also folds flat. So for cargo space, you got all kinds of ways to carry something wide or long."

Carla pulled her top lip between her teeth. They were crossing the freeway. Still no black Durango in sight.

"These are really popular cars. They're our bread and butter on the lot. Very fuel efficient. It's got a four-cylinder engine, with one hundred fifty horsepower. In 1998, Daimler-Chrysler merged with Mercedes, did you know that? They've parted ways now, but still, with this Cruiser, you get Mercedes parts and performance at a Chrysler price."

They hit a red light and stopped. Carla checked the visor mirror for cars behind them. No sign of Thornby.

Brandon turned to face her, amused fascination on his face. He ducked his head, shoulders hitching. "So ... tell me. Who we hidin' from?"

Carla's eyes snapped to his. He looked as calm as she felt fried. She tried to follow his lead, willing her muscles to soften, her breathing to even out. Easier thought than done. Adrenaline still rushed through her like a freight train. "Nobody."

"Really." He pointed his nose toward the road, looking at her from the corner of a half-opened eye.

"Okay. Somebody then. Is that enough?"

The light turned green. Brandon drove forward. "Boyfriend?"

Carla hesitated. "Yeah."

Concern flicked across his face. He gestured toward her ankle. "He didn't do that to you, did he?"

"No. Yes."

Brandon aimed her a disconcerted look.

Carla blew out a breath. "Can you just drive and stop asking questions?"

"Okay." He nodded slowly. "But something tells me you're not all that interested in hearing about this Cruiser."

No judgment in his voice, or anger. No, *Hey, lady, let me take you back; I've got cars to sell.* It struck Carla that she'd done to him what Thornby had done to her. Lured him to a potential sale under false pretenses. Not that she wanted to kill this likeable guy, but still. He'd have a right to be mad. He worked pure commission like she did.

She pressed her head back against the seat. "How old are you?"

"Twenty-four. Why?"

She shrugged. "Just wondered."

"How old are *you*?"

"Thirty-two."

He gave another of his slow nods. Checked her left hand. "Not married."

"No."

"Me either." He sniffed. "I was engaged once."

"What happened?"

"She called it quits."

"Oh. I'm sorry."

He lifted a shoulder. "It's okay. For the best, I guess."

Carla folded her arms. Normalcy was beginning to return to her body, largely, she suspected, due to Brandon's easy manner. It just sort of rolled off the guy, pulled her in.

They reached an intersection and he turned left. By now they were far from the dealership. Another long gaze in all directions told Carla that Thornby was not around. She'd really done it. She'd shaken him. She exhaled loud and long, then dared to sit a little straighter in her seat.

"So." Brandon checked the side mirror before changing lanes. "Want me to take you back now? Apparently you got away from . . . whoever."

Take her back. That was just it—she couldn't go back. Carla gazed ahead through the windshield, trying to figure her next move. She was going to have to convince this guy to let her off somewhere else, allow her car to sit in his parking lot—in the middle of all the new models, where it wasn't supposed to be.

Best not mention where she'd parked.

Brandon lifted his hand. "You want to tell me what's going on?"

Oh, boy. "It's a long story."

He shrugged. "I can take a longer route."

Carla managed a little smile. In the next second it faded as tiredness swept over her. This was the first time she'd been able to let down in hours. She rubbed her forehead, dropped her head in her hands. Breathed in, breathed out.

"That bad, huh."

She pulled her fingers away. Pressed her head back against the seat. No lies would come to mind, nothing to placate him as to her strange behavior. She simply had no energy to create. "You want to know the truth? It's not a boyfriend. Someone's trying to kill me."

Silence. Carla could almost hear the wheels in Brandon's head turn as he wondered whether to believe her. "Really." He emphasized the first syllable. "Why?"

"I don't know. That is, not completely. I kind of know."

"Kind of?" He threw her a questioning glance.

"I know who, and I know what I did to make a certain person feel . . . at risk, but that was years ago. Why he sent a hit man after me now, I can't entirely say."

Brandon gave one of his slow nods, then mushed his lips, as if trying to decide between the first of a dozen follow-up questions. "Have you called the cops?"

"I can't."

"Why?"

She closed her eyes. "I don't know which ones to trust." She told him about the state trooper.

"Wow." He lifted his eyebrows. "You think the *police* are in on this? Must be some mighty powerful person who wants you dead."

Carla surveyed him from the corner of her eye, unsure if he was placating her. She'd slept in her clothes, her makeup had to be a wreck, her hair barely combed. She was sweaty and no doubt smelled. He probably thought she'd escaped from some loony bin.

She sighed, searching for some other topic of conversation. How about the weather? Football? How goes the car business? Her focus landed on Brandon's left hand, the third finger unnaturally curved against the steering wheel.

"What happened to your finger?"

He glanced at it, a rueful expression crossing his face. "It's a long story."

"Thought we were taking a longer route."

He threw her a half smile—*one for you.*

They drove without speaking for a couple of blocks. The awkward quiet tugged at her ears. This kid had saved her life. He deserved ... something.

"So, Carla. Think it's safe to take you back to the lot now?"

She cleared her throat. "I can't go back there. I can't get back in my car. He'll be looking for it."

He processed the news. "Where do you want to go?"

"I don't *know.*"

He shot her a concerned look. "A friend's house? A relative?"

"No. I can't run to anybody. He told me if I did, he'd kill them too." She lowered her head, felt her chin quiver. Exhaustion swept through her again, leaving her weak-limbed. You know what—she just wanted to go *home.* Let Thornby find her in her own bed in her own little blue house, let him shoot her as she slept. At least this would all be over.

Brandon fell silent. No doubt ruing the moment he ever laid eyes on her—*what did I do to inherit this crazed woman?*

Carla inhaled deeply and dabbed the corners of her eyes. Okay. Enough self-pity. Use up any more of this guy's time, and she'd owe him a car commission. She blinked, taking in their surroundings. They'd followed Sprague back toward Spokane and weren't far from the downtown area. Her sluggish brain shook itself off, thoughts and plans forming.

"See that bank up there?" She pointed. "Will you give me a sec to run to the outside ATM?"

"Sure."

He pulled into the parking lot and close to the machine for the sake of her ankle. Carla murmured her thanks and slipped from the Cruiser, clutching her purse. That bag and its contents—including the diary—were all she had, now that she'd abandoned her suitcase and car.

At the machine she withdrew her bank's ATM limit—five hundred dollars. Tomorrow she could withdraw another five hundred.

Back in the car, she thanked Brandon profusely. "Look, I know it's a little farther out of your way. But could you take me to the Hampton Inn near the airport?"

He mushed his lips, looking her straight in the face. Carla saw her reflection, blue and disheveled and tiny, in the lenses of his sunglasses. "Okay." He put the car in gear and backed out of their parking space.

"Know how to take city streets over?" she asked. "So we don't have to get on the freeway?"

"Yeah."

Carla tilted her head, observing him. Brandon's even-temperedness hadn't changed. Probably thinking *anything to keep this lady calm*. A few more minutes, and he'd be rid of her.

They didn't speak again until they were within a mile of the hotel. Remorse stabbed at Carla for the problems she'd cost the guy. And she couldn't bear to think of any harm coming to him for his help.

"Brandon, I need to tell you a couple of things. They're important."

"Shoot."

"I parked my car in the middle of all the new ones on your lot. I knew I wasn't supposed to, but it was the perfect place to make it blend in. I don't think I remembered to lock it. And I left my suitcase on the front seat. Could you lock the doors for me?"

He lifted a shoulder. "Yeah. But we can't let the car stay there. The boss is going to want to know where it came from. You got a key hidden on it by any chance? So I can move it to the street?"

"No!" Fear sloshed around inside her. "If the guy who's after me happened to see you driving that car, he'd *know* you've talked to me. You wouldn't be safe. Just lock it up and be done with it. Tell the owner you don't know where it came from. If it's towed, it's towed. That's the least of my worries right now."

"What about your suitcase?"

She shook her head. "I wish I had it. But I don't. And it's too dangerous for me to go back and get it. I keep thinking that Thornby—that's the name of the guy who's after me, at least the one he told me—is going to figure out what I did and come looking for my car on your lot. If he shows up, Brandon, you've *got* to play dumb. He's driving a rented black Durango. And you can't tell *anybody* you saw me, talked to me, much less where you brought me. Understand?"

"Yeah, okay. And I'll lock your car." He spoke lightly, and Carla knew he didn't understand the danger, not at all.

He pulled into the parking lot for the hotel, then to a stop outside the lobby. Carla turned to him, sudden loneliness washing over her. He put a gentle hand on her shoulder and pressed. The loneliness surged.

She swallowed hard. "You know, you really ought to meet a girlfriend of mine. You two would get along great."

"Oh, really, who's that?" His tone was dry, as if meeting any of her insane friends was the last thing he wanted.

"Leslie Brymes. She's just a few years younger than you."

His head pulled back. "*The* Leslie Brymes? As in hot reporter from Kanner Lake Leslie Brymes?"

Carla smiled. "Yeah, that one."

He pushed his sunglasses up on his forehead, his translucent blue eyes widening. "*You* know *her*?"

"Hey, don't you read our Scenes and Beans blog? I thought everybody did."

"Huh?"

"You know, the Java Joint blog. She writes posts for it; so do I." Carla took in Brandon's blank look. "Okay, never mind. Just...

know I'm not the mad-woman-escaped-from-the-asylum that you think I am."

He dipped his head, his playful smile returning. "Well, hey, count me in for meeting Leslie. I'm good anytime."

Carla nodded. Her hand found the door handle and pulled. "Thanks so much for everything you've done. I hope I don't get you into trouble for being gone so long."

He shrugged. "I'll be fine." His forehead creased. "How about you? I feel bad, leaving you here by yourself. No suitcase, no anything."

Nice to know he felt sorry for her, even if he did think she was nuts. "I'll be okay."

He gestured toward her ankle. "You gonna put that foot up?"

"Yeah."

"Okay. Well, let me at least help you inside."

Brandon slid from the car, came around, and pulled her door open. Allowed her to lean on him as she limped through the hotel door into the lobby. Only when the young man behind the counter affirmed there was a vacancy for her and assigned her a room on the first floor did Brandon take his leave. Carla paid in cash and checked in under a false name—Sally Aimes. First one that popped into her tired mind.

At the lobby door Brandon turned back, gave her a little wave and a wink. "Take care now, Sally."

She watched him drive away, thinking Stella-esque thoughts of the kindness of strangers.

Minutes later in her room, Carla finally took care of her throbbing ankle. Carefully she removed the plastic cover off the ice bucket and hobbled down the hall to fill it at the machine. Back behind her locked and bolted door, she wrapped some of the ice in the plastic, then rolled it up in a hand towel. That done, she pulled the pillows from the second double bed onto the bed nearest the bathroom. Then and only then did she collapse upon the mattress. She fussed the two extra pillows into place beneath her ankle, positioned the ice packet, then layered the two pillows from her bed behind her head.

She checked the digital clock. Almost two-thirty.

Two-thirty. Hard to believe twenty-four hours ago she'd been in her office, researching comps for a client.

The adrenaline pulsing through her veins began to recede. As she finally allowed herself to relax, every inch of her body sagged into the mattress. Carla closed her eyes. *Breathe in … breathe out. In … out.* So quiet. So still. She could feel her emotions, shoved to a cool back burner, now shift to the front toward heat. Somebody turned up the temperature.

Better watch out. After all she'd been through, this just might be a good time for a meltdown.

But Carla fought it. Fear held her back. She wouldn't. *Couldn't.* After sixteen years she had so many things to cry for. So many hurts, guilts, losses. If she let go now she might not stop until the next century, and she hardly had that kind of time. A few hours of rest, and she was out of here …

Her thoughts fuzzed. It took some doing to pull them back into focus.

… On the run to who-knew-where …

Carla's mind blurred again. Her body settled further into the bed, gravity dragging her down, down.

… With no plan … No friends…

No … life …

Exhaustion rocked her, sang its siren song.

Carla tumbled into a dark, dream-haunted sleep.

FORTY-EIGHT

I'm shaking all over. Gravity's pulling me down so hard I wonder if I can ever get off this bed.

Today was the last day of school before the Christmas holiday. And my last day of work until after New Year's. I went into the office around 3:00 as usual. Bryson wasn't there. He's been gone for a week. As for Mrs. My-Husband – I haven't seen her for a long time. She quit coming to the office weeks ago.

Maybe she's just avoiding me.

Jilke pounced on me the minute I walked in the door. He stood up and towered over me. "Sit down."

His voice sounded so harsh. I was feeling tired already and in no mood to fight. I sank into my chair.

He pulled out the ledger I use to record our petty cash. I do it in pencil like he taught me, so I can erase if I make a mistake. Jilke shoved the ledger under my nose and jammed his finger on the figures for the current month. "I can't believe you would do this. I've been going over these figures. You've been stealing money for the past five months."

My jaw dropped. "Are you out of your mind?"

"*Don't* get cute with me. You've been after more than just a job ever since you came here." His eyes flicked toward Bryson's office. "Well, you got it in more ways than one. I've sat back and watched it all go on, unable to stop it. *This* I can stop. I will not let you steal money from the very man who's done so much for you."

"I *didn't* steal any money! I don't know what you're talking about!"

"Then how do you explain this?" He smacked his finger against the page.

I leaned over the ledger, knowing everything would add up. It always did. And wouldn't Jilke be feeling the fool in a minute. But as I looked at the numbers, I could see erase marks. Inflated costs for stamps and paper and other supplies. The numbers still computed, but it showed we'd spent ninety dollars more than we really had. I looked up at Jilke with widened eyes, then grabbed the petty cash box from inside my top drawer. It had just the amount of money the ledger said it should. Ninety dollars missing.

Panic shot through me. I stared at Jilke—with his smug faked indignation—and understood.

I shoved the petty cash box back in my drawer, my fear turning to rage. "*You* did this. You've wanted me out of here for months. Well, guess what, I'm not leaving. Bryson will never believe your little trick."

"*Senator Hanley* believes it, all right. I spoke to him on the phone last night. He agrees you have to go."

"I don't believe that!"

He sat on the edge of my desk and leaned close to my face. "Believe what you want as long as you believe this—you're *out* of here. *Forever.* Now get your stuff and be gone, or I'll call the police to take you out."

My face flushed hot. "You can't get away with this! You're lying to Bryson. As soon as I tell him what you did—"

"Get out!" He stomped around to my chair and yanked it back from my desk. "Get out now. And stay out of Bryson Hanley's life." He grabbed my arms and pulled me up. I pushed him away.

"I'm going to tell Bryson. He *won't* believe you!" Tears stung my eyes, and that made me all the madder. I didn't want to give Jilke the satisfaction of seeing me cry.

"You *will not* call him, get that?" His voice fell to a whisper that sent ice running through my veins. "I don't think you understand your situation. You've been stealing from a *state senator*. He's got a few friends on the police force. Friends who would believe his word over yours any day. Count yourself lucky all you have to do is leave. I promise you this—you say *one word* about Bryson Hanley to anyone, and we'll press charges. You want to have your baby in juvenile hall?"

One word. He didn't have to explain.

That did it. I couldn't help sobbing. It's one thing to pull such a dirty trick on me, but to try and harm my *baby*. All I could do was grab my purse and leave.

Four hours later, I'm still on my bed. I'm done crying for now, but my eyes feel like they're going to burn out of my head. I still can't believe Bryson would think I'd steal from him. That hurts me worse than anything. I *love* him! I would never take anything from him. *How* can he think that of me? No matter how well Jilke lies? And how will I ever see Bryson now? At *all*?

There's no way I'm just sitting back and letting this happen. *No way*. I'm going to talk to Bryson. Tell him what a lying little punk he has for a manager. Then we'll see who stays in the office and who goes. Bryson loves me. He won't let this happen to me. And he certainly would never let me go to jail.

He's gone until after the new year. Somehow I have to hang on until I can call him.

Merry Christmas, Carla.

FORTY-NINE

Two-thirty. Too late.

Tony pulled off Sprague into the parking lot of a strip mall and stopped in a space far from other cars. He turned off the engine and sat there, staring at nothing. He was past screaming curses. Past pounding the dashboard, the console. If he wanted to save his family, he had to keep his wits about him. He'd looked and looked. Done everything he could think to do. But he'd lost his target. Again. By now she could be miles away, headed anywhere.

With a deep breath, he pulled out the cell phone registered in his real name and called his boss. The line picked up after the first ring.

"Tony. About time. You're pushing the hour."

Tony clenched his jaw at the disdain in the voice. "Just want to tell you it's done."

"Really. Well, now, you've made my day. I was beginning to wonder if I had to come out there myself."

"No need." Tony focused across the parking lot at a couple exiting a store, the woman with a toddler boy in her arms. A rush of emotion deflated his chest. He couldn't *wait* to see his son.

"What took so long?"

Tony dropped his head back against the seat. "Complications involving her work. I wanted to wait for the safest time. Now you can rest easy. She'll never be found."

A low chuckle filled his ear. "Ah, Tony. I knew I could count on you."

Yeah, right. Tony cleared his throat. "I've got some details to finish up here, then I'll be on my way back."

"Fine, take your time." A long inhale—and Tony knew something was coming. "You'd have loved the way Timmy looked today, by the way. He wore a red sweatshirt to preschool that said 'My dad rules.'"

Tony's lungs went cold.

"And your wife was lovely in her black jeans."

"You gave me until three o'clock." The words pressed from Tony's throat.

"Oh, no problem, you got it. I imagine your son's happily playing games or napping now—whatever children do midafternoon. Still, I'm so glad you called. I was beginning to sweat."

Tony's fingers nearly bent the phone. Sending some underling all the way out to watch his family had been nothing less than a display of power. And absolutely *unnecessary.*

"I'm coming home." He ground out the response. "My family had *better* not be harmed, and completely unaware of any of this."

"Or what, Tony?" Dark amusement writhed through the words. "You'll tell on me? Expose me for all my sins? Don't forget you have a few of your own."

Wouldn't matter if his own were exposed. *Nothing* would matter if he lost his family.

Tony opened his mouth to spit a reply, then bit it back. That wouldn't help, not now.

"Gotta go. See you soon." He clicked off the line.

For a moment he sat, empty gaze roaming the parking lot. He knew he'd catch up with his target again; already he had some ideas. Meanwhile his boss wasn't likely to find out Carla Radling still lived. After all, she was keeping herself pretty scarce. Still, he couldn't take the chance ...

With a defeated sigh, he punched in the number of his wife's cell phone. When she answered, he would speak the dreaded words they had agreed upon long ago. The words he would say if his "CIA job" posed a sudden threat to her and Timmy. At the message, Robyn would immediately pick Timmy up from preschool, drive to the airport, and take the first flight to a friend's house in San Diego. There she would wait—without calling him—until he contacted her.

"Hi, sweetie!" Robyn's voice sounded in his ear. So unsuspecting. Tony almost changed his mind. He didn't want to frighten her like this.

"Hi." He kept his voice light. "Guess what, I bought a new suit."

Silence. He could hear the shock, the unspoken questions tumbling through the phone. *Come on, Robyn, hang in there.*

"That's nice." His wife's voice trembled, and for a moment he was afraid she wouldn't continue. "Oh, honey, um ... someone just walked in my office. I need to go. Call you back, okay?"

"Okay. I love you."

"I love you too." The words choked. Then the line went dead.

Tony lowered his phone and caressed the keypad with his fingertips before folding the cover shut.

FIFTY

Just want to tell you it's done.

Paul Jilke hung up the phone and pushed back from his cluttered desk. Beyond his closed door he could hear other phones ringing, the voices of assistants and clerks. Bryson Hanley's Seattle-based office, one of three in the state, was a busy place. Tomorrow it would be busier with Bryson's presence. Friday, the US Senate was not in session, and Bryson would be home for a long weekend, meeting with voters.

Jilke swiveled in his black leather chair to gaze out the window at the Seattle skyline, his long fingers steepled. There'd been something in Tony Derrat's voice during their conversation yesterday—something tainting his claim that Carla Radling hadn't shown up to their meeting. Enough to make Jilke want to mention Tony's son. Now this. Jilke didn't believe a word of what the man had said today. Jilke had been around a long time, ever since Golden Boy Bryson had begun his climb to fame. He knew expressions, had learned how to look into a person's eyes and tell if he was lying. And he knew voices. Like subtle body language, vocal tone could give away not only deception, but hidden agendas and half-truths.

Jilke would bet Tony had flat-out lied.

He laced and unlaced his fingers, feeling the dry rub of skin against skin. Understandable why Tony should lie today, but hardly forgivable. Jilke tightened his mouth. What could have gone wrong? The target was a mere unsuspecting woman.

Clearly, Tony was losing his touch.

Jilke sighed. He didn't have time for this. Bryson Hanley's campaign manager didn't know the meaning of extra time. Every minute was spent toiling for the campaign. Hectic days, nights of little sleep. And it was only going to get worse.

But this was too important. Carla Radling could bring down everything he'd spent his entire life working for. And that *would not* happen.

Pushing a curse through his teeth, he swiveled back toward the desk. Picked up his cell phone and dialed. He got an answer on the first ring.

"Yes, sir."

"You still watching Derrat's wife's place of work?"

"Just like you told me."

"Good. I want to know if she leaves early. And whenever she does leave, follow her."

"Right. No sweat."

Jilke clicked off the line and returned to work. Not five minutes later, his cell phone rang with the news. Robyn Derrat was in the company parking lot, making a beeline for her car.

Jilke slammed a palm against the desk. *I knew it.* His mind roiled with repercussions. For the first time real fear edged up his spine.

"All right, listen." His voice was low and tight—a sign to the man on the line that he'd better follow his assignment *perfectly.* "She'll be going to the preschool to pick up their kid. Stop them in the parking lot. Tell them you've been sent by Tony's boss to take them out for ice cream. She won't believe you, but whatever you do, *don't* let them get away. And call me the minute you've got them."

"No problem."

Jilke smacked off the call, resisting the urge to throw the phone across the room. Fury settled deep in his chest. Everything within him wanted to call Tony Derrat *now*. If the man were here, Jilke would choke him with his bare hands. And enjoy every minute of it.

But no. He knew how to wait. He knew how to plan. When the wife and kid were captured—*then* he and Tony would have a nice little chat.

FIFTY-ONE

Brandon eased back in the PT Cruiser's driver's seat, knees spread, steering with one hand—the casual way he liked to drive when a customer wasn't with him. But he hardly felt relaxed. All the way back to Spokane Valley his mind had spun questions about Carla-the-Crazy-Woman. One minute he thought she might be telling the truth, and the next minute he thought she was nuts.

If Brandon knew one thing, he knew women couldn't be trusted. They could be all lovey one minute, downright insane, even dangerous, the next. He had the scars to prove it. He glanced ruefully at the crippled third finger on his left hand. Never healed right after the tendon below it had been cut almost through, even though he'd had surgery. The knife-wielding chick had been a girlfriend.

Still, Carla seemed different. Smart, first of all, and nice. Well, she could be nice if she hadn't been so uptight. And she had a sense of humor. Brandon liked that.

He flicked on the blinker and moved to the far right lane on the freeway, preparing to exit. Hoping no one had discovered Carla's car yet. Pretty big lot. Just depended on where the salesmen had met customers. Brandon figured the chances were fifty-fifty.

He veered off onto Sprague and up to Elizabeth, then turned left. He pulled into the Spokane Chrysler parking lot and returned the Cruiser to its empty spot. Out on the pavement, the Cruiser locked up, Brandon looked around for Carla's car. He found it farther up the aisle, still unlocked, with a small red suitcase lying on the passenger seat.

He opened the driver's door and slid inside. Before he locked up the car, he intended to check a few things out.

Leaning over the console, he ignored the suitcase for the moment and opened the glove box. Rifled through its contents. He discovered a white envelope that looked promising and pulled it out. Checked the papers inside. There they were—registration and insurance. Also some receipts for work on the car. He unfolded the papers and looked them over. *Radling*, that was her last name. Carla Radling. From Kanner Lake.

He pressed his lips together, processing the information. She hadn't lied about her first name. And—hey, Kanner Lake. Maybe she really did know Leslie Brymes.

Replacing the papers, he returned the envelope to the glove box. Then he unzipped the suitcase. On top was a jumble of clothes, shoes, and toiletries. Underneath, a laptop case. He moved it around. Heavy. Computer must be inside. He spotted a cell charger. Oh, man, bad news. Carla's phone wouldn't last long without that.

He rezipped the case and sat back, thinking. The contents sure were messy—like someone had thrown in stuff in a hurry. Also, the laptop case seemed strange. Most people would carry that separately.

Brandon ran a finger back and forth across his lips. Couldn't say he was totally convinced about her story, but . . .

He pictured Carla's face, so tired and full of pain, as she stood at the hotel counter. He'd felt so bad for her that he hadn't wanted to leave. Didn't matter whether she was right on in everything she said or whether she was crazy. Either way she just looked lost. He'd wished he could do something for her.

Sighing, he focused on the suitcase. If he locked this car, that would be it—the suitcase would be locked up with it. Meanwhile Carla was in that hotel room with nothing but her purse and too afraid to come back here. At least that's what she claimed.

Brandon rubbed his hand down his face. He should take the suitcase to her after he got off work at eight. He'd wanted to help her—well, here was a way. Still, he wasn't real happy about the thought. How did he get himself into this?

Before he could change his mind, Brandon slid out of the Toyota, walked around to the passenger seat, and took out the suitcase. He yanked up its long handle, pulled it all the way down the lot to his car, and placed it in the trunk. His manager or some team member was probably watching from the showroom, wondering what in the world he was doing. He'd have some fancy explaining to do. Normally he'd be dying to tell everybody about his weird experience, expanding it in all the right spots. *Can you believe it? I took this crazy lady for a test drive, and she flat-out insisted some hired hit man was looking for us.* But a voice inside his head told him to keep quiet. Sometimes things weren't always what they seemed—he'd learned that well enough.

Yeah, he had a great story to tell. But not yet. Not today.

He closed the trunk. For now, back to work. He really needed to sell a car this afternoon. How about two. So far he was top on the board for the month, and he aimed to stay there. Bringing in the most revenue would mean a $500 bonus.

Seeing no customers wandering on the lot, he set off toward the showroom—then slid to a stop. His chin dropped. *Man.* After all that, he'd forgotten to lock Carla's car.

Irritated with himself, he veered back up the long aisle of cars. By the time he reached the Toyota, his thoughts had gone through a number of loops and ended up on another question. As long as he'd returned, was there anything else in the car Carla might need?

He dumped himself back in the driver's seat, leaving one foot on the pavement, and reopened the glove box. Rummaged through its contents. Nothing much there he hadn't seen the first time. He looked around the car—in the back, felt under the front seats. Nothing. And really, enough was enough. He had to get back to work.

Mumbling to himself for his idiocy, he swiveled toward the door to get out—and came face-to-face with the barrel of a gun.

FIFTY-TWO

An hour and a half east of Seattle, Tanya still could not relax. No matter that she was almost positive no one had followed. No matter that she sat high in the cab of a borrowed black Ford pickup, where she could keep an eye on all cars around her. The tension in her muscles went deeper than fear for her physical safety, even for her life. It went down to her soul. And it wouldn't be loosened until she told Carla Radling everything.

She'd taken a taxi to a friend's house, checking cars behind them all the way. Colleen worked at home, and her son was away at his freshman year at college, his pickup truck left behind despite his protestations so he'd "have more time to study," according to his mom. Colleen, being the good friend that she was, had asked Tanya a few questions, then knew when to stop. Tanya had merely told her she needed to make a sudden trip, that it was personal in nature and couldn't be discussed until it was all said and done. For reasons of privacy, she wanted to borrow a car and a cell phone. Colleen had given her both.

Tanya could only hope she'd be able to return them in one piece.

Part of her knew it was no use driving to Kanner Lake. If no one had heard from Carla Radling after all these hours, she was probably dead. Tanya knew it, but still wouldn't allow herself to believe it. She *had* to see Carla. She *had* to tell her what happened all those years ago.

The traffic on Interstate 90 had thinned once Tanya had gotten well away from Seattle. She hadn't been able to call Leslie Brymes's cell phone yet—she'd been too busy watching traffic. Now it was time.

Eyes on the road, she rummaged in her purse for the phone and the piece of paper with Leslie's number. Holding the phone in one hand, she used her thumb to punch in the numbers.

"Leslie Brymes."

"Leslie, it's Tanya."

"Tanya!" The voice blended relief and anxiety. "Whatever you do, don't hang up on me again!"

"I won't. I have time to talk now."

Tanya told her what had happened in the last two hours. Leslie related events in Kanner Lake. Checking Java Joint for extra bugs—none was found. A missing person's bulletin issued for Carla. Leslie had been by Carla's work, and the receptionist had allowed her to look through Carla's desk. "The police were already here and did that," the receptionist told her. "But maybe you'll see something they didn't."

Leslie found nothing. Nor did she see anything that might hint where Carla had gone when she drove by Carla's place. She'd talked to a few of Carla's friends, but they knew no more than anyone else.

The last appointment Carla had kept was with some out-of-towner who'd wanted to see the Edna San estate the previous evening. But it didn't appear she'd run into trouble there, because she'd spoken to Bailey this morning on the phone. In that conversation she talked like something had happened but wouldn't say what. That was the last anyone had heard from her.

Tanya's heart stalled at the news. Still she clung to stubborn hope. Somewhere, somehow she would find Carla—alive.

"Are you going to tell me what this is about?" Leslie asked.

Tanya hesitated. How much did Leslie know of Carla's past? If Leslie knew nothing, it wasn't her place to tell. "I can't. It wouldn't be fair. Carla needs to be the first to hear what I have to say."

"Tanya." Leslie's tone was low. "I just hope you have the opportunity to see her."

"Me too," Tanya whispered. "Me too."

They fell silent. Tanya's gaze bounced to the rearview mirror, the freeway lanes on either side. The constant checking had become habit.

"Look," Leslie said. "You might not want to talk to me, but you do need to tell Chief Edwards what you know. I promised I'd tell him when I heard from you again. He's got nothing to go on right now, and if you have information about who's after Carla and why, you are obligated to tell the police."

Dread sifted through Tanya. She understood her obligation to tell. She'd pledged to confess to Carla, hadn't she? But a policeman was another matter. What would become of her once the information she'd guarded all these years left her lips? Who would Chief Edwards feel obligated to inform? Her life would so quickly unravel. How would the world judge her? Punish her? And Curt, her son. She couldn't bear to think of hurting Curt.

What was she thinking? She couldn't *do* this.

"Tanya?"

She clutched the steering wheel, sickness rising in her gut. Maybe she should just hang up right now. Take the next exit off the freeway and head south. Disappear ... somewhere. Anywhere.

"Tanya, *do* you understand you need to talk to Chief Edwards?"

"I ... Yes."

"Will you do that now? Please? You should call him, at least tell him who's after Carla. He has no leads, Tanya. What if your information could help find her?"

Of course she would call the chief. She was a responsible citizen. Someone who would never want to break the law. Someone who was always concerned for the helpless, had volunteered countless hours to prove it . . .

Her fingers curled around the steering wheel. If only she could play Superman, turn the world back sixteen years.

"Okay." Tanya's voice was pinched. "I'll call. But I'm not going to tell him what I have to tell Carla. Not unless we find her *dead* will I tell anyone else first. *Understand* me?"

"Yeah. Yeah, okay." Leslie drew an audible breath. "But it makes me wonder what on earth you know. And I have to tell you, you're scaring me to death."

"Make that two of us."

Tanya couldn't write down the chief's number while driving. Leslie told her she would call Chief Edwards right now, tell him everything Tanya had told her. He would contact Tanya for the rest of the information.

"He'll phone in just a few minutes, okay?" Leslie sounded as if she wasn't sure Tanya would answer the phone. With good reason. If only she knew how close Tanya felt, even now in the face of reason, to veering off the freeway and disappearing.

"Okay. I'll be here."

Tanya closed the cell and laid it on her lap. Knowing that its next ring would unravel years of tangled deceit—and more than a few lives would never be the same.

FIFTY-THREE

Where do I begin? How can I write down all the lies? My life will never be the same.

Yesterday I finally talked to Bryson. I called him at the office on his private line. When he heard my voice, he hesitated. *Hesitated.* My whole world came down to that second. Right then I knew he believed Jilke.

Bryson told me how sorry he was, and how he'd have given me the money if I'd asked for it. He might as well have cut me in a million pieces. I sobbed to him that Jilke set me up. That I still loved him. That's when he said we couldn't talk anymore—and hung up on me.

I'd lost him. For real. For good. Just like that.

Think that's enough for one afternoon? Oh, no. God had more planned for me. I knew one day I would pay for my sins. Well, that day is now.

I had a meeting scheduled with Mrs. Demarco. I called her to say I couldn't come. I was sick. Truth was, I couldn't get up off my bed. She said we had to meet today—and she'd come to my house.

As soon as we sat down Mrs. Demarco told me. The Hanleys don't want my baby anymore.

Right then, the baby kicked me hard.

I couldn't even say anything. I already wanted to die. I just sat there while Mrs. Demarco told me the Hanleys felt it would be "awkward" to adopt my baby after I'd been fired for stealing from his office.

She patted my arm as I cried. "Don't worry, honey, we'll find other good parents for your baby. And the Hanleys said they'll continue paying all your medical expenses to the end. Isn't that kind of them? You don't have to worry about a penny."

Oh, yeah, so very kind.

Jilke did this to me. All of it. He never wanted me in Bryson's life – now he's got his wish.

If I could find a way to kill him, I would.

FIFTY-FOUR

Brandon froze, widened eyes focused on the gun pointed at his nose. Then to the fingers that held the weapon. The arm ... shoulders ... the face of a man he'd never seen before. Movie star looks, except for the bad sunburn. Dark hair. Mean, twisted mouth. Guy looked like Pierce Brosnan on a very bad day.

Brandon's hands rose to chest level, fingers spread. "Hey, man, *what* are you *doin'*?"

"Where's the owner of this car?" The question pushed through gritted teeth. Nothing but the lips on the man moved, not the slightest twitch of his head. Brandon felt like a rabbit cornered by a salivating fox.

"I don't *know*." He poured disgust into his voice, as if he couldn't believe this guy's rudeness. "Would you turn that thing away from my face?"

The man's expression blackened. "I'm going to ask you one more time. *Where* is the owner?"

Only then did Brandon get it. Maybe he was a little slow, but shock would do that to a person. This was Carla's Thornby. The guy in the black Durango. The hit man was *real*.

"That's a fine question. I'd like for *you* to tell *me*." Brandon wagged his head. "I see this Toyota parked here in the middle of all our new Chryslers—not exactly where it's supposed to be. Nobody on the lot or in the showroom knows anything about it.

So I slip inside and have a look around. If the owner doesn't show up soon, we're going to have to tow the thing."

"You're lying."

Brandon's heart hammered against his ribs—*let me out!*—but danged if he was going to show any fear. This guy seriously ticked him off.

"Look." He lowered his hands a little. "How about if I get out of the car? Then I don't have to get a crick in my neck talking to you." He started to shift his weight onto his foot on the pavement.

The gun barrel met his forehead. He stopped moving.

"I could kill you right here," Thornby spat. "Leave your body in this car and be long gone before anybody even found you."

The metal of the barrel felt cold. In his mind, Brandon saw the scene. The bullet firing into his skull, his body crumpling. His hands rose up to his shoulders.

"Yeah, and what good would killing me do? If I supposedly know something about who drove this car here, you wouldn't hear it then, would you?"

"Maybe I'll just shoot you through the knee. Leave you begging for me not to do the other one."

Brandon licked his lips. He'd seen that one in a movie or two. Didn't want to go there. "Man, it wouldn't do any good. I *don't know anything* about the owner of this car."

"I'm a desperate person." The words seethed. "You understand? Desperate people do desperate things. You're not leaving here 'til you give me what I want."

Okay, maybe this wasn't Thornby. Maybe it was some crazy new reality show. Brandon resisted the urge to look around for a hidden camera. "I *don't know* the answer to your question."

Air sucked in and out of the man's throat like some mad dog. Forget logic; this guy's finger could flick the trigger any minute.

"Get all the way behind the wheel," he commanded. "We're going for a drive."

"That'll be a little hard without the key."

"You've *got* the key. In your pocket. Somewhere."

Brandon sighed. "I *don't* have the key. You want to pat me down, go right ahead. You won't find it."

The man slid the gun away from Brandon a couple inches. The tendons on the back of his hand ridged solid and hard. "We'll take the new car right behind me then." His tone turned sarcastic. "Make it a nice, friendly test drive."

What *was* it with test drives today? Had to be a better way to sell cars. "Sure. Fine. But you're going to have to let me stand up."

From his pocket, Brandon's cell phone rang—a tone he knew well.

"Don't answer it."

"It's Shawn, my manager. If I don't answer, he's going to wonder what's going on and come out here. Don't think he won't. Shawn cares a lot about his salesmen. He checks up on me even when I'm home."

Thornby moved back two steps. "Let it be. Get out of the car."

Brandon obeyed. As the cell rang again, he raised his hands high above his head, hoping someone in the showroom just might see what was going on. Why did this have to be such a slow day? Where *was* everyone?

"Get your hands down! Waist level."

Third ring. Brandon lowered his arms. Anger buzzed up and down his limbs. No wonder Carla was running from this dude, scared out of her mind. If Brandon saw his chance, he was taking it. Thornby would be toast.

Fourth ring. The call went to voice mail.

Thornby gestured with his chin. "Get the key and get us in this car." He stepped back more, giving Brandon room to move to the passenger door of the new Chrysler.

Brandon edged toward the lockbox on the car, then narrowed his eyes at Thornby. "I'm going to have to get the key for the box in my pocket."

"Do it slowly." The gun remained pointed at his chest.

Brandon slipped a hand into his right pocket and withdrew the key. Held it up so Thornby could see, then inserted it into the lock. He pulled the Chrysler key out of the box and turned to Thornby. "Who's drivin', you or me?"

"Unlock all the doors. Then get behind the wheel."

A press of the electric button clicked open all the doors. Brandon's thoughts spun. No way was he getting in the car with this guy. He'd heard the statistics on killers separating a victim from others. Wasn't exactly so they could go off and share a Happy Meal. If he got in that car, he wasn't coming back alive.

He stepped toward Thornby as if to move past him on the way around the front of the car. Thornby stiffened. "Go the other—"

A cell phone rang—this one from Thornby's pocket. Thornby started, and his hand jerked.

Brandon saw his chance. He ducked to the right and swung his left arm. He connected at Thornby's wrist. Thornby's hand careened up, the gun flying away. The cell phone rang again as the gun landed on the hood of the Chrysler with the crisp sound of metal on metal, then slid down over the side. It landed with a muffled thud on Brandon's left shoe.

He kicked it under the car.

Thornby's fist flew. Brandon bent low and charged, head-ramming the man in the waist. Thornby stumbled back, bounced off the Toyota hood, and shot forward, swinging both arms.

Brandon had never been much of a fighter. But something in him cracked. Manly way or not, this guy was going down, and it was going to *hurt*. Brandon braced himself against the Chrysler and shot out a foot. The heel of his shoe buried itself in Thornby's groin.

"Ahhhngh!" Thornby's face contorted. He sank to his knees, clawed fingers pulled between his legs.

The impact knocked Brandon off balance. He stumbled to the right, tripped an awkward two-step, and fell. His right palm and chin scraped pavement. He raised his head an inch and hung there for a moment, slightly dazed. His eyes focused on a circle of pebbled asphalt between his hands. *Get up, man, get up!*

Behind him, Thornby shuffled and moaned.

The sound of sliding metal sliced through Brandon's ears.

He scrambled to his knees, swiveling to face Thornby. The man clutched his gun, swinging it up to aim. Thornby was bent over at the waist, face livid purple, breath sucking through clenched teeth, but he kept on coming. How was the guy moving in all that pain?

The barrel aimed even with Brandon's chest. In that stretched second, he knew he was gone. Regrets flooded his mind—things he hadn't done, and had. Words he hadn't spoken. Then time rushed in like a freight train.

Brandon's mind exploded. With the yell of a wild man, he jerked to the right, vaguely registering as the gun went off. He pivoted left and launched himself at Thornby's shoulder. Thornby jumped to his right, hitting the side mirror on the Chrysler. Brandon sailed through the air where Thornby's body should have been, hit the Chrysler hood with a whacking *thud*, and rolled down its length. He tumbled onto pavement in front of the car, all breath knocked from his lungs.

Shouts sounded from the direction of the showroom. Brandon lay on his side, struggling to breathe. The afternoon turned cottony, with muffled sounds of running. Help was coming—Shawn, coworkers, somebody.

And Thornby was getting away.

Brandon sat up, sucking in air. By the time his manager and two salesmen drew up, puffing, he'd swayed to his feet.

"What happened, what happened?"

"Did I hear a gun?"

"Who was that guy?"

The questions bounced in his throbbing head. Brandon waved a hand in the direction his attacker had gone. He turned, searching up the lot, then on up Sprague. Thornby was nowhere in sight. Man couldn't be far. Most likely he was crouched behind parked cars up the street, slowly but surely making his getaway.

"Crazy guy had a gun. He tried to kill me."

Brandon leaned over, hands on his knees, and breathed. Didn't matter. Let the guy get away; Brandon had no energy for a chase. He was scraped up and bruised, not to mention not much good for selling a car the rest of the day. As if lost commissions weren't bad enough, now he faced a long explanation with his manager, including why a brand new car in the lot had more than one dent in its hood. Shawn would insist on calling the police. Brandon would have to file a report.

But, hey, at least he was alive.

"Come on, let's get you back inside," Shawn said. "Your chin's bleeding."

One thing for sure, Brandon thought. As much as he'd love to walk away from this mess, he couldn't now. Carla had to know what happened. And, seeing as how it had almost cost his life, that suitcase was *absolutely* getting to her.

As he started the long, weary trek back to the showroom, Brandon slapped a coworker on the shoulder. "Listen, man. Next time a single chick comes in wanting to test drive a PT—*you're* taking her."

FIFTY-FIVE

Vince Edwards leaned over his desk at the Kanner Lake police station, yellow pad pulled close, pen in hand. Photos of his family lined the front of his desk. Nancy, his wife. Tim, their son who had died in Iraq, a victim of a bomb. Heather, their daughter who lived in Spokane with her husband and little girl, Christy. Outside the front station window ran Main Street. Through that window Vince could watch people come and go, see the seasons change. Vince loved his family and town. Would give his life for either one. The tragedies in Kanner Lake within the past fifteen months had seared his heart. Life had been wonderfully quiet since the horrible murders of last March. Now this. And he wasn't even sure what *this* was.

"Ms. Evans, you still there?"

"I'm ... yes."

"I asked if you have any idea why these threats are happening now. Since you say the events in question took place sixteen years ago."

In the first few minutes of their conversation Tanya Evans's vocal inflection had told Vince many things. She sounded intelligent, compassionate, fearful. And she sounded like someone carrying around a lot of guilt. The woman had told him details about Carla Radling's past that he never would have guessed. That Carla had clerked for Bryson Hanley (a man Vince had hoped to vote into the presidency) when she was sixteen. That

Hanley had seduced her—probably as one of his numerous conquests, although Carla might be the only minor. That she had gotten pregnant. And now Hanley's campaign manager, a focused, power-hungry individual who would stop at nothing to get his man in the White House, had appeared uninvited in Tanya Evans's home last night, threatening her life if she told what she knew.

Now she feared Paul Jilke had sent someone to kill Carla.

It took a moment for Vince to absorb all the information. When the shock settled, he understood one thing—there was a lot more to the story than Ms. Evans was telling.

"Things ... got stirred up recently," she said. "Someone came to me asking questions, someone who'd uncovered information that didn't look right. And, of course, this is during the last year of campaigning for the presidency—a position Hanley has sought all his life. His people aren't about to let that slip through their fingers. At least Jilke won't."

"Who came to you, and with what information?"

"I can't tell you that yet." Her voice pinched. "I owe it to Carla to speak to her first."

Vince hoped with all his might she would get the chance. Already with what little he knew, his heart was sinking. Men seeking power made for powerful foes.

He could wear down Tanya Evans until she told him everything. Years of questioning suspects and reticent witnesses had taught Vince the tricks of the trade. But they weren't face-to-face. He couldn't study her body language, employ subtle "power" movements of his own. Nothing but a phone line connected them, a line that could be cut by one flick of her finger. He *would* get all the information in time, but for now he shouldn't push her.

"How does Jilke know this person came to you?"

"I told him." Ms. Evans's tone flattened, as if she couldn't believe her own stupidity. "I was trying to get to Senator Hanley himself, but he was out of town. Jilke pulled the information from me. Believe me, he knows how to do that. I had no idea that I was talking about something he didn't know. That is, he knew some of it—enough to convince me he knew it all. He knew about Hanley's affair with Carla and that she had become pregnant. But he didn't know the end of the story. If he had, he may have tried to kill Carla and me long ago. But hearing it *now*—when Hanley's on a rocket launch to the White House—Jilke obviously decided he couldn't let it sit. We're a time tomb, Carla and I. We're his worst nightmare."

Vince asked a few additional questions, but Ms. Evans would say no more. That would have to do for now. She was on her way to Kanner Lake. His immediate task was to get her there in one piece.

"Ms. Evans, I want to send a state trooper out for you. He'll make sure your car is left in a safe place—and more important, he'll make sure you arrive here safely. Okay?"

"No. *Don't.*"

"Why?"

"I don't know if I can trust a Washington trooper. This is Bryson Hanley's state. How do I know who might be working for him?"

Vince's gut churned. It was one thing to consider dirty politics, but a dirty cop was something else. After all the years he'd given to his career, he couldn't tolerate the thought.

He tapped his pen against the desk. "At least tell me what kind of vehicle you're driving."

She hesitated. "A black Ford pickup truck. I don't know the model."

Vince made a note. "Happen to know the license plate?"

"No."

"Okay. And your approximate location?"

"You're not going to send someone out for me, are you?" Fear hitched Tanya's voice.

"Not if you don't want me to. I can't make you get into a trooper's car against your will. But under the circumstances, I'd sure feel better at least knowing how far away you are."

"Okay." She paused a minute, then read him the name and number of the nearest exit.

Vince wrote it down. "Thanks. I'm going to call about every half hour to check on you. And please don't hesitate to call me anytime. If you change your mind, I'll send someone out for you right away."

"I won't . . . I *can't* change my mind."

When they ended the call, Vince lowered his forehead into both hands. *Bryson Hanley—and Carla?* The thought of a young, impressionable girl seduced by a powerful man made him sick. He couldn't imagine such a thing happening to his own daughter at that age. And a *pregnancy*? What happened to the baby? How had Carla lived with such terrible secrets as she'd watched this man rise to fame?

Vince's head swirled with questions and doubts. Part of him couldn't believe Ms. Evans's story, even though she sounded so believable. If it hadn't coincided with Carla's disappearance and the bugging of Java Joint's phone, he might think she was a crackpot. Of all politicians, Bryson Hanley was *known* for his protection of families and children. For supporting education and the underprivileged. The man was constantly photographed with his wife and children. The quintessential husband and father—everything the country wanted in a man who would be president.

The other side of Vince knew that Hanley wouldn't be the first powerful man to fall victim to his own sexual weaknesses.

But a US senator. One on his way to the White House. Not exactly the kind of man whose office Vince could waltz into with mere allegations. Especially during the campaign. The media would rip into the story like a pack of hungry wolves. Talking heads would have a heyday, the Republicans crying scandal, the Democrats screaming the senator's defense. Hanley would deny everything, claim smear tactics. Vince and his family, Carla, Kanner Lake in general—so many people he cared about—would be caught in the middle.

Vince lifted his head, pinched the bridge of his nose with thumb and forefinger. Time to get to work. He needed to find one missing woman and protect another. And if all these allegations were true, in the end—bottom line—he would need proof.

FIFTY-SIX

Three miles from the car dealership, Tony lay in the Durango, knees drawn up, dragging in oxygen. He'd driven to safety, then crawled into the backseat and collapsed like a marionette with cut strings, groin still spiking pain. Murderous rage chewed a hole in his heart. By the time this was over, he was going to kill *everybody* involved. Carla Radling, Paul Jilke, that car salesman—and anyone else that got in his way.

He screwed his eyes shut, remembering every detail of the salesman's face. The kid was lying. Tony *knew* it.

His cell phone rang—Jilke's tone. Tony lifted his head off the seat and growled. Let the man call 'til doomsday, he didn't care. Tony would answer when he was good and ready.

Except that Robyn and Timmy were fleeing town about now.

Anxiety streaked through Tony. He fumbled in his pants pocket for his phone. Willed his voice to sound normal.

"Hello."

"Hello to *you*, Tony." Jilke's voice was low and cold. "Guess what—a friend of mine picked up two people you know. Your wife and son. Seems they were about to fly the coop. Any idea why they'd want to do that?"

The words hit Tony like an avalanche. He sat straight up, ignoring his searing pain. "Jilke, you hurt my family, and you're *dead*, you hear? I'll tell everything I know, I'll expose everybody, including your favorite man, Hanley. I don't care if I go down, I *don't care,* but you *will not* hurt my family and get away with it!"

"Temper, temper." Jilke pulled in a slow, smug breath. Tony wanted to reach through the phone and rip out the man's vocal cords.

"Let's get down to business, shall we." Jilke's tone turned to steel. "I want to know it *all.* Everything you've done, every lie you've told me. And *maybe* if you come clean with me, when you've done your job you'll get your family back. Otherwise, you can count on not seeing them again."

Tony ground his teeth. Rage told him to hurl the phone out the window. Rationality told him to keep cool, do whatever Jilke asked. They would sort this out later, man to man, once Robyn and Timmy were safe.

He slumped back against the car seat—and told Jilke what he wanted to know. Every bit of it. Jilke listened without interruption.

When Tony was done, silence pulsed over the line like blood from a wound.

"Listen to me, Tony." Jilke's words were the dead calm of a man beyond fury. "Change cars fast, then get back and start surveillance on that dealership. I think you're right—the kid knows something. He's your only link to our target right now. *Don't* let him out of your sight. I've got to check into a few things here, and I'll call you back. Don't even *think* about not answering the phone."

"Wait, I want to talk to my—"

The line clicked in Tony's ear.

FIFTY-SEVEN

Paul Jilke's hand trembled as he punched in the number to one of his men. The men no one else knew about, nor did they even know each other. He'd found them over the years as situations warranted—people he trusted, ruthless enough to carry out his commands without complaint or question. Greedy enough to allow their silence to be bought.

Jilke knew he was not alone in what he did. Successful politicians like Bryson Hanley didn't rocket to the top without someone watching their backside. "Protect your man" was the ancient philosophy of those in Jilke's shoes—and with Bryson Hanley he'd had a lot to protect. A brilliant politician, charmer of the voter. And Hanley cared about the common folks; he truly did. He would make a strong president, the kind the US needed. Jilke would be at his side when the last votes were counted, when the victory was announced, when the confetti fell. Like Hanley, he had worked all his life for those glorious moments.

But like many men of strength before him, Hanley's soul had been woven with a fatal flaw. Fatal, that is, were it not for Jilke's protection.

The phone rang once in his ear. Jilke pictured Hanley coming in the door of his Washington office tomorrow, heady with the poll results, confident in his trajectory. Ignorant of those things of which he must remain ignorant.

Hanley had committed a most egregious error, one that stunned even Jilke, who knew his chameleon abilities so well. He had kept a fact—a very important fact—from Jilke for sixteen years. Only the blurting of a flustered and frightened Tanya Evans had enlightened Jilke with the news.

He'd acted immediately, confident that fate had alerted him at the right moment. Any further in the campaign, and were such news to leak it would devastate the entire Hanley camp. Jilke had not told Hanley he'd learned the truth. He simply took it upon himself to clean up the mess.

The phone picked up. "Bruce here."

Jilke kept his voice even. He would need a double dose of antianxiety meds tonight. "Where's your target, Bruce?"

"At work. Been watching all day."

"How do you know?"

"Her car's still in the parking garage."

Jilke closed his eyes. "You telling me you've been watching her *car*?"

"That's how she got here."

He flexed his jaw. If his fear proved true, this guy was as good as dead. "Do me a favor if you value your life." His tone flattened. "Call her office and see if she's there. I don't care what story you give the receptionist, just get to her. Call me right back."

He snapped his phone closed and waited an interminable three minutes. Too long. By the time his return call came, Jilke knew what he would hear.

"She's not there." Shock wavered Bruce's voice. The guy knew he'd pay. "They said she left at lunch and never came back."

Jilke raged then. Yelled and screamed at the man's pure, unadulterated *stupidity*. He knocked papers off his desk, stalked around his office. Spewed every cuss word he'd learned since childhood. When his anger finally drained, leaving him spent and breathless, he threw himself in his desk chair, head pounding.

"Get to her house, see if she's there. Then report back." Jilke smacked off the line and slammed the cell down on his desk.

She wouldn't be. He knew that. By now Tanya Evans, a.k.a. "Ellie," would be halfway to Kanner Lake. Looking to meet up with Carla Radling, who *also happened to be missing.*

Two men after two women—and *both* of them screwed up? *How* could this happen? What dark fate had set such an unthinkable situation in motion?

If those two women met, Carla Radling would no longer keep silent. A mother's wrath was the most furious of forces. Hanley could kiss his campaign good-bye.

Jilke yanked up his desk phone, punched in the two digits to his secretary. Not for years had he needed to do his own undercover work. But now all bets were off. Either those two women died—today—or his life, all he'd ever dreamed of, was over.

"Get me on a plane to Spokane. *Now.*"

PART THREE

Collision

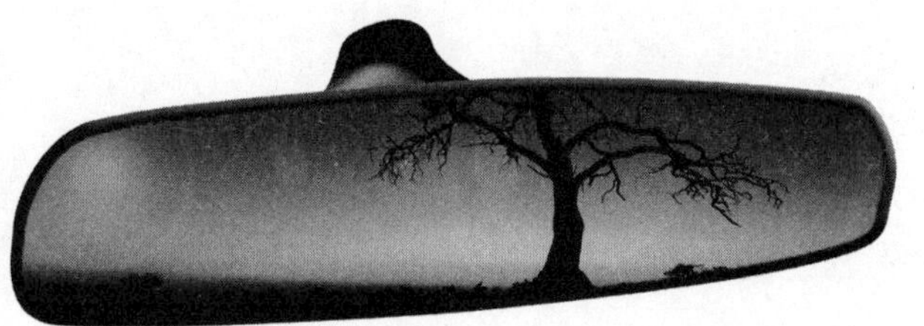

FIFTY-EIGHT

Carla drifted in the murky waters of half-sleep, the shore now near ... now not ... A wave lifted her up, edged her forward. She felt the swish of sand around her legs ... the brush of soft ground beneath her ...

Her eyes opened.

She blinked at a TV set, a white wall with a watercolor print of purple-grey mountains. A dresser with three drawers.

Reality flooded back.

Carla jerked her head toward the clock radio near the bed. 3:59. She'd been asleep for an hour and a half.

Her ankle felt wet. She sat up, examining the towel wrap she'd so carefully placed. The ice had melted and run out of the plastic, soaking the cloth. She moved the soggy pack aside and examined her ankle. A little less puffy. Throbbed less too. But not totally better, not by a long shot.

Sighing, she sank back against the pillows.

She needed to get up, get out of here. Rent a car, drive ... away. Carla closed her eyes, searching for the energy to move. Every limb felt weighted to the bed, her blood like water. Her stomach rumbled. No doubt part of her tiredness was due to hunger. If she could just eat, she'd find the strength to get up. But this hotel didn't have room service.

Carla laid a hand against her forehead. A tear blurred one eye and rolled down her temple. Where was she supposed to go? What could she do to make this end?

How long before Thornby found her here?

No reason he should find her. No one knew where she was but Brandon.

That's one person too many.

What had she been thinking, letting him hear the false name she used, the room she'd been assigned? She'd just been too exhausted, in too much pain to care.

But so what if Brandon knew? He'd helped her here. He'd been kind. Beyond that, he didn't believe her story. The guy thought she was nutty as a loon and probably wouldn't give her a second thought. He had cars to sell.

She told herself to get up. But still couldn't do it.

Carla shifted her head on the pillow, and her eyes fell on the television remote, sitting near the clock radio. Absently, she picked it up, clicked on the power. The screen spritzed to life—some talk show. Keeping the volume low, she flipped channels until she landed on CNN. Two talking heads were discussing the presidential campaign. The picture switched to a scene of Bryson Hanley in a crowd, smiling and shaking dozens of the faithfuls' hands, thrust toward him in hope of a touch.

Carla's heart turned over.

She watched him grasp fingers, remembering when he'd held hers with such gentleness. Watched him gaze deep into the eyes of one voter after another, his expression the epitome of sincere promise. She'd seen him in action so many times over the years, and always she reacted the same. Remembering him in love, remembering him in hatred. Pulled toward his charisma, even as she knew it was all a sham.

How could he have gotten away with his two-facedness all these years?

At age sixteen she'd believed she was the only one. That's what he'd wanted her to think. But as she learned the truth about Bryson Hanley, as she grew into adulthood, Carla saw clearly what she could not see then. Hanley was a womanizer. He'd no doubt had many affairs. Were any others with teenagers? Had he gotten anyone else pregnant?

Carla thought back to the iciness of Bryson's wife. The woman had mistrusted her from the moment they met. That too could have tipped Carla off, if she hadn't been so starry-eyed. Mrs. My-Husband had known, all right. Probably not about the affair with Carla, or she'd have found herself without a job in a hurry. But the woman knew about her husband's dalliances. She took one look at Carla's face, her youth, and reacted with jealousy and fear. Carla smiled bitterly. Mrs. My-Husband had no doubt been thrilled to hear she'd gotten pregnant by her teenage boyfriend.

The news flashed from scene to scene of Bryson while the pundits discussed his rise to fame. Bryson at his desk in DC. Speaking to a group of business people in his home state of Washington. Addressing a college graduating class. Breaking ground on a new building that would house unwed mothers and their children. Laughing with his son, his arm around his daughter's shoulder—

Carla snapped off the TV.

She needed to go to the bathroom. She needed a drink of water. She needed to *leave.*

Carla pushed herself up, swung her legs to the floor. The left ankle immediately throbbed. She winced.

Jaw set, she stood up, refusing to make a single sound in her pain. She rested on her right foot, left one barely touching the floor. Hobbled a step toward the end of the bed, then a second and a third.

The ring of the hotel phone shattered the silence.

FIFTY-NINE

Mrs. My-Husband is pregnant.

I heard it on the news tonight. How she and "State Senator Hanley" are ecstatic. How they've been wanting to be parents for a long time. The news said a "source" from Bryson's office confirmed the report. The source—obviously Jilke—explained this is why Catherine Hanley hasn't been seen in public for the past two months. She'd had infertility problems, he said, and the Hanleys didn't want to announce the pregnancy until she was well into it.

Her due date is in April. The baby is a girl.

April.

She got pregnant almost the same time I did.

Maybe they didn't know right away. Probably not, since Bryson told me her periods weren't regular. Still, they've probably known for at least three months.

Now it all makes sense. They've known for some time they didn't need my baby. Bryson needed to get rid of me. Jilke found a way.

What I wonder is—does Bryson believe Jilke's story about my stealing? Or was Bryson in on that setup from the very beginning?

I can't bear to think that's true. That he would lie to me, and act so betrayed and everything when we talked on the phone.

If you say one word about Bryson Hanley, we'll press charges. That was Jilke's final word to me. If I ever tried to get back at Bryson, like tell anyone I'm carrying his baby, they'd put me in jail. Tell the police and everyone I'm just trying to cause trouble because I got fired. And who would ever believe me over Bryson Hanley? Especially now that everyone's so happy for Mrs. My-Husband's pregnancy? Washington's favorite son—going to be a father at last. The whole state's grinning.

I'd be squashed like an ant.

What they can't possibly understand is, I would never tell anyway.

I do think Bryson was in on the setup. I think this is his way of protecting himself.

Don't you worry, Bryson Hanley. I can protect myself too. *And* my baby. You don't know everything. You can't keep me down. I'm going to have this baby. I've named her Rebecca. (Somehow I know it's a girl.) And Scott and I will raise her, just like it should have been in the first place.

I don't need you, Senator Hanley. Mr. Golden Boy. We both know you're not all that golden, don't we?

Someday I hope the rest of the world knows too.

SIXTY

Carla jerked to a halt, heart knocking against her ribs. Who could be calling? Thornby?

Maybe it was the front desk.

Brandon.

No one else knew she was here. It had to be Brandon, checking up on her.

She hoped.

Carla stared daggers at the phone, as if her will alone would silence it. A second ring, and a third. Her nerves jangled. She limped to the bed stand and snatched up the receiver just to stop the noise. Slowly she brought it to her ear, then stilled.

She heard voices in the background. Felt a presence holding the phone, waiting for her to talk.

Seconds ticked by. Carla closed her eyes. It was Thornby.

"Carla?"

A voice she recognized. Not Thornby.

Carla bent over, feeling weak, then sat down hard on the bed. "Brandon."

"Yeah. You okay? Didn't think you were going to answer for a minute."

"I'm . . . fine."

"How's your ankle?"

"Not good." Carla mouthed rote answers, her mind still trying to wrap itself around her relief.

"Oh, sorry. Listen up, though, I gotta tell you something. I had a little visit from your friend Thornby." He told Carla about the gun, the fight, Thornby running off.

Carla brought a hand to her face, thoughts whirling. If she hadn't fled that car dealership, she could have been caught. Brandon could have been killed. *Any friend who helps you is dead.* All the more reason now why she couldn't call *anyone.* Why she was truly, completely *on her own* …

"Brandon"—her throat cramped—"I'm so sorry. I never should have gone to you for help. I knew better; I just … had nowhere else to go."

"Hey, don't be worrying about that. I'm not calling to make you feel bad. I just want you to know this guy's still after you. Don't think he'll come back here, though. My manager's called the police, and they're on their way over here. I'm going to give a full report and a description of the guy. The cops'll be looking for him. Plus we need the report for our insurance claim on the dented car."

Carla's fingers tightened on the phone. "Please don't tell the police about me!"

"Why? You're obviously in trouble, and you need help. Plus, how am I going to explain what happened? I have to tell my manager where your car came from."

She rubbed her forehead, trying to work coherent thought into her brain. Her stomach felt so empty, her body so tired, and her ankle throbbed. She couldn't begin to *think.*

"Wait." Carla edged back to rest against the headboard and lifted both feet up on the bed. The ankle pain eased off a little. "Okay. Tell them you took a crazy woman for a test drive if you have to. But don't tell them where I am. I can't trust the police, Brandon! Remember it was a state trooper who helped Thornby find me."

"So what am I supposed to say?"

"That you dropped me off on the street and have no idea where I went."

Brandon hesitated. "I don't know. I don't want to lie to the police. And Shawn—that's my manager—I sure can't lie to him."

Fear edged Carla's voice. "Listen to me—you tell them where I am, it won't do any good. I'll just leave. Be gone before any policeman gets here. I'll have to do that, don't you understand? I *can't* trust the police!"

Brandon sighed. "Yeah, okay, I hear you. There's been a few times in my life I wondered about the police myself. I'll tell them I let you out, and I don't know where you went."

Carla's body went limp. She sank her chin toward her chest. "Thank you."

They were silent for a moment.

"Look," Brandon said, "I'm going to get this suitcase to you if it's the last thing I do. I get off work at eight. I'll bring it over then. So *don't* leave, okay?"

"You're staying at work? Haven't you had enough for one day?"

He gave a little snort. "Thought so for a while there, but hey, I haven't sold a car yet. Besides, I'm thinking this huge Band-Aid on my chin's going to make people feel sorry for me. Somebody'll buy from me for sure."

Carla smiled. Then checked the clock: 4:30. It would be a long time until he arrived. "You have to be careful when you come. Keep an eye out for a black Durango."

"Oh, I'll be watching, all right." Disgust tinged Brandon's voice. "I see it, I'm leading the guy straight to the police station. I've had *enough* of him."

Carla's stomach growled. "Brandon, when you come—do you think you could bring me something to eat?"

"Sure. What do you want?"

"Doesn't matter. Anything. I haven't eaten since lunch yesterday, and I don't want to show myself in the restaurant here."

"You got it."

Carla heard muffled words in the background. Brandon's voice dimmed, as if he'd turned his mouth from the phone. "Okay, be right there." He came back, louder. "I gotta go, the cops are here."

Apprehension spiraled through Carla. "Remember what you promised."

"Hey, listen, no worries. You think I want anything happening to you? I got a bit invested now, know what I mean?"

"Yeah, guess so. Thanks. Call me when you're on your way over, okay?"

"All right."

They clicked off the call, Carla staring at the receiver in her hand. Not sixty seconds passed before reality hit. She couldn't stay here now. She dared not trust anyone, including Brandon. His manager, the police, coworkers—someone was liable to pull from him the whole story. And who knew how the information could spread from there?

Tears bit her eyes. She was so very tired. But she had to rouse herself, call a cab, go to a car rental agency—and drive off again. To some unknown destination, full of unknown people and an unknown life.

The receiver began to beep. She leaned over and smashed it down, wishing it were her fist in Bryson Hanley's face. This was never, ever going to end. Not unless she told everything and exposed him. And that, for her own sake, and the sake of Hanley's children, and for Scott, she would not do.

Carla blinked back the tears. No time to cry now. She had more important things to do. Like save herself.

SIXTY-ONE

I am so huge. I look like a barn. I feel like a barn. I have to go to the bathroom all the time.

Worst of all, I keep having these early contractions, called Braxton Hicks. Dr. Hughes says they're not real contractions and the baby's not really ready to come yet. But they sure feel real. They *hurt.*

I had a doctor's appointment today. Dr. Hughes says everything looks good. I had an ultrasound again—and the results are the same as last time, no question. It's a girl. I *knew* it! Scott and I are getting excited! I can't wait to finally hold Rebecca. Touch those tiny hands and fingernails. See the color of her eyes and hair.

Scott and I have decided I'll live with Mom for another year. Somehow I'll try to finish my senior year while taking care of a baby. There are agencies to help me. Then after we graduate, we'll get married.

Sometimes I feel so guilty for what I've done to Scott. I just have to shove it back down. No way can I let myself think about it. I just have to go on and make a life for the three of us. This is really, finally going to work out. Just like I never went to Bryson in the first place. Just like it should have been.

Lisa, the nurse in Dr. Hughes's office, is still so nice. The first time I had an appointment after hearing about Mrs. My-Husband's pregnancy, Lisa was all worried for me. She could tell I was upset, even though I tried to hide it. After my appointment was done, she came outside in the hall and hugged me. Told me she was proud of me, and that I'd make a good mother. She promised she'd be my friend after the baby comes. Not just a nurse but my friend.

I need someone like her.

My old friends have all fallen away. I hardly even talk to Mary Kay anymore. It's my fault, I know. I can't tell anyone the truth about what happened, and all the lies make me pull away from people. I just have to try hard not to pull away from Scott too. I *need* Scott. Rebecca needs a father. And he's still been so wonderful to me. He doesn't deserve to be hurt.

As for my mom—forget it. She tolerates me, that's all. I think she hates my baby already. She'll never lay a hand on Rebecca, that's a promise.

Not that many more weeks, and I'll have my baby. She's all that matters anymore. If I can be a good mom, maybe I can make it up to God for all the lies I've told. For everything I've done. And maybe He'll stop punishing me.

Just a few weeks. I *can't wait* to hold Rebecca. She'll be the one good thing to come from all of this. And she'll get all the love from her mother that I never got from mine. All she deserves and more.

Hurry up, April, and come!

SIXTY-TWO

It took twenty minutes for Brandon to tell his story to the cop—a tall, broad-shouldered guy with suspicious brown eyes named Officer Criggen. Brandon had to be careful what he said. Tricky thing, remembering what you told the police if it all wasn't on the level. Twice, he almost blurted out the truth about where he'd taken Carla. Worry tugged at him. Carla had no one to help but him, and he was stuck here for hours.

The entire time he walked the new car aisle with the policeman and Shawn, as he pointed out the dents in the Chrysler and reconstructed the events, Brandon thought about Carla. One thing he could honestly tell the police—he had *no idea* why she was in trouble. "I asked, and all she'd say is, 'It's a long story.' "

He told Criggen his attacker's name was supposedly Thornby—at least that's what the guy told Carla. And that he was driving a rented black Durango.

The policeman wrote it down. "We'll check that out with local car rental agencies. Just may lead us to him."

"All *right.*" Vengeance beat in Brandon's chest. Thornby wasn't going to get away with this. No way.

Officer Criggen pulled on gloves and went through Carla's car, checking her papers. From there he confirmed her full name. That much Brandon had told him, knowing he'd soon discover it anyway.

Before the officer left, he radioed into headquarters to run Carla's name. He came back to Brandon and Shawn with the news—a missing person's bulletin had recently been filed on her.

Missing person. Brandon stared out the showroom window. He imagined family and friends who missed her. How scared they must be—

Leslie Brymes.

The name echoed in his brain. *Leslie.* Carla's friend. And a reporter. Sounded like Carla trusted her. Still, Carla refused to call her, for fear of bringing her trouble.

But he could.

Brandon smiled.

Yeah, he could. He should. If ever Carla needed a friend, it was now.

And, of course, there was that other part Brandon had to admit. He wouldn't mind introducing himself to the hot Leslie Brymes. Nope, he wouldn't mind that at all.

SIXTY-THREE

Leslie hung up from talking to another of Carla's friends—who like the rest knew big, fat *zero*—and dropped her head in her hands. It was almost five o'clock. Her interview with the developer of the new hotel was supposed to happen two hours ago. Of course she'd cancelled it, on the fast track to find Carla. Instead she'd found *nothing*. Every hour that passed only made her feel sicker. She knew Carla was dead. Knew it as surely as she'd found Vesta Johnson's body last March in her car.

Why? Why would anybody want Carla dead? And why would Carla talk to sweet Bailey in such a mean way when Bailey had tried to help?

If only there was more Leslie could do right now. But for the moment they were all stuck in a waiting game. Tanya Evans was on her way to Kanner Lake. There she would talk to Chief Edwards. Leslie could only hope she'd manage to hear Tanya's full story too. This not knowing was driving her *crazy*.

Leslie swallowed a lump in her throat. Still, she longed to know the truth more for Carla's sake than her own career. The lessons she had learned during the March murders had been hard won and humbling. Driven by stark ambition to succeed, Leslie would have done anything to get a story. She'd reacted that way when the infamous actress Edna San went missing from her lake estate fifteen months ago. But in March, when her own friends were killed, Leslie had recognized the darker side of her ambition. She'd shoved it aside to help the investigation, her craving for justice far greater than "getting the story." Not to mention she'd also learned more than she ever cared to know about the evil that existed in this world—an evil that sent her careening straight into the arms of Jesus. Where else could a person go in the midst of such darkness?

"God," Leslie whispered, "it's dark again. Please help. I don't know what to *do*."

It was so quiet in the office. Jared was out, seeing what he could discover about Carla. Which must not be much, or he'd have called. Part of Leslie wanted to run home, jump into bed, and throw the covers over her head. Hide from hearing the truth she so feared. She and her roommate, Paige, could rent a silly movie, stuff themselves on popcorn with lots of butter ...

Leslie raised her head. Her face felt cool in the absence of two warm palms. Her eyes roamed over the worn office—Jared's desk and computer, the stacks of past newspaper editions, the grey metal file cabinets—as if seeking an answer in the clutter.

Her desk phone rang. She grabbed the receiver, hoping for something. Anything.

"*Kanner Lake Times*, Leslie Brymes."

"Leslie, hi. My name's Brandon. You know somebody named Carla Radling?"

Panic and wild hope seared her chest. She hunched forward, gripping the edge of her desk. "Do you know where she is?"

"Yeah. I saw her a little while ago."

Leslie's shoulders slumped. Her hand rose to her mouth, instant tears welling. Questions crowded her mind as to who Brandon was, or how he knew. But those could wait. All she cared about now was Carla. "Where is she, is she okay, what *happened*? Everybody's *looking* for her!"

"Whoa, whoa. She's okay. Sort of. I'll tell you everything."

And he did.

Sometime during his story, the reporter in Leslie made her pull a pad of paper near, begin taking notes. By the time Brandon finished, she'd covered two pages. Two pages of *very crazy stuff.*

Brandon told her where Carla was hiding. The name she'd used to register, and her room number. Three times he emphasized how *no one else* could know. "She keeps saying she can't trust the cops. I can see why, after that state trooper stopped her."

Leslie bit her cheek. Could that be true? Maybe the trooper's stop had just been coincidence ...

At any rate, how did all this fit with what Leslie had heard from Tanya Evans?

"I'm going over there in about three hours to take her suitcase," Brandon said. "But I figured she could probably use some company now. Do you think you could at least call her or something?"

"*Call* her?" Leslie's words pinched. "You kidding—I'm over there *now*! Brandon, I can't thank you enough. I was so afraid she was ..." The word caught in her throat.

"Hey. No problem." Brandon made sure Leslie's caller ID had recorded his cell number, and Leslie gave him hers. "Will you call me when you get to Carla?" Brandon said. "Just let me know she's okay. Oh, and she'll need some food. She hasn't eaten since yesterday."

"Okay. We'll keep in touch. And if that Thornby guy comes back, you need to let me know. As well as the cops, of course."

"Yeah, don't worry."

Leslie plunked down the receiver, her heart in her throat. "Thank You, God, thank You, thank You ..."

Grabbing her cell, she punched in 411 for the number of the Hampton Inn.

SIXTY-FOUR

Tony had never felt readier for blood.

From a parking place near a Mexican restaurant at a long diagonal across Sprague, he kept an eye on the Spokane Chrysler lot. Not easy from this distance, but he couldn't risk getting any closer. Tony had only one job until Jilke showed up—keep the car salesman in sight. Which could get tricky if the kid took some customer for a test drive. Good thing Tony had changed cars. He'd found a nearby Enterprise agency, ditched the Durango in a strip mall parking lot, and rented a white Ford Taurus. If Carla had come crying to Blond Boy for help, she'd have told him about the black SUV. Car salesmen knew cars. The kid would have spotted the Durango on his tail in no time.

Tony had watched a policeman come and go from the dealership. Taking notes, examining the dented Chrysler on the lot. Blond Boy no doubt gave a physical description of his attacker. Not good.

Jilke's plane arrived in Spokane at 5:58. He'd rent a car, drive out to Spokane Valley, and pick Tony up. By that time it would be around 6:30—an hour and a half from now. Tony could only thank whatever gods existed that business on the Chrysler lot was slow. *Ninety minutes with no test drives—that's all I need.*

Tony knew Jilke was mad enough to kill him. But he needed Tony to hunt down Carla Radling—and now a second woman.

Tanya Evans, a.k.a. the mysterious "Ellie from the past." Meanwhile Tony could practically taste the vengeance of strangling Jilke. But he needed the man to secure his family's safety. *Nothing* was more important than that. With his bare hands Tony would tear apart Carla, Tanya, Blond Boy, and half of Spokane if he had to. Anything to get his family back.

But once their targets were dead, he knew this love/hate dance between him and his boss would be over. Only one of them would be left standing.

And it wasn't going to be Paul Jilke.

SIXTY-FIVE

Perched on the edge of the bed, Carla reached for the phone to call a cab. Before she could pick up the receiver—it rang.

She snatched her hand back and stared wildly at the phone. A second jangle chewed through her head. Her brain flashed crazy thoughts of third time's charm gone bad. First Bailey, then Brandon—now Thornby?

Steeling herself, she picked up the receiver and held it to her ear.

Silence.

"Carla? Is that you? Talk to me, it's Leslie."

Leslie!

Carla's jaw creaked open. "H–how did you find me?"

What a stupid question. The minute the words left her lips, she knew.

"Well, it sure wasn't thanks to you." Leslie's tone pulsed with frustration. "How could you *do* this to us—don't you know all your friends are looking for you?"

"I couldn't . . . I didn't—"

"Never mind, it doesn't matter. Nothing matters now that I've found you. Listen to me. You stay *right there*. You hear? I'm coming to get you."

"No!" Carla's stomach tightened. The emotion of the past twenty-three hours rushed her in a cold wave. The running, her fear, reading the diary. Hadn't she been through *enough*? She couldn't watch her friends die too. "You *can't.* I won't let you put yourself in danger."

"Don't worry about me; sounds like *you're* the one in trouble."

"But I can't go back home, Leslie; he'll find me there."

"Fine then, we'll camp out in your lovely hotel room."

"You don't—"

"Carla, *be quiet!* I've got things to tell you, things you've got to know. An old friend of yours is on her way from Seattle. She has something desperately important to tell you. Sounds like it's some kind of confession. She's the one who called Java Joint this morning, saying her name is Ellie. Her real name's Tanya Evans."

Tanya Evans.

The name twisted a knife in Carla's heart. She hadn't thought of that name in well over a decade, but the mere mention popped sweat on her forehead. As if some tornado whisked her up and plunked her back sixteen years, she could hear the soothing voice, smell the hospital room, feel the racking pain.

She slumped over, head resting at an awkward angle against the headboard.

"Carla, you okay?"

"Yes." Her voice was a whisper. "No."

Leslie hesitated. "Who is she?"

Carla swallowed. "Somebody I knew only one day. And never saw again. But it was a very ... important day. Hard. Terrible."

"Oh. Can you think why she'd want to talk to you?"

Something desperately important to tell you ... confession. The words finally registered. What could—

A horrific thought pierced Carla.

Rebecca.

Stunned, Carla pushed upright. No. *No.* The idea was so heinous, so *nauseating,* it snatched all breath away. It couldn't be true. Not *possible.*

Her gaze fell on the blue window curtains and snagged there. "No. Can't think of a reason." The words came out thick, pleading to be true.

Silence. Carla knew she hadn't convinced Leslie any more than she'd convinced herself. She pressed a hand over her eyes, wanting to shut out the room, the world.

"Okay. Well." Leslie took a breath. "Tanya's driving. She'll hit Spokane about six-thirty. I'm in touch with her by phone, and I'll direct her to where we are. I'll be with you by then. Also—you should know somebody's after her too, but it looks like she gave them the slip in Seattle."

After her? Someone Bryson had sent?

That would only be true if Tanya knew something...

The thought stabbed again. Carla doubled over, chest against her legs. She froze there, feeling the rush of blood to her head, the spin of her mind back in time.

Rebecca.

She could hear the sounds of that day—the tap of steel instruments, Dr. Hughes's footsteps in and out, her own grunts and screams. Saw the IV bag, Tanya's misty eyes, her own knees up and spread, shaking, her skin goosebumped. Felt the misery and grief that ground her up and spit her out.

Carla hunched over like a broken puppet, shoulders drawn in, arm wrapped around her legs. At that moment, everything she'd thought vital in her world dried up and blew away. Suddenly none of it—not exhaustion or hunger or fear or even saving her own life—made a difference. Only one thing remained: the pulsing, writhing need to *know*. Whatever else happened, whether she lived or died, Carla wanted only to hear what Tanya Evans had to tell her.

"Leslie." Her voice croaked. "Just get her here. *Now.*"

SIXTY-SIX

I couldn't write before this. Today is my seventeenth birthday.

Rebecca was born last Tuesday. March 31. Three weeks earlier than the due date Dr. Hughes gave me.

I saw him just the day before. I was having lots of Braxton Hicks contractions and didn't go to school. Scott took off work to drive me to Dr. Hughes's office for a checkup. He examined me and said the baby didn't look ready to come yet. I was so disappointed. I just wanted it to be over with! Lisa squeezed my hand. "It won't be long now." She gave me a big smile. "When you get to the hospital, I won't be there, but the nurses on staff will take good care of you."

I hugged her hard.

All that night, more contractions. The next morning I stayed home from school again. I knew the baby was coming. I called Dr. Hughes around nine, and he told me to come into his office. Scott left work to take me.

This time Dr. Hughes said it was time to go to the hospital. The next thing I knew, I was in a delivery room bed. I was *so scared.* I had wanted it all to be over, but now that I was in labor, and the pains really came hard—I was just petrified. The only good thing was I had a wonderful nurse. Her name was Tanya. She said she'd never leave my side. She held my hand and helped me through the pain. Tanya was so caring, it almost seemed like she felt the contractions as much as I did.

Scott stayed in the waiting room. He couldn't stand to see me suffer. And I really didn't want him there, watching and worrying. I'd put him through enough. Tanya would help me.

Labor went on and on. For the first few hours, I had contractions at pretty even intervals, but they didn't get any closer together. Dr. Hughes said I wasn't moving fast enough, and he wanted to give me Pitocin. He took Tanya out of the room to talk. When she came back she looked upset. I asked her what was wrong, but she said it was nothing – she just didn't like to see me in pain.

She put an IV line in me and started the Pitocin. She said it made contractions come faster. We both hoped the anesthesiologist would get there before the contractions got too bad.

About an hour and a half later – *boom.* The contractions came hard and fast. I was amazed how sharp the pains were. Not aching and low like cramps, but cutting like a knife. In the front and also in my back. Every time one peaked, I screamed. I mean it, I was panicking. I didn't know pain could ever be that bad, and I wasn't going to live through it.

I just kept telling myself it was for Rebecca. She would make it all worth it.

Dr. Hughes checked me often. Tanya kept holding my hand. I saw worry in her eyes for me.

Finally the anesthesiologist came and gave me an epidural. After that, the pain stopped. It was so weird. I felt numb below the waist. I also felt – I don't know. Strange. Like I wasn't totally there. I think it was just all the hurting and tiredness. I'd hardly slept at all the night before. I felt like cotton was wrapped around my head.

The baby finally came.

I wanted so badly to hold her. I kept asking, "Where's my baby, where's my baby? Let me hold her!" I tried to push up on my elbows and see what was going on at the bottom of the bed, but the doctor made me lie back down. I think he was afraid I was getting too excited. He gave me some more medication, and I got real tired.

Then I fell asleep.

When I woke up, Scott stood beside me, tears streaming down his face. I tried to talk, but my mouth wouldn't move. My body felt weird and empty. Finally I croaked out, "Where is she?"

Scott swallowed hard and shook his head. That scared me. Oh, so bad. I lay there in that bed and felt a fear go through me like I've never felt before in my life.

Dr. Hughes nudged Scott away. He took my hand. I looked around but didn't see Tanya.

"Carla." His face looked grim. "I'm so sorry to tell you we lost the baby. She was born with the umbilical cord wrapped around her neck, and that apparently choked her as she was coming down the birth canal. We did everything we could to bring her back, but ... we couldn't."

I stared at him, feeling concrete pour over me.

No, no, no-no-no-no-no ...

Right then something inside me died too.

It was awhile before I could form any words. I can't remember what I said. Or what I did. The whole world just went numb. The concrete hardened, and I couldn't move. Not an inch. Then it poured over my face and shut out everything. All sound, all light. All hope.

Vaguely, I remember Scott leaving the room. I don't remember how long I lay there. Tanya came in. I could tell she'd been crying.

I asked Tanya to see her. My Rebecca. Please, just let me see my baby!

Tanya tried to talk me out of it. She said it would be too hard for me. I got mad then. Anger rushed me, sending cracks right through all the concrete until it fell away. If I hadn't been so weak I'd have jumped off that bed and choked her. "She's *my* baby and I *have* to see her!" I screamed and sobbed until the doctor came back. He finally said okay and told Tanya to bring the baby in.

So Tanya brought Rebecca to me. Tanya was shaking and white-faced. Her eyes were rimmed red. She could barely look at me. She laid Rebecca in my arms and whispered, "Take as long as you need, Carla. I'll be just outside the door whenever you call me."

I waited until she left. Then I looked into my baby's little face—and died all over again.

God, You did this, didn't You? It's my punishment. How could You have taken her from me?

She was blue. And so tiny. But she was made perfect. Thin arms, teeny hands, and fingernails like pearly drops of water. Lots of dark hair. The cutest little button nose. And sweet little lips.

I unwrapped her completely and marveled at her legs, her toes, the funny round stomach. I cried so hard over her, I washed her body in my tears.

No way could I give her back.

I never did call Tanya. I cried myself to sleep, holding Rebecca like I would never let go.

When I woke up, she was gone.

Just like that. It's over. All this. All the hurt and fear and pain. And my baby's gone.

We had a little service for her at a nearby church. I sat with Scott. He cried all the way through it. My mom didn't come.

Now here I am. Back in this ratty house. Empty, unloved. And I feel *so old.*

I haven't been back to school. Who cares? Haven't talked to any friends, barely even talked to Scott. He keeps calling. I know he's hurting too. I should hold him, comfort him. He deserves that. But I can't look into his face, knowing this is all my fault. Knowing that he lost his chance to be a father because God chose to punish me for my sins.

Mom just says it's for the best. I wasn't ready to be a mother anyway. She's always been such a blessing of help.

The next day after I got home from the hospital, I turned on the television and saw the news. Mrs. My-Husband had given birth to a healthy baby girl. She and Senator Hanley were so happy, the reporter said. And the state of Washington was celebrating with them.

You did this too, didn't You, God? Arranged the timing so perfectly. Gave them their baby almost the same time You took mine. You stuck a knife in me and twisted it.

Bryson used me up, then kicked me away like a mangy dog. Isn't it enough for me to see him with his wife and their baby? Why did You have to take mine? Why did Rebecca have to pay—with her life? *I'm* the one who should have died. Rebecca deserved to *live.*

Happy seventeenth birthday, Carla. Happy, happy rest of your life.

SIXTY-SEVEN

After Leslie's call, Carla's quiet hideaway turned into Grand Central Station. She received two more calls in a row. Each time, robotlike, she picked up the phone and waited for the person on the other end to speak. But her mind was somewhere else. Her mind dragged itself through the muddy, soul-griming day of her baby's birth—and death. All her present movements, her thoughts and words, were carried out in the shadowed haze of the past.

The first caller was Chief Edwards, insisting that she contact Spokane police to pick her up for safety. "No!" Carla didn't even try to hide her irritation. "Don't you *understand* I don't know who I can trust? Hasn't Leslie *told* you that?"

"All right, I'll come myself, then. You trust me, don't you?"

"Chief, I *can't*. I have ... to talk to someone. I have to set some things straight."

"That's fine, but in the meantime I'm concerned for your safety."

"My safety." Carla's voice withered. "It doesn't matter now. Besides, you can't make me come with you. I'm not a 'missing person' anymore. I'm here of my own free will, and you *can't make me do anything!*"

"Okay, I hear you." Chief's voice sounded worn but calm—and for that calmness Carla wanted to smack him. Didn't he understand that what little was left of her life was about to come undone?

Chief cleared his throat. "Tell you what, though. I'm going to check up on you regularly. If you change your mind, I'll be there. You have your conversation with Ms. Evans. But understand, this Thornby has now allegedly attacked the car salesman who helped you, and Spokane police are looking for him. You *will* need to come on record with what you know."

What she knew. That had once frightened her more than anything. Now the terror lay in what she didn't know. What Tanya Evans was going to tell her.

The second call nearly knocked her flat.

Tanya Evans.

Carla smashed the receiver against her ear, elbow digging into the mattress. At first no words would come. She could hear Tanya's breathing, cars whooshing in the background. Could in some inexplicable way feel the hurtle of this woman toward her on the freeway, their two lives careening into each other as they had all those years ago.

"You remember who I am?" Tanya sounded as wary and tired as Carla.

"Yes."

Tanya's voice cracked. "I have thought of you every day since I last saw you. Not one day has passed. Not one ..."

So many things Carla wanted to say, so many questions. Not the main one that plagued her—she couldn't begin to form those aching, desperate words. But—why now? Was Tanya driven here only because her own life was in danger? Was this meeting, some sixteen years late, not chosen, merely compelled?

"Someone told you?" Carla whispered. "About me and ... *him*?"

Tanya sighed. "Yes. Dr. Hughes knew. He told me who the father was."

Dr. Hughes *knew*? Carla had never guessed that. Why did he have to know?

Suddenly she understood. All of it—the whole, dark, horrible plan. Of *course* the doctor had to know. Tanya wasn't the one so close to Bryson Hanley. Dr. Hughes was ...

The horrifying question begged to be asked, but Carla couldn't do it. Not over the phone. She and Tanya needed to look into each other's eyes. "How far away are you?"

"Not too far. I think less than an hour."

An hour.

Carla hung up the phone and fell back on the bed, pressed under the weight of an impossible wish. That the next hour, however terrible her imaginings, would stretch out all the way into eternity. Because once she heard the truth, if her newfound dread came true, she could never, ever go back. And what would become of her then?

SIXTY-EIGHT

Leslie arrived at the hotel at six o'clock. She parked her yellow VW bug around back and scurried inside, bearing a bag of food from Java Joint—a roast beef sandwich, chips, and one of Bailey's biggie lattes. Bailey had made it extra hot, praying aloud it would get to Carla without cooling too much. The woman had cried tears of relief when she heard Carla had been found.

S-Man had hung around Java Joint all day, working on *Starfire* and hoping to hear news of Carla. When Leslie whisked in with her information, chomping at the bit to jump in her car and *go*, he'd been adamant about driving with her.

"No, Ted." Leslie turned to him at the counter, trying to rein in her adrenaline as Bailey made the sandwich. "You can't, really. There are ... things that are going to be discussed in private. I don't even know what they are. Big, bad things. Woman things."

Ted placed his hands on Leslie's shoulders, concern creasing his features. "I can't let you go alone. I didn't last time."

"I know." Leslie reached up and stroked his cheek. Odd, how naturally that came—as if she'd done it dozens of times. "But now it's different. Chief Edwards knows where we'll be. He'll be checking on us. If we ended up needing police, they'd be there in minutes."

Ted's eyes locked with hers. For a moment she thought he wouldn't take no for an answer. An unreadable expression moved across his face, then was gone, replaced by the look of a long put-off decision finally made. He gave a slow nod. "Leslie, it's about time you and I go out to dinner. Let's do it tomorrow."

Whoa. Hadn't expected that right now. But somehow it felt right.

Leslie gave him a lopsided smile. "You got it."

Ted hugged her long and hard before she left, and she hung there, pressed against his chest, gauging the feel of it. Bailey bustled about, pretending not to notice.

During the drive to Spokane, Leslie relived the comforting feel of Ted's arms around her. Funny. When she pictured his face, the image of Frank West—who'd been in her dreams for so many months—sort of blurred.

Thoughts of Ted bounced to Carla ... Tanya ... And somebody else, although Leslie had no idea who. Some powerful, faceless presence who pulled the strings of this puppet show. Chief Edwards apparently knew, after talking to Carla. Clearly, Leslie was the least informed of all. A pretty lousy situation for a reporter.

Logistics pulled her attention. Leslie picked up her cell phone. First, a call to Paige to let her know Carla was okay, and that Leslie didn't know when she'd be home. Then a call to a friend who lived in a little rented house in Spokane Valley. Katy helped care for her mom, who had breast cancer, and often slept at her parents' home. Leslie wanted to move Carla to Katy's house. It would be a more comfortable place for Carla and Tanya to meet. Plus they'd have access to a kitchen, be able to make dinner.

"Sure," Katy told her. "I'm with Mom now and won't be coming home tonight anyway. You know where I hide the key."

Plans in place, Leslie called Tanya, giving her directions to Katy's house. It wasn't far from the freeway and would be an easy find.

Now at the door to Carla's hotel room, Leslie held the latte in one hand and stuck the bag of food under her arm so she could knock. "It's me!"

Carla whisked back the door, pulled her inside, then closed and rebolted as if monsters awaited in the hall.

The room pulsed with … something. Fear. Oppression. Grief.

They looked at each other.

Carla was a wreck. Mascara smeared, limping, bags under her eyes, clothes disheveled. But none of that compared to the world-weariness on her face. It was a change no mere twenty-four hours could make. Leslie felt in her gut what she'd only recently understood. She didn't know this woman at all. No matter their seeing each other almost daily at Java Joint, no matter that they would recognize each other's voice in a crowd. Leslie could not remember one time they'd really *talked,* one time when Carla had said anything of significance about her private life, her dreams, her childhood.

Sadness welled in Leslie's chest—for what, she couldn't quite define. Then, just as suddenly, anger bubbled. Despite Carla's obvious vulnerability, Leslie didn't know whether to hug her or slug her for the fear she'd caused.

Leslie thrust the bag of food toward Carla. "Here. Bailey made you a sandwich."

"Oh. Thank you." Carla took it from her hand.

Leslie walked farther into the room, set the coffee down on the dresser. "She made you a latte too. Extra hot. It's still warm."

Carla hobbled to the first bed and set down the food bag, then to the dresser to pick up the coffee. She grasped it with both hands, as if pulling comfort from an old friend. She took a sip and closed her eyes. When she reopened them, they were misty.

Never had Leslie seen Carla anywhere close to tears.

Leslie touched her arm. "Come on, I'm getting you out of here. I have a house where we can go."

Fear radiated over Carla's face. "I don't want to go out. What if Thornby's around? He's out there somewhere. Besides, Brandon's bringing my suitcase."

"I'll call Brandon. We'll be a lot closer to where he is, anyway. Look, it'll be better. You and Tanya can have more room to ... talk."

Carla's eyes locked with hers. Then she nodded, as if too tired to fight. "Okay."

Leslie carried the coffee and pulled the suitcase, going slowly as Carla limped down the hall beside her, eyes darting in all directions. Carla's fingers gripped her purse and the bag of food as if they might rocket away. At the door, she hung back until Leslie checked the parking lot. Once inside Leslie's VW, she slid far down in the passenger seat. Leslie could hear her strained breathing.

"You okay?" Leslie started the engine. "It'll only be ten minutes or so."

Carla nodded.

On the freeway, Leslie called Brandon, then Chief Edwards. She gave both of them the phone number and address of Katy's house. Brandon would be stopping by later with the suitcase. And Chief Edwards would be alerting Spokane Valley police to do drive-bys.

"Do you see a black Durango?" Carla's words squeezed out.

Leslie checked the side and rearview mirrors. "No."

Carla pulled in a shuddering breath, brought both hands to her face. "I'm so scared."

Questions crowded Leslie's head. Where even to start? "This Thornby. Where did he come from?"

Carla's voice came muffled through her fingers. "He posed as a client. Said he wanted to buy the Edna San estate. I met him there. He pulled a gun on me."

Whoa. Leslie threw her a glance. "How'd you get *away*?"

"I pepper-sprayed him. Got him good too. He turned into a slobbering idiot."

"Oh."

How *terrifying.* But the description was so Carla. Leslie couldn't help but giggle.

Carla gave her a shocked look, then managed a raw laugh. "Well, he was. You should have seen him."

"I believe you."

They fell silent. Carla's head swiveled as she checked out her window, then peered into her visor mirror to check behind them.

"Carla, are you praying about all this?" The question popped from Leslie's mouth, surprising her. Definitely not something she'd have asked before last March.

Carla focused on her lap. "God and I aren't exactly on speaking terms."

Oh. "Well, maybe you should be."

A shrug. "I'm in so deep now, Leslie, even God couldn't get me out."

The excuse sounded familiar. "He may not whisk you out of the situation, but He'll help you through it. It's like … like stumbling around in a dark room. You'd turn on the light, right? You'd still be in the room, but at least you could see where you're going."

No response.

Their exit approached. Leslie veered off and turned right. Up four blocks, another right—and they pulled into Katy's driveway at the end of a cul-de-sac. "Stay here for a minute, okay?" Leslie slid out of the car, walked around to the right rear of the house, and pulled the hidden key from beneath a loose brick at the edge of the small patio. She unlocked the back door that led into the kitchen. Once the door was open, Leslie replaced the key, then walked through the kitchen, down the hallway, and into the garage. She hit the button for the door. As it slid up, she ducked out and got back into the car to drive it inside.

"We made it." Carla sounded as if she couldn't quite believe it.

Leslie laid a hand on her arm. "Yeah, we made it. You're gonna be okay, Carla. At least... you're not alone anymore."

She helped Carla get her suitcase inside, took the food bag and coffee into the kitchen. "Now we can microwave this for you." She held up the biggie cup. "You go into the living room, put your foot up on the couch. I'll bring the food to you. And I want to ice that ankle."

Carla did as she was told. Fifteen minutes later, ice in a zipped plastic bag against her ankle, the latte mostly finished, Carla lay propped against pillows on a couch by the front living room window, staring toward the entryway. Face pale. Waiting. Tension crackled from her very stillness. As if she knew Tanya's information would change her life forever.

"Aren't you going to eat your sandwich?" Leslie asked.

"I can't. Not now."

At Carla's insistence, Leslie walked through the house's rooms. Katy's place had an open floor plan, its small tiled entry area separated from the living room on its right by a four-foot-long, waist-high wall. On the left side of the entryway, as one entered through the front door, was a coat closet. Straight off the living room lay the kitchen, the two areas divided by a long eating counter lined with four stools on the kitchen side. A left turn from the entryway led to three bedrooms—a master suite on the rear of the house, and two smaller rooms, sharing a bath between them, on the front. Beyond the two smaller bedrooms was the door leading to the garage.

All looked well and safe. Katy kept a neat house.

Leslie checked and rechecked that every window and door was locked. All curtains in the living room and on the entire front of the house—including the two bedrooms and bath—were drawn. As she walked around, she prayed for Carla. For Tanya. For all that would take place here. *God, let Carla somehow see the clear truth of You, not the muddiness her own choices have made You to be.*

The sun was setting. After clearing away Carla's coffee cup—the roast beef sandwich remained untouched—Leslie turned on the porch lamp, then lights in every room of the house. When night fell, there would be no darkness here.

At 6:25, they heard a car pulling up to the curb out front. An engine cut, the slam of a door. Leslie sidled around the couch to the front window and edged back a drape.

A woman hurried up the sidewalk toward the porch, clutching a purse, fear and relief hunching her shoulders, dread cross-stitching her face.

Leslie turned to Carla. "She's here."

Carla nodded, then started to shake.

SIXTY-NINE

Tony's cell rang at six-fifteen. Paul Jilke was on his way from the airport and needed directions.

It would take every bit of willpower Tony possessed not to choke him on sight.

Ten minutes later Jilke turned into the Mexican restaurant parking lot, driving a white Ford Explorer. Tony slipped out of his Taurus and climbed into Jilke's car.

"Well, there's the mighty hunter." Jilke's sarcasm screeched like nails on a chalkboard.

"Where's my wife and son?"

"Oh, they're fine, fine." Jilke waved a hand. "Being watched over. And fed. You do your job here, Tony, and they'll be none the worse for wear."

Tony's blood boiled. Kidnapped, held against their will—and *none the worse for wear*? He thrust his heels against the SUV's floor, jaw tightening.

Jilke shifted in his seat. *Ah, so ever-in-control Paul Jilke was finally nervous.* Tony felt a righteous satisfaction at that. Those two women must be one powerful threat.

"Tanya Evans hasn't been found yet." Jilke knocked a knuckle against the steering wheel. "We're following her credit card. She uses it, we're on her. Meantime"—he pointed toward the dealership—"this guy's our man. I feel it in my bones."

"Yeah? What if your bones are wrong and the kid just goes home? All the hours you had me sitting here will be one royal waste."

Jilke glared at him. "He knows something, count on it. Wherever the guy takes us, we follow. After I get through with him, he'll tell us everything he knows. And some things he doesn't."

They waited. Watched car salesmen come in and out of the showroom, meeting people who wandered onto the lot. Blond Boy appeared and greeted an older couple. Soon he was leading them from car to car. A blue sedan seemed to interest them in particular. Eventually the three of them moved into the showroom.

Minutes stretched on, people coming and going into the Mexican restaurant. Jilke said little to him, and that was just fine by Tony. Any more of his arrogance and Tony just might have to shove his teeth down his throat. Jilke's phone rang numerous times, his "men" checking in. Apparently they had no information on Tanya Evans. With each call, Jilke's anger grew. By the time Blond Boy got off work—whenever that was—Jilke would be downright toxic.

At 7:45 Blond Boy walked out of the showroom with the couple, shook their hands. The woman got into the car in which they'd arrived. The man headed for the new blue Chrysler sedan, a bounce in his step. Tony and Jilke watched him drive it off the lot and down Sprague.

"One for our side," Jilke sneered.

Tony said nothing. High and mighty Jilke thought he knew so much. About desk jobs, maybe. But how often had he done his own dirty work on the streets? In fact, the sale *was* one for their side. A deal at the end of the day would make the kid happy. Help him forget the afternoon's unfortunate occurrence. On the way home he'd be a little more relaxed, a little less cautious. Thinking his rotten day had turned out decently after all.

Too bad for him. His rotten day had only begun.

SEVENTY

Carla used her iced ankle as an excuse not to get up to greet Tanya. Truth was, she doubted her legs would hold.

Tanya hurried over the threshold as she and Leslie exchanged quick greetings. Leslie closed the door and bolted it. Then leaned against it, hands cupped, looking from Tanya to Carla as if not sure her presence would now be wanted.

Gazing over the half wall, Tanya drank in the sight of Carla as if she'd waited for this meeting for years. Her breathing came fast and fluttery. She dragged fingers through her hair, mouth open, but no words coming. Carla wouldn't have recognized her. The nurse she remembered was young and golden-haired, a little chunky, with a compassionate, round face. This woman looked thin and worn, her jawline sharp. Deep crow's feet at her eyes and trenched smile lines made her look older than her—what—fifty years?

Carla couldn't speak. One hand gripped the couch cushion, the other hugging the part of her where Rebecca had once grown. *I can't do this, I can't do this!* As if her world hadn't been ruined years ago, then turned upside down again yesterday. This woman would now break it in two. Carla knew—*knew*—what Tanya would tell her. And she could not bear to hear it.

"Carla." Tanya breathed her name, already making her way around the low wall and into the living room. She crossed halfway, then stopped.

"Hi." Carla felt like she was wrapped in gauze. This couldn't be real. Maybe she was dreaming this. Maybe she'd dreamed the entire last twenty-four hours.

Tanya angled toward an armchair by the half wall and perched upon it. Leslie pushed away from the door. "Can I get you some water, Tanya?"

"Yes. Thank you." Tanya's gaze did not leave Carla's face.

Leslie moved into the kitchen and opened a cabinet. Picked up a glass.

Carla pulled in a breath, crossed her arms. "You've driven a long way. I imagine you need to use the bathroom."

"Yes. Actually I do."

"It's down the hall." Leslie leaned over the long counter and pointed. "Second door on your left."

"Thank you."

Tanya headed down the hall. Carla watched Leslie put ice in the glass, fill it with water. She brought it into the living room and placed it on a small table by the chair. Then looked to Carla, biting her cheek. "What do you want me to do? Stay with you? Go into another room?"

Carla focused on the burgundy-colored carpet at Leslie's feet. The scene felt so surreal. Where was the earthquake? The crack in the heavens? Sixteen years of hiding her terrible, soul-wrenching secret—and it all came down to this. A revelation in some stranger's living room.

Leslie's feet blurred. Carla blinked hard, then raised her eyes. Before this night was over, the guilt would kill her. If she'd made different choices, her daughter would be alive today. "You sure you're ready for this, Leslie? Because it isn't pretty." Carla's voice was thick.

Leslie nodded.

"Okay, then, you asked for it. The story of my life in a nutshell." She took a deep breath. "When I was sixteen, I clerked for Bryson Hanley. He seduced me into having an affair. I got pregnant. The baby died at birth."

Leslie's jaw loosened, then dropped. Her eyes rounded. She pulled back her head, gave it a small shake of disbelief.

"Tanya was the nurse in the delivery room." Carla saw Tanya appear in the hall, stop at the entryway tile. Her eyes were bright. She had been crying. How good of her. She should be crying *rivers* of tears. "The nurse who was so kind to my face. Who I *trusted*."

Carla pushed herself up on one elbow. Her gaze locked with Tanya's, even as she continued to talk to Leslie. Her throat squeezed until words could hardly pass. "The doctor told Tanya the father was Bryson Hanley. Senator Hanley, who feared he had so very much to lose, even then, by the birth of that baby. *My* baby."

Carla's gaze shifted to Leslie's wide-eyed face. "Now she's here to make a 'confession.' At the same time someone connected to Bryson Hanley is trying to kill me." Sickness rose in Carla's stomach. "Now tell me, reporter Leslie, the gal with the nose for news—what do you suppose she could possibly have to confess to me? The nurse who helped Dr. Hughes—Hanley's old friend and confidant—deliver my baby? The *healthy*, perfect baby who *died while I was asleep*."

Leslie's face drained of color. Disgust flattened her forehead. Slowly she looked to Tanya.

A cry seeped from Tanya's throat. She flung herself into the living room, across to the couch, and sank to her knees before Carla.

"No, no, you don't understand!" Tears fell in fat drops down her face. She brought up both hands, fingers laced in a desperate plea. "And you have to know who Dr. Hughes *was*. He was the chief of staff at the hospital, the head doctor. And like a father to Bryson Hanley. Dr. Hughes ordered everybody around, and everybody obeyed. The whole hospital ran by his word. *Nobody* questioned him, *ever.* And who was I? A young single mother who *loved* being a nurse. I never wanted to do what he forced me to do, Carla, and I almost didn't. But I *had no choice.* He won my silence, because Dr. Hughes *always* won."

Leslie teetered to the armchair and sank into it. Carla couldn't move. Tanya knelt one foot away, head down, shoulders shaking. Like a penitent. Close enough for Carla to lay a hand on her head and soothe her, as for so many years Carla had longed to be soothed. *No way.* This woman had smiled in Carla's face—while she *let them kill Rebecca.* And for what? Just because of "who Dr. Hughes was"? Rage and grief knocked through Carla. Well, get this, world. The charade was *over.* Make no mistake—Carla Radling would keep quiet no more. This woman would pay.

Most of all, Bryson Hanley would pay.

Tanya choked off the tears and lifted her head. Grim determination settled over her face. She shifted off her knees and sat on the floor, a strand of hair caught on her wet cheek. "I am *so sorry.*" She searched Carla's face. "I've carried this for years. The guilt was so strong, I fell into depression. Quit nursing within a year and never went back. I know this is nothing compared to the pain of losing a daughter, nothing at all. But I want you to know it changed my life too." She inhaled a shuddering breath.

"Now it's time I told you the truth ..."

SEVENTY-ONE

Tanya clenched her jaw as sixteen-year-old Carla Radling thrashed. Head thrown side to side, moaning, legs churning against the delivery room bed. And the worst of her labor was yet to come. Carla was only four centimeters dilated, with contractions five to six minutes apart, but in the last two hours, the pain that lashed her body had brought her no closer to giving birth.

Tanya gripped Carla's fingers. "It's all right. This one's almost done now."

Soon the girl's writhing slowed, then stopped. Carla swallowed hard and gazed at Tanya, her deep brown eyes full of fright. "How much longer?"

Tanya tried to smile for her. "It'll be a few hours yet. But we've paged the anesthesiologist. Once you have an epidural, it'll be so much better."

Carla's brows knitted with weariness. "How long before he comes?"

Tanya's heart panged. This young girl was so brave even in her fear. Sixteen was too young to give birth.

"Soon, I hope."

In truth, it would be longer than that. This was no big Seattle facility. At the small Terrin Hospital anesthesiologists were hardly a dime a dozen. And the one they needed right now was tied up in surgery.

And where was Dr. Hughes? The man had come in and out of the room twice, looking harried, mind elsewhere. Not that he was needed yet, with so little happening. Still, Carla should have the comfort of knowing her doctor was near. She wasn't some woman in labor with her fourth child. She was no more than a *kid*.

Carla licked her lips. "I'll be okay. This is for Rebecca. I can't wait to hold my baby. Seems like I've waited forever."

Before Tanya could reply, Dr. Hughes strode in. He went immediately to the bottom of the bed to examine Carla with a mere "How we doing here?" Tanya bit back her disapproval. What was wrong with him? He usually had far better bedside manner. He could have held Carla's hand for a minute, looked into her eyes. Let her know he saw her as a person, not just a pair of spread legs and uterine contractions.

Dr. Hughes felt around, then pulled back, holding his gloved hand out from his side. He shook his head. "She's not progressing fast enough. I want to start Pitocin."

He moved toward the door with a jerk of his head for Tanya to follow. Silently, she padded out behind him. She had her reservations about the Pitocin. It would be given intravenously, monitored until contractions came more frequently. That would still take awhile, but it could also mean some very hard labor. Speedy dilation came with a price. Tanya wanted to make sure the anesthesiologist would show before it was too late.

In the hall, with the door to Carla's room closed, Dr. Hughes spouted his orders. When she started to question, he cut her off with a finger pointed in her face. "Get the IV—*now*."

Seething inside, Tanya scurried to obey. Nobody crossed Dr. Hughes. Soon Carla was hooked up to a bag. The monitor indicated the baby was doing fine.

The Pitocin worked. Over the next hour and a half, the contractions increased. Carla was barely hanging on. Her fingers dug into the bedcovers, sweat standing on her forehead. "Please, please, *please*," she sobbed. "I can't *stand* it. *Do* something!"

Tanya wished she could take the pain for her. When the anesthesiologist finally showed, Tanya nearly cried. The epidural brought fast relief to Carla. She eased back against the pillows, breathing hard. Shivering started. Epidurals affected some patients that way. Tanya did her best to keep her comfortable.

"Soon." She stroked Carla's arm. "Soon you'll be a mom. Rebecca is a beautiful name."

"I know." Exhausted, Carla gave a feeble smile. "Rebecca."

A contraction set in. The monitor showed its progress and peak. Carla, numbed below the waist, watched the screen, clearly feeling nothing. When it passed, she focused on Tanya. "Please tell me the pain won't come back. I thought I was going to die."

"It won't. We're watching your medication, and we won't let it."

Tanya left Carla for a moment to visit the waiting room at the end of the hall, telling Carla's very worried boyfriend that she was doing better and in no more pain. His gratitude nearly brought fresh tears to her eyes.

Back in Carla's room, Dr. Hughes hurried in, all business. He greeted Carla distractedly, said he and "Nurse Evans" had to step outside for a minute. Before Tanya knew what was happening, he'd guided her all the way down the hall into a private office and shut the door. He gestured toward a chair. "Sit down."

Tanya sat, her heart tripping double-time. Whatever this was, it couldn't be good. Had she done something wrong? Her thoughts fled to her seven-year-old son, Curt. She couldn't, *couldn't* lose this job.

Dr. Hughes stood by the door, hands clasped, feet apart. The white coat, the grayed hair of his sixty-plus years, the furrows in his forehead were as Tanya had always seen him. But the raw grimness on his face scared her to death.

"What's about to happen stays here, understand?" He raised his eyebrows for emphasis. "I won't have to spell out the consequences if it doesn't."

He stabbed Tanya with a stare. She managed a nod.

"Good. We have little time, so I want you to listen to me, then *do what I say.*" His words came clipped and low. "In a little while I will be calling Bryson Hanley's wife to tell her that tests I took this morning have indicated she needs to come in immediately for a C-section. She's three weeks early. She came into my office for an exam this morning, mentioning she hadn't felt the baby kick in a while. I was concerned enough to do the ultrasound myself. It appears the baby is dead."

Tanya's jaw unhinged. "Oh, *no.*" Like everyone else, she had followed the Hanley's happy story of pregnancy after so many years of trying.

"I managed to distract Catherine enough that she didn't realize what was happening. I wanted to inform Bryson first, let him break the news. No question it would devastate Catherine. I told Bryson we should take the baby as soon as possible, but at the moment I had to hurry and get back here to check on Carla. Bryson hadn't known she was in labor."

Tanya frowned. Why should it matter? Did he know Carla?

A shadow crossed Dr. Hughes's face, as if he was about to speak the unspeakable. He swallowed—and in that horrible moment, Tanya had a crazy thought.

No. No way. Bryson Hanley, protector of the family and children, could never do such a thing.

"At the news about Carla, Bryson decided not to tell Catherine her baby is dead."

Tanya could hardly breathe. Her mind filled in the horrific blanks. No, no, no. This couldn't *be.* But she saw the truth. As much as she and all the other staff at Terrin Hospital kowtowed to Dr. Hughes, he served the state's Golden Boy. She pictured the scene. The serendipity of fated timing turning over in Bryson Hanley's brain. The dawning idea of salvation for him and his wife. His silver-tongued words to convince the doctor ...

Dr. Hughes's jaw flexed defensively, as if he saw her horror. "As soon as Carla's baby is born healthy and well, I will call Catherine and tell her the 'tests' indicate her baby may be in danger and should be taken now. Everything will happen very quickly and with as few people knowing as possible. I will insist on that, saying it's to protect the senator's privacy. I will use the largest operating room—you'll soon see why. Carla will be medicated—nothing to hinder labor, but to make her woozy at the birth. Catherine will be under full anesthesia. You will bring Carla's baby to the Hanleys and take Catherine's baby away."

Nausea hit Tanya. In that moment she saw it all. Her helplessness, her bleak future. She couldn't refuse, or she'd lose her job. And Dr. Hughes could make sure no one else hired her. How would she provide for her son? But the guilt she would bear if she went along! Tanya pictured the grief in Carla's eyes. How could she let that young girl believe her baby was dead?

How could Bryson Hanley *do* this? The politician that everyone loved and trusted. What kind of *monster* was he? And how could Dr. Hughes ever agree to it?

Tanya pushed to her feet, throat nearly swelling shut. "I *will not* do it. You can't make me!"

Fear and anger blackened Dr. Hughes's expression. Tanya knew he was already in too far; there was no letting her off easily now. He closed the space between them in three steps, his face thrust in hers. "You *will* do it. And you *will* keep quiet. I can't do this alone. I will inform Bryson you had to know. You'll be well rewarded."

She stared at him, stupefied, then laughed bitterly. "You think this is about *money*? How about morals? A clear conscience for the rest of my life. I *won't do it*."

A terrible stillness came over Dr. Hughes. He glared at her with the fierceness of a demon. "You will." His words turned to gravel. "And here's why. Because Bryson Hanley is the father of Carla Radling's baby."

Tanya froze. She ogled him, unable to speak.

"Yes, Tanya, it's true. Bryson told me himself today. He brought Carla Radling to me in the first place—it all fits. I should have seen it before. So we are simply giving the baby to her *own* father. Which set of parents do you think can better raise that child? An unwed mother from the wrong side of town, or Bryson and Catherine Hanley? You want the baby uneducated and neglected, or loved and nurtured—and likely one day the daughter of the president?"

Tanya's head shook back and forth, back and forth. She couldn't believe this. Bryson Hanley—and sixteen-year-old Carla? It was too awful to imagine.

"I can't. I just *can't*."

Dr. Hughes clenched his teeth. "Yes, you can. And you will. And let me make this *very* clear—if you walk out this door and spout off, Bryson and I will absolutely deny it. *No one* will believe you. You'll be out of this hospital before the day is over, and I'll make sure you never nurse again, anytime, anywhere. And *that*"—he stabbed the air with a finger—"is the end of this argument."

Defeat weakened Tanya's knees. She pulled her arms across her chest and stared at the floor, mind numb.

"Look at me now, and listen."

Somehow she raised her heavy head. Dr. Hughes proceeded to tell her exactly what she would do. "Got that?"

She nodded dully.

The doctor took a deep breath, rearranged his face, and opened the door. Tanya followed like a robot. With each step away from that hated office, her mind churned. One word now to the head nurse on duty, and she could stop this. No one would believe her, but the stunning accusation would keep Bryson Hanley and Dr. Hughes from trying to carry out their plan.

But your career will be over.

Tears bit Tanya's eyes. She focused on her shuffling feet. Wasn't the doctor right? Carla's baby *would* have a better home with the Hanleys. Carla was too young to be in labor—and too young to be a mother. She would mourn, yes. But she was young. She would get over it. When she was older and settled, she could have all the babies she wanted, while the Hanleys may never have another chance ...

Outside Carla's room, Dr. Hughes turned and stared at Tanya. She flinched, then slowly, knowing she would pay for this her entire life—nodded once more.

From that moment on, there was no turning back.

The timing was tricky. If they had not been in a small hospital, with Dr. Hughes's word as gold, if others had questioned why he had so few professionals in attendance at the C-section, the events could not have occurred. But who would ever begin to imagine such an evil thing?

Somewhere along the way Tanya lost all ability to feel. Young Carla Radling, drugged by Dr. Hughes, succumbed to wooziness as she gave birth. Even so, with only half her faculties she alternately cried and laughed as the baby crowned, then launched from her in a smear of bloody fluid. "Where's my baby, where's my baby? Do you see her, is she okay?" Carla started to push up on her elbows to see.

"No, no, lie still now." Dr. Hughes cut the cord and thrust the infant, silent and shaking, into a blanket held by Tanya's waiting (and equally shaking) hands. "Hang on, Carla, I'm going to give you a little more medication now." Quickly he injected a dosage of relaxant in Carla's veins. She fell asleep almost immediately.

He performed the afterbirth procedures while Tanya stood back, gazing in Rebecca's face. She was a quiet little thing, and so perfectly made. Fuzzy tufts of dark hair. Tears scratched Tanya's eyes. "Rebecca," she whispered behind the doctor's back. "You *are* Rebecca."

Dr. Hughes finished up and hit the door. "Watch the time and be there when I told you." He jabbed a finger toward Tanya, perspiration on his face, his movements abrupt. Creases on his forehead revealed the truth—for Bryson Hanley the respected doctor had crossed a river whose other shore lay beyond his morals, beyond everything he stood for. And no bridge could ever secure his return. For the first time, Tanya felt a twinge of sympathy for him.

In the silent room, Tanya dropped two tears on Carla Radling's still arm and wiped them away. The baby made no sound, blinking in stunned wonder at the world into which she'd been thrust.

After the agreed-upon time had passed, Tanya pulled the blanket over Rebecca's head and hurried down the back stairs toward surgery, where Catherine Hanley's C-section was being performed. Outside the door she carefully laid the baby down and put on a surgical mask and shoe covers. Then, Rebecca in her arms, she peeked though the glass window of the door. This moment, she thought, was when she would be caught. There was no reason this crazy plan should work. And if she was seen entering surgery with a newborn baby, the blame would be hers alone. Dr. Hughes would deny all knowledge of such unprofessional, unconscionable *stupidity*. She'd be fired on the spot.

Tanya had no choice but to make this work.

Dr. Hughes glanced toward the door and spotted her. Then he looked at Hanley.

The senator sat to the right of his wife's head with a view of the door, the anesthesiologist on her left. A free-standing separator rose from Catherine Hanley's chest up about three feet—a typical device that allowed a father to be present without having to watch the mother's body cut open.

As the doctor reached into the womb to lift out the baby, the senator jumped to his feet in excitement and looked over the separator. "Can you see the baby? Oh, I just can't—" He pulled back, feigning instant dizziness at sight of the blood. "Oh. Oh ..." His legs buckled.

Through the door, Tanya heard Dr. Hughes curse. "Don't let him hit the floor and bust his head!" He jerked his chin toward the anesthesiologist and nurse. "Take him over to the corner where he can't see and get him to sit down." He pointed to the metal stool upon which Hanley had sat. "Everything's stable here."

With a flurry of chaotic movement, the two rushed to catch Hanley. He played his part well. They pulled him and the stool backward, then wrestled him—a near dead weight—into a sitting position. Made the good senator put his head between his knees. The nurse and anesthesiologist hovered over him, their backs to the operating table.

Hanley continued his act as, watched by no one but Tanya, Dr. Hughes cut the cord on the dead infant. Tanya unwrapped the blanket from Rebecca. Hughes turned with the baby, and at that moment Tanya entered. They switched infants and Tanya slipped out. The whole thing was over in seconds. Tanya almost wondered if she'd dreamt it all. Before she knew it, she was ripping off the surgical mask and shoe covers with one hand. She covered the delicate, dead child in the blanket still warm from Rebecca's body and scurried up the stairs back to the labor and delivery floor. She cleaned the baby up and carried her into Carla's room, where the girl still slept. Laid the infant in a waiting bassinet. Then she tiptoed back out to the hall to call an orderly with the sad news that an infant needed to be transported to the morgue.

It was over. She'd done it. Dr. Hughes and Bryson Hanley had pulled off their horrific plan, and now she would be forever tied to them in guilt. The thought made her *sick*. Why had God allowed this? Why hadn't He sent some interloper at just the right moment to stop them?

I don't know how I'll live with this.

Tanya needed to inform Scott that "his baby" had died. First, she stumbled to the bathroom and threw up.

By the time Carla awoke and demanded her baby, the infant had already been taken away. Tanya thought her very soul would crumble. How could she perpetuate the lie to this trusting child? The rush of fear and adrenaline behind her, Tanya was already facing the bleak rest of her life, each ticking minute adding weight to her remorse. But it was too late to turn back now, far, far too late.

When Carla became nearly hysterical, crying to see her dead child, Dr. Hughes needed to calm her down. At his orders, Tanya descended to the morgue herself and brought the infant to Carla, then stood outside the room's closed door and listened to the young girl wail. The grief Tanya heard twisted a garrote around her heart. Despite her own agony she forced herself to stay and listen to every sob. She deserved to hear the pain.

Not until Carla quieted some time later did Tanya peek in to find she'd cried herself into an exhausted sleep.

Tanya slipped inside to take the baby. Before she left, she laid a gentle hand on Carla's forehead and promised she would always keep watch over Rebecca.

As she carried the pitiful, dead infant away, Tanya passed an exuberant Bryson Hanley in the hall, regaling the beauty of his new baby girl to another nurse. His eyes grazed Tanya's face and the wrapped bundle in her arms. He turned his back on them both as she walked by.

SEVENTY-TWO

When Tanya finished speaking, the room fell into the silence of a tomb.

Weights laid upon Carla's closed eyes. The world floated out there, just beyond her body, but she couldn't bear to look at it.

Strange, her thoughts. She could almost believe she had died from the shock and landed in some weigh station for homeless souls. Except that she felt the couch beneath her, the throb and chill of her ankle. Her throat was achingly tight, and her limbs felt like water. She focused on these sensations, knowing that to dwell on what she'd heard would turn her inside out.

But reality pushed through. And with it surged emotion that would rip her chest apart.

Rebecca was *alive.*

Brittany, the beautiful little girl she'd watched grow up on TV, now a teenager—was *her* daughter. Rebecca.

A hurricane of reactions raged inside Carla, even as she couldn't move. She could only hang on and pray she wouldn't blow away. Fury and elation, relief and shock. She was a *mother.* Her daughter *lived.*

She wanted to dance. She wanted to sing. She wanted to run to the end of the world and hide. How to grasp something so earthshaking? Her grief had exploded into a thousand jigsaw pieces, falling back to form a new, stunning picture.

Did she feel less pain—or more?

She had a daughter. But one who could never know or love her real mother, who was safe in the world Bryson Hanley had created for her. To learn the truth—all of it—would cost the girl everything she had ever known.

Somewhere beyond Carla's scrunched eyes, Tanya sniffed.

That one, small sound plunged a hand into Carla's blackness and pulled her out. Her eyes blinked open, still dry. She was beyond crying.

Numb, she looked at Tanya sitting on the floor, hugging both knees, head bent. Awaiting forgiveness.

Well, she could just wait—forever.

Carla focused on Leslie. The young reporter's eyes glazed with disbelief, a slow dread of the truth's repercussions whitening her face. They stared at each other until Leslie shook herself out of her stupor. Her face hardened with disgust.

"Did they pay you, Tanya?" she demanded. Accusation in her voice stung like a wasp.

Tanya's shoulders slumped further, as if she couldn't bear to confess any more. "Paul Jilke, Hanley's campaign manager, sent me checks over the years. I never asked for it, and didn't want it—but he warned me not to reject the money. As long as he paid and I accepted, they knew they had me under their thumb. I could live."

"How much, Tanya?" Leslie wouldn't let it go. "How much *blood money* did they pay you?"

"Enough for a house," she whispered. "Enough to provide for my son when I fell into depression and couldn't nurse anymore. I eventually pulled out of that. Went to work for a health insurance company. But it took a long time. Meanwhile, Dr. Hughes would never talk, Hanley knew that. The doctor retired in 1997. Three years ago he died from a series of strokes. After that only Bryson Hanley and I knew the truth."

Leslie glared. "What about Rebecca? Did you 'watch over her' like you promised?"

"Yes. Terrin is a small town. I volunteered in Brittany's school, made friends with her at a young age. I became like an older sister, taking her places, hanging out with her now and then as she became a teenager. She knew I was on duty during her birth. More than once I told her, 'I was one of the first to see you.'" Tanya's breath shuddered. "That made us closer. Bryson Hanley approved of our friendship. He's so ... crafty. He knew the more involved I was with his daughter, the more I loved her, the less likely that I would ever do anything to upset her happiness."

"So why *did* you?" Carla blurted. "Why have you come now?"

Tanya raised her head and looked at Carla. Her eyes were red-rimmed and worn. Old. Her jaw flexed as if she prepared herself, and in that instant Carla knew there was more. Something to even further rock her world.

Tanya's gaze drifted above Carla's face. "It was such a chance thing. Brittany had to do a major project for science. She chose one in hematology—the science of blood. She studied the various blood types, learning the percentages of each within society, what mixtures cause what types. She looked at her own medical records and found her blood type is A. Then she researched the types of her parents. Her mother's was O, the most common. Brittany had learned the variants of recessive and dominant types. She knew, due to recessive factors, two A parents could make an O, but two O's could never make an A. Brittany assumed her father's blood type would be the A. It wasn't. Bryson Hanley is also an O." Tanya's eyes pulled back to Carla. "*You* must be the A."

Carla's face felt frozen. She drew her arms across her chest.

"Brittany was devastated. Three days ago she came to me, since she knew I used to be a nurse. Ironically, she thought her *mother* must have had an affair. How else could this have happened? She cried in my arms, begging me to find some way to scientifically explain it. I was tongue-tied. I wanted to lie just to soothe her, but couldn't find a way at first."

Carla's throat cramped. *Oh, Rebecca.*

"Finally I said there had to be some rare occurrence in nature neither of us had learned about. We *knew* her father and mother were her real parents. But Brittany saw the lie in my eyes. Probably wasn't hard—my face couldn't have contained a drop of color. She stormed out, her faith in me shattered, crying that she'd make her mother tell her the truth." Tanya drew a shaky breath. "I knew that would be terrible. To this day, I fully believe her mother has no idea what happened."

Carla gripped the edge of the couch. Brittany—her Rebecca. A teenager's world coming unglued, just as her own had done. The daughter, fated to suffer for the sins her mother had committed.

Tanya wiped a tear from her cheek. "I rushed to Bryson Hanley's office, wanting to warn him. Somehow he had to talk to Brittany before she confronted her mother." Tanya shook her head. "He wasn't there. Jilke stopped me, demanding to know what was wrong. I told him."

Tanya's hands lifted to cover her face. She hung there, shoulders rising with each breath. Carla stared at her, wondering what could possibly come next.

Tanya dropped her hands. "I thought Jilke knew everything. How could I *not* believe that? He was the one signing the checks all those years." She locked eyes with Carla. "But he didn't. That evil man thought he was paying me for my silence about how your baby *died*. That's what Hanley led him to believe. Hanley would rather have Jilke think he had ordered the baby killed than to know the truth—that proof existed of his affair with you."

Carla's mind had gone numb. She couldn't hear anymore.

Leslie leaned forward. "*That's* why all of a sudden Jilke wants Carla dead!"

Tanya nodded miserably. "He was ready to kill me too. Maybe he would have, if he hadn't feared that Brittany might suspect something, given the timing. He threatened me, had me followed. But Carla, if Jilke had known this years ago, I truly believe you would be long dead." Tanya swiped the back of her hand against her cheek. "Today everyone knows about DNA. One test would definitively prove Brittany's parentage. Jilke knows that. In 1992, it was different. DNA testing was new, and most people hadn't heard of it yet. We knew about mixing of blood types, sure, but how many people learn what their parents' types are? With no thought of DNA, the risk Hanley took then was not nearly the risk it's become now."

Rebecca. The terrifying thought spun through Carla. Rebecca was searching for answers, stirring the waters. Would Jilke find a way to kill her too? Maybe stage a car accident. A drowning. Would he *do* that, just to see Bryson in the White House?

No way, he wouldn't.

Yes, he would.

No, no, no.

Nausea rose into Carla's throat—and all the emotion locked inside rode with it. With a sudden sob she jerked up, pushed off the couch. She jumped to her feet. Pain knifed her ankle, but she didn't care. She flailed her arms, raked fingers through her hair. The world tilted, and she didn't know where to go, how to get off. Only that she had to *move.* "I won't let him ... He's not ... He can't hurt *Rebecca*!"

Carla's gut churned. She had only coffee to vomit, but nothing would stop it from coming. Wild-eyed, she pushed her way around Tanya, stumbled toward the hall. Leslie called her name, but she barely registered, didn't *care.* All she wanted was to get to the bathroom, as far off by herself as possible.

By the time she hit the hall, tears gushed and her vision blurred. The pent-up sobs of sixteen years finally erupted—deep, loud, ugly sobs from the depths of her being. Her arms waved, smacking against the walls. She saw the first door on the left, the second, leading to a bathroom—but kept going. Farther on, away from everyone, everything. Into the master suite, slamming the bedroom door, lurching across the carpet. She wobbled onto the linoleum floor of the bathroom and banged its door behind her. Punched in the lock. Teetered to the toilet and threw back its lid. Sank to her knees.

Carla heaved and cried, heaved and cried, hanging onto the porcelain for all she was worth.

SEVENTY-THREE

Five minutes after eight.

Darkness had fallen, street lights glowing up and down Sprague, the private lamps bright in the Chrysler dealership lot. Tony sat stiffly behind the wheel of the Explorer, one nervous finger about to rub a hole in his jaw. He and Jilke had traded places so Jilke could make phone calls once they started to tail Blond Boy—*if* the kid ever got off work. Tony was beginning to wonder if the dealership stayed open until midnight.

The two men had planned what to do when they found their targets. Tanya Evans would be shot on sight. She had nothing to tell them, Jilke said. Anyone else in the vicinity—wherever that might be—would be shot as well. Hit fast, hit furious, and leave no witnesses behind. Carla Radling would stay alive only long enough to tell them what she'd taken from her house, where it was, and who else knew about it. Forcing her to talk would not be hard. Tony had pulled a small black duffel bag from the Taurus. In it lay the knife he'd bought that morning and other important items—rope, duct tape, a cloth, a small bottle of chloroform. No flashlight. Its beam across windows in a darkened house just might spook the neighbors. Tony also had two guns—the compact Chief Special he'd almost lost in the Chrysler parking lot, and a powerful Marui Glock 26 with a GB-Tech AAC Scorpion Silencer. With fifteen bullets in the magazine and a solid safety feature that blocked the trigger, the

Glock was the perfect weapon in situations that required speed and maneuverability.

"There he is." Jilke gestured with his chin toward the dealership. Blond Boy was coming out of the Chrysler showroom, making a beeline toward what they assumed was his own car. He glanced around more than once.

"He's looking for you." Accusation coated Jilke's voice. He'd already made it very clear that Tony's two screw-ups spelled the end of his fat paychecks. Tony didn't care. He just wanted to get himself and his family out of this alive.

Blond Boy got in his car, started the engine, and pulled out onto Sprague. Tony counted to five and followed. His heart rattled against his ribs. If the kid failed to lead them straight to Carla, Jilke just might shoot Tony in pure rage.

On the cell phone, Jilke read off the kid's license plate to one of his men. Blond Boy turned onto the freeway, heading west. A few miles up, he exited and veered south. By the time he turned right into a short cul-de-sac of fairly new homes, Jilke had the kid's name and address. His house was not on this street.

"Come on, Brandon, you're our boy. Lead on." Jilke leaned forward, drumming his fingers against the dashboard.

Tony passed the cul-de-sac, made a U-turn, then pulled over to the left curb, facing the wrong way. He cut the SUV's lights and edged forward until they could see the salesman's car in front of a house at the bottom of the street, some four homes down. Brandon had pulled up behind a dark-colored pickup. A streetlamp some distance away provided just enough light for them to watch Brandon open his trunk and pull out a suitcase. He closed the trunk and wheeled the case up the short sidewalk. Rang the bell. His body was now fully lit under a porch light, as was the suitcase. It was red.

Bingo.

SEVENTY-FOUR

When Carla ran down the hall, Leslie jumped up to follow and make sure she was all right. Tanya shook her head. "Let her go. It's too much, she needs time."

Much as she didn't want to admit it, Leslie knew Tanya was right.

Fingers clenched, Leslie sank back into the chair. She stared at Tanya, rage knocking around her ribs. For all Tanya's tears, Leslie couldn't stand the sight of her. All these *years*, living her lie. Costing Carla her own daughter. Forget what Tanya said; nobody forced her to do what she did. *"Why didn't God do anything to stop it?"* What a crock. *Maybe He did, Tanya—maybe He put* you *there so you could stand up for the truth.*

A car door slammed out front. Leslie pushed from the chair and moved to the window behind the couch, nudging aside the curtain. A blond guy was pulling a suitcase from the trunk of his car.

Brandon. She'd almost forgotten.

She stepped back. Wiped her eyes, ran fingers through her hair as she headed for the door. The bell rang before she could open.

The guy stood on the porch, overhead light spilling on his short hair. He had sky blue eyes and a large Band-Aid under his chin. "Hi," Leslie said. "You must be Brandon."

He smiled. "And you're Leslie. I recognize you from TV."

She nodded. Peered around him up the street. No one visible, no cars.

He glanced over his shoulder, then turned back. "I didn't see a black Durango anywhere. And believe me, I know what they look like. Used to drive one."

"Good." Still, after what she'd just heard, Leslie knew Carla and Tanya were in terrible danger. They were ants against a roaring lion.

"I tried to call you on the way over," Brandon said. "No answer. Good thing you'd already given me directions."

"Oh. Yeah." Leslie forced her overfilled brain to think. "I put my phone on vibrate awhile ago when ... we didn't want to be interrupted. And it was in my purse, so I didn't hear any buzz."

A vague sound filtered from the other end of the house—a sob from Carla.

Brandon's eyebrows rose. "Everything okay?"

Leslie licked her lips. "Look, an awful lot's happening here. I'd ask you in but I can't. Thank you for bringing Carla's suitcase."

He mashed his lips together and tilted his head. "Okay." He pushed down the long suitcase handle, picked up the bag. Leslie caught sight of another Band-Aid on his right hand. "Let me just stick this inside for you."

Leslie stood back to allow him in, willing him to *hurry.* Only a minute or two had passed since she opened the door, but already she felt exposed, as if the night sprouted eyes. "Thanks. I really am sorry I have to rush you."

He stepped back onto the porch. "Can I call you tomorrow? Make sure everyone's okay?"

"Yeah, sure. Just—please don't tell anyone where we are. Although we won't be here much longer." The minute Carla calmed down, Leslie needed to get her and Tanya in the car headed to Kanner Lake—to Chief Edwards and safety.

Chief Edwards. Had she missed a phone call from him too?

"Okay." Brandon gave her a lopsided smile. "I just hope someday I get to hear what this is all about."

Leslie thought of Brittany Hanley. Rebecca. Had the girl confronted her mother? Teenagers were stubborn. Would she drive this thing until she learned the truth? Leslie swallowed. "You just might." *Along with the rest of the world.*

Brandon turned to leave. Leslie watched him walk halfway down the sidewalk, then closed and bolted the door. As she wheeled the suitcase to the corner of the hallway leading to the bedrooms, she heard his car door slam and the vehicle drive away.

SEVENTY-FIVE

Tony and Jilke watched as Brandon stepped back onto the porch—without the suitcase. Tony narrowed his eyes. "That gal who answered the door. Was that Leslie Brymes—the reporter from Kanner Lake?"

Jilke growled. "I do believe so. And no doubt a friend of Carla's."

Brandon got back in his car.

"Looks like he's cutting out." Jilke worked his long jaw side to side, then shrugged. "We know where he lives. We'll catch up with him when we're done here. He's bound to know too much." Jilke glanced over his shoulder. "Turn back around. Let's circle the block, see where we can leave the car. We'll go in from the rear."

Minutes later they rolled down the dark street behind the house where Brandon had gone. Here, older houses had been turned into small businesses—a gift boutique, a massage clinic, dental office. All was now quiet. One streetlamp down the way did little to light the area in which they stopped. They cut the engine and got out. Tony carried the duffel bag, the Chief Special in his front pants pocket. Jilke demanded the Glock. Tony had no choice but to give it over, even as he knew he was probably sealing his own death warrant. Jilke handled the weapon with familiar precision, checking the safety, running admiring fingers down the silencer.

He caught Tony's expression, and his smugness returned. "You think I've spent *all* my life behind a desk?"

They hurried onto the massage clinic's parking lot and around to the back. A fence bordered the yards for the cul-de-sac homes. They came up to it, measuring the houses' positions against their memories of the street.

Tony pointed left, to a house where every light blazed. "That one. Next door."

"Yeah."

Tony tossed the duffel bag on the other side of the fence and climbed over.

SEVENTY-SIX

Leslie stood near the suitcase, her mind on overload. What to do now? The last thing she wanted to do was talk to Tanya. She turned down the hall, went into the bathroom, and closed the door. Sat on the closed toilet seat and stared at the wall. She still couldn't believe what was happening. Where would this all end? If this news got out—the *world* would change.

Some time passed—Leslie wasn't sure how long. She wandered back toward the entryway, thinking she really should check on Carla soon. If she didn't appear in five minutes, Leslie was going in after her. They needed to get out of here.

Tanya was in the kitchen, pulling a mug from a cupboard. She moved to the sink. What was she going to do, make tea? Leslie closed her eyes, rubbed her forehead. She needed to get her cell phone. Check in with Chief Edwards.

Where was her purse anyway?

Kitchen table.

She headed forward to walk around the long eating counter when a sound stopped her cold. A puncture of glass from the side kitchen window.

Tanya's head jerked. Her hands flew up, the mug clattering from her fingers into the sink. She collapsed to the floor with a sickening thud.

Shot. She'd been *shot.*

Every light in the house clicked off.

SEVENTY-SEVEN

Leslie froze in her steps. Her brain flashed white, unable to process. Then thoughts flew in like locusts buzzing her head. Her skin crawled.

Tanya—dead?

Carla?

Cell phone.

A muted *pfft, pfft.* Metal clanging onto kitchen floor. The back door lock? Glass shattering. A door pushed open. A footstep.

Leslie fled. Down the hall she ran on silent feet, right hand trailing the wall for guidance. Her fingers hit the wood of the master bedroom door, felt for the knob. The cool metal turned in her hot hand. She slipped through the door, locked it. Stumbled forward, arms waving through thick, claustrophobic air. Where was the bed, the dresser, the bathroom? *Get to Carla, get to Carla.*

No, 911!

How far away was Thornby? How long before he explored every room and shot through this door?

Leslie's forearm banged a piece of furniture. *Dresser.* She was on the right side of the room. Leslie reached out, grabbed its corner, feeling her way down to its other end. Hit blank wall, exploring with her palms. She reached a doorway.

Bathroom. Carla.

Her fingers skittered across wood, seeking the knob. Tried to turn it.

Locked.

She shook the door. "Carla!" She could only spit a vehement whisper. "Carla!"

Sound on the other side. The door opened. Leslie could barely make out Carla's shape.

"What's happened? The lights?" Carla sounded like a lost child.

"Thornby's here."

A cry sounded in her throat.

"There's a window in here, isn't there?"

"Yes. But . . . it's high."

"Open it and get out. *Now*. I'm dialing 911, then I'm right behind you."

"But— "

Leslie shoved her. "Go!"

Swiveling, Leslie struggled for her bearings. She needed to cross the room at an angle. The phone sat on the nightstand to the right of the bed.

She stumbled three steps. Four, five. Six. Her knee brushed fabric. She felt around. The small armchair against the back wall. Too far.

Leslie veered left. After an eternity her leg hit bedcovers. She bent over, sliding her hands to the right toward the head of the bed, up, up, until she touched the nightstand.

Her hands fumbled for the phone.

She felt books, a pen, a glasses case. Lamp base. Her heart beat up her throat. She dragged in air, fingers reading the foreign Braille world of the table. Her hands moved toward the back of the nightstand. Nothing. Around the front of the lamp, toward the back on the other side. She hit the hard plastic phone base. Small, the kind that housed an upright extension phone. She jerked her hand up to grab the receiver—and knocked it off its stand. It rattled off the back of the table.

Oh, God, oh, Jesus, please help me!

She staggered a step, feeling for the wall, slipping her hand down between it and the nightstand, hitting baseboard … carpet. Her spider fingers scrabbled forward. Touched the receiver. She yanked it up.

Hunched over, she ran her fingers over the surface, searching for the "talk" button. She punched one after another. Nothing. Forced herself to slow down, *think*. Remember the layout of a normal phone. She slid her hand toward the top of all the keys, found the button that must be right and pressed. Nothing. Punched again, one, two, three times.

Nothing.

Thornby had cut the phone wires.

In a suspended second, her body reeled back to the murders of last March—to the cabin that flipped into blackness just like now. With her inside.

This time there would be no one to help.

The bedroom door rattled.

Leslie gasped. Flung the phone to the carpet and dropped to her knees. She flattened herself down, lying parallel to the bed and facing the bathroom. Lifted the floor-length coverlet and pressed herself as far beneath the bed as she could get—which wasn't far. She pulled the coverlet over the rest of her body.

Pfft.

Wood splintered. The door flung open.

SEVENTY-EIGHT

The bathroom smelled like vomit. At least Carla was done throwing up. Before the light went out, she'd staggered to her feet, rinsed out her mouth and splashed her face. Then she'd slid to the floor again, her back against the cold side of the bathtub, utterly worn. When the world went black, her mind didn't grasp the obvious possible reason. She'd been too immersed in thoughts of her daughter.

Thornby is here.

Her body shook. She had no more energy. No more. Any minute now she would pass out. Part of her didn't care. Too much, too fast. She just couldn't handle it all.

Rebecca. Do it for Rebecca.

Carla's eyes were growing accustomed to the darkness, her vision aided by the dim filter of light from a parking lot beyond the backyard. She closed the toilet lid and stood on it, holding onto a towel rack above it with her left hand. The window began on her right, at the edge of the toilet, and ran over to the bathtub. She unlocked it, then reached for the crank at the bottom of the window and turned it hard. Heard the gentle creak of opening. The glass swung out, away from her. She cranked until the thing would turn no more, thrust her hand into the opening. Hit wire mesh.

A screen. She needed something to knock it out. What?

A shoe. But she'd taken hers off in the living room.

She scrambled down from the toilet lid, yanked open a deep drawer beside the sink. Pulled out the first thing her fingers closed upon. A blow dryer. She jumped back up on the toilet and punched the screen with the side of the dryer. It held fast. She hit it twice more. The screen crunched, then fell away. She heard a slight whoosh, then a muted metallic clang as its frame hit ground. Sounded like it landed on grass.

I hope.

Noise from the bedroom—Leslie knocking against something? She should be here any minute.

The window was about chest high. Could she even make it?

Carla grabbed the sill with weak hands and launched herself into the air.

She hit the wood hard, knocking air from her lungs. The hard crank rammed against her breastbone. For an interminable moment she hung there like a scarecrow, then pushed herself farther over the sill. There she balanced, feet dangling in the bathroom, head tilted toward dark lawn six feet below.

From the bedroom, the sound of a man's voice.

Where was Leslie?

She wriggled, thinking to go back, save her friend. But she lost her pivot point... teetered forward.

Carla tumbled into the night.

SEVENTY-NINE

Leslie dared not move.

"Hey. In here." A man's voice.

She stiffened. *Two* of them?

Brandon.

Could that be? Was he a ruse all along?

Surely Leslie's heart would give her away. It pounded so hard the floor beneath her shook. Blood whooshed in her ears. Her body sucked up oxygen, wanting more, more. The heavy coverlet cocooned her in heat, every breath stifling. She longed for fresh air, her mouth wide open, inhaling, exhaling, chin trembling against the carpet.

She could see nothing, could only listen to the sounds of two killers mere feet away. They'd moved into the bedroom, one behind the other. This she knew by the sounds of footsteps following shuffling footsteps, the lineup of breathing.

Please, Carla, be gone!

The men approached the bathroom door. They wouldn't see her from its threshold. Not unless they checked around the bed or moved to look out the back window . . .

One set of footsteps hit tile. Crossed the floor.

Leslie held her breath.

A string of curses erupted from the bathroom. "They've gone out the window."

Air hissed from the other man's throat. "That's *your* fault, Jilke. I *told* you we should have come in from opposite ends of the house."

Paul Jilke? He was *here*?

"Shut up and *move*."

The footsteps hurried away. Out of the bedroom, up the hall. Leslie pictured the men trotting through the kitchen as fast as they could in the dark, into the backyard. Was Tanya still lying on the floor in front of the sink? Was she dead?

Where was Carla?

Leslie rolled out from underneath the cover.

For a minute she lay there, breathing hard. Willing her heart to calm. She raised her head, tilted an ear toward the bathroom, listening for sounds outside the window.

Nothing.

Could she even hear backyard sounds from here? If they found Carla and pumped a silenced bullet in her heart, how would Leslie know?

She pushed to her knees and swayed. Shook her head and began to crawl toward the door. She wouldn't get up for fear they'd somehow spot her shadowed form through the window.

Out from the blackness beneath the bedspread, Leslie could now see better in the darkness. She scrambled across the room to the threshold. Stopped. Leaned out toward the hall, straining to hear the tiniest sound. All was quiet. She swallowed. Once she started up that hall, if the men returned, she would be caught.

What choice did she have?

At least they'd already checked the house. Maybe if she heard them coming she could slip into another room, and they wouldn't think to look for her.

Leslie crawled into the hall, then staggered to her feet. Stooped over, she moved swiftly toward the kitchen.

At the corner of the entryway, a shape appeared on the floor. Leslie slid to a stop, legs shaking. She steadied herself against the wall, peering at the object. Rectangular. Upright.

Carla's suitcase.

Her feet moved on. At the entryway tile, she bent over and crabbed her way forward, down, down the long length of the eating counter. She could feel cool air coming from the open back door. At the end of the counter she hesitated, heart pounding. What if one of the men waited for her around the corner? Inches away. Gun barrel ready and aimed at her face.

Help me, Jesus. Please, keep me alive.

She leaned out, peered with one eye around the corner. Saw only the kitchen table against the right wall, the back door hanging open.

Leslie shuffled into the kitchen.

On the floor by the sink she spied a form. Still, crumpled. *Tanya.*

Leslie's mind replayed the second of bullet impact, Tanya's head jerking. She'd never had a chance. If Leslie had been in the kitchen at that moment, she'd be dead now too.

She veered right, scrambled toward the table. Every second counted. She was an open target in the middle of the floor. She reached the table, banged into a chair. Its legs stuttered across linoleum—as loud as an avalanche.

Leslie stilled, air backed up in her throat. Listening. When she heard nothing she half rose, threw her hand across the table, and grabbed her purse. Sank to the floor.

Her pulse ground in one long, continuous beat as she scrambled around the counter. There, back against the wall, knees up, she dug feverishly in her purse, seeking the phone. Her fingers closed around it, pulled it out.

Her head swiveled toward the table. She should put the purse back. What if they returned and noticed it was gone?

Clutching the purse in one hand, the phone in another, she lunged across to the table, jammed the bag upon it, and jumped back behind the counter. She sank to her knees and crawled, phone grasped in her palm, fingers protecting it from banging the floor.

At the entrance to the first front bedroom, Leslie veered inside. Crabbed her way around a dresser on her immediate left and hunched between it and the wall.

Were Spokane Valley police doing drive-bys? How long since they'd been around? They'd see the house in darkness …

She held her phone low and flipped it open, blocking its light as much as possible with her hand. She started to press 911, but hit 51 instead, the auto dial for Chief Edwards. He answered on the first ring.

"Leslie! Where have you been, I've called twice!"

"Send cars." Her faint whisper wobbled. "They're here—two men. Tanya's dead."

Chief's shock vibrated through the line. "Where are you?"

"In the house. Carla got away through a window. They've gone after her."

"Stay with me." Chief had recovered his terse, professional tone. "I'll radio."

Leslie waited.

Had the men found Carla? Was she dead? Leslie leaned her head against the wall. Would they come back here and kill her too?

A sickening reality kicked her in the gut. Bryson Hanley could actually get away with everything he'd done. With all three of them dead, no one would be left to tell.

"Leslie?"

"Yeah."

"They're on their way. Running code. Sit tight and stay on the phone."

Running code. With lights and sirens blaring. What if Jilke and Thornby heard them coming and slipped away?

"Chief, I need to tell you— "

A shuffle filtered from the hallway. Leslie's head jerked up. She lowered the phone, snapped it closed, every muscle in her body twisting into a knot.

A figure moved into the room.

EIGHTY

Carla hit the ground with her head and right shoulder, and rolled. For a second—*too long, too long!*—she lay there, breathless. The muscles she'd landed on cramped in pain. An energy beyond herself forced her to her knees. She cast wild looks left, right. Where to go? The men could be right behind her. No time to run across the open backyard and jump the fence, especially with her ankle. No time even to reach the neighbor's back door.

She veered left. Her ankle screamed in agony, but she paid it no heed. She headed toward the back corner of the house and stumbled around it to the side yard. There she stopped, pressing her back against the wood. Listening over the rattle of her heartbeat.

A man's curses spewed through the bathroom window.

Jilke!

Carla hadn't heard the hated voice in years, but she'd never forget the sound. Paul Jilke was *here.* With Thornby.

Her knees buckled. She caught herself halfway down, forced her body to straighten. Every fiber in her body vibrated with fear—and *rage.* This was the man who had signed her death warrant. The man who would do anything to protect Bryson Hanley.

No more sound from the window. The men must know she'd escaped. They'd come after her. The two of them could go in different directions.

Where was Leslie? Had she called 911?

They'd killed her; Carla knew it. Either that or wounded her badly. Carla couldn't leave her friend. She *couldn't.* It was her fault Leslie was hurt. Hadn't Thornby *warned* her? What had she *done*?

Hurried footsteps sounded from the back of the house on the far side. The men were coming out the kitchen door.

Carla hobbled toward the front yard. Her thoughts spun. Where to go? Too many streetlights; she could be spotted on the sidewalk. One bullet, and she'd be gone.

Tanya's pickup truck at the curb. Should she hide behind it?

Then what? She'd be trapped.

At the front corner, she ducked left, hunching down, limping along the house. Past the garage, around the porch, by the living room windows. At the next corner, left again, down the side yard. Any minute now her left leg was going to give way.

She reached the back corner and slid to a stop, pulse throbbing in her throat. Cocked her head.

No sound of the men.

Were they back there, waiting?

This was it. Either she would die in the next moment, or she would go the only place where she could hide—back inside that house of death. They wouldn't think to look for her there. She could get to a phone. She could get to Leslie.

Rebecca—if I'm killed, and you ever learn the truth, I hope somehow you'll know how much I loved you.

Carla leaned forward, weight on her right foot. Closer to the corner ... closer ... her body shaking, her mind already visualizing the pointed gun. She peered around the house.

She made out the vague shape of a man running through the neighbor's backyard, his back to her. Where was the second?

No time—go!

She slipped around the corner of the house, fully exposed should the man whirl around. Stumbled to the back patio and inside the open door. Carla dropped to her knees on the linoleum.

So dark—her eyes had gotten used to the streetlights out front. She blinked, trying to assimilate. Ahead would be the living room, to her right, the kitchen sink and cabinets. There would be no outlet there. Just a peninsula floor with cabinets and walls on three sides.

But there will be a phone on the counter. And knives.

She crawled right.

Her shoulder brushed the cabinets, making a *shooshing* noise. She inched left, away from the wood. Where were the knives? She'd have to get up, risk being seen through a win—

Her palm hit something. An arm?

She jerked back, ice in her veins. Motionless, one hand in the air. Her legs shook. Was it Thornby, taunting her?

The person didn't move. Carla squinted in the darkness, the outline of a form taking shape. Crumpled. Not moving.

Tanya.

With trembling fingers, Carla reached out, felt her limb, a shoulder. She touched hair, the side of Tanya's head. A crusted hole.

Carla's stomach roiled. She pulled in one deep breath. Another. Then forced herself to crawl around the body. Trying to force her mind from Tanya, who had given her life to finally speak the truth. Tanya Evans—her daughter's friend.

Rebecca would mourn.

Tears filled Carla's eyes. She swiped them away. No time to think; she had to *see*, had to find a knife.

Beyond the sink lay a distance of all cabinets, no back window. There was a window behind her, near the table, but Carla had no choice. She pushed to her feet, peering at the countertop, frowning as her eyes and hands worked together to discover its contents. She saw/felt a toaster, blender. Coffee maker, a large fluted bowl. Where was the phone? A small plant, another bowl with fruit.

There—a telephone.

Soundlessly, Carla removed the receiver. Heard nothing. She punched buttons and waited, then punched more. Still dead.

No dial tone.

Slowly, she replaced the receiver.

No phone. The thought sank in. Leslie had never called the police. She wouldn't have been able to reach her cell before the men ran into that master suite.

Where *was* her cell? It was now Carla's only hope.

Her distracted gaze fell upon a rectangular shape and stopped. *Wooden knife block.*

Carla reached out, ran her fingers over the handles, searching for—what? The biggest? Smallest? The reality of using a knife rammed her. Could she really stab someone? What if she dropped the knife, and *he* stabbed *her*?

She pushed the thoughts aside, forced her concentration on the girth of the knife handles. She pulled one halfway out. It felt too light, too small. Carla thought of Rebecca, of Tanya, dead—*where* was Leslie?—and knew she wanted the biggest knife in the block. She tried another, a third, and heard the firm swish of a French chef's blade.

She slid it all the way out, grasped the handle with both hands.

Now to find Leslie's cell phone. And Leslie.

Muted footfalls sounded outside the open door. Someone hurrying across the brick patio. Headed inside.

Carla did the only thing she could do. Laid the knife on the counter, jumped to the right—and threw her body on top of Tanya's.

A man stepped into the house.

Carla held her breath.

Beneath her she could feel the warmth of Tanya's body. Cheek to cheek, temple to temple. Life pressing death. Carla felt a strand of Tanya's hair against her skin. The ragged circle of the bullet hole against her own head.

Horror surged through her. She jerked in reflex, had to force herself to stay *down*. Crazy as it was, she visualized the bullet drilling backwards into her own brain.

God, I'm not ready to die!

The man moved across the side of the kitchen, the silhouette of a gun before him. Carla knew her vision was more adjusted to the inside blackness than his, could only hope he would not veer her way. She rolled her eyes up, toward the man's face—and saw Jilke's aged but recognizable profile.

His head never turned. He moved toward the living room, then swerved right. Carla stayed still as he passed the long eating counter. If he looked her way, if he took the time to peer into darkness . . .

Jilke's footsteps hit tile, then softened. He was heading down the hall.

Leslie.

Carla lifted her head from Tanya's, listening.

Seconds ticked by.

Jilke's voice rolled into her ears.

EIGHTY-ONE

A long-barreled gun pointed down at Leslie's face.

"Don't you know how bright that phone's light is in the dark—even through curtains?"

Leslie's world ground to a stop. She stared at the man's dark figure, mind frozen.

"Who did you call?"

Was this Jilke? Thornby?

As if it mattered.

She pressed her fingers into the carpet. "I just . . . I . . ."

"*Who* did you *call*?"

"The police."

The man seethed. She couldn't see his face, but she could *feel* the anger. It was live and sizzling.

"What do you know about Carla Radling?" He moved closer, the weapon not two feet away.

She swallowed. What did she know? What did *that* matter? "She told me everything."

"Who have you told?"

Understanding seeped in. The cell phone may have led this man to her, but it was also saving her life—for the moment. He needed to contain the information. As soon as he learned she'd told no one, she would be dead.

Leslie forced venom into her voice. "Five friends. In five different countries."

He slammed her head with the side of his gun. Pain tore through her brain. Leslie's body swayed left. She slumped against the wall, dazed.

The man leaned over her. "Get up. We're leaving."

Leslie couldn't move, the smell of her own sweat-sticky fear filling her nostrils. How long since Chief Edwards radioed in the call? Two minutes? Three?

She blinked blurry eyes up toward the man—and saw him split in two. One figure in front, one behind. The one in back clutched something long and flat in both hands, raised it—and plunged it high in the first one's back.

Carla.

A scream gurgled from the man's throat. He jerked up straight, both hands flying out. His fingers uncurled from the gun. It dangled … dropped to the floor. He staggered back two steps, then found his footing, as if fury itself drove strength into his limbs. He swiveled toward Carla. Leslie could see an outline of a huge knife protruding from beneath his left shoulder blade. It hadn't gone in very far. Not a wound to kill, only drive him like a maddened beast.

Leslie pushed away from the wall, threw her hand around the man's lower leg and yanked with all her might. He crashed headlong toward the floor. Carla screamed and jumped out of his way.

Where was the gun? Leslie searched the carpet in vain. The man's foot twitched. He was already rising. As he pulled forward to kneel, the gun appeared beneath his leg. Leslie grabbed for it.

The weapon felt hard and warm in her hand.

The man lunged for Carla. Leslie raised the gun, trying to aim, but she didn't dare pull the trigger for fear of hitting Carla. He rammed Carla's body, shoved her against the wall, fingers circling her throat. The frantic movement of his shoulder muscles loosened the huge knife. It worked its way out and fell to the carpet. He felt it with his foot, back-kicked hard. It tumbled across the floor and under the bed.

Leslie's hand cramped around the gun. If she shot, wouldn't the bullet go through the man into Carla?

Choking sounds spilled from Carla's lips. Fury shot through Leslie. She pushed to her feet and launched herself across the room and into the man, hitting his back right shoulder at an angle. He stumbled to his left, away from Carla. She slipped to the floor, wheezing in air.

Leslie raised the gun and fired.

Nothing happened.

She tried to pull the trigger again.

Something was blocking it. A safety? What, where?

Her trembling right hand struggled to keep aim at the man while her left fingers explored the gun. The barrel, underneath the trigger, around the handle. What was she supposed to *do*?

The man rose up, a monster in the darkness, his shape outlined against the dim spill of streetlight through the bedroom's curtains. Leslie backed up, still fumbling with the gun. Carla hacked and coughed, struggling to get on her knees, crawl toward Leslie and the door.

Leslie felt something on the bottom of the gun handle. A piece that moved.

Hard, running footsteps filtered from up the hall. Reflex whipped Leslie's body around, jerked her finger on the trigger.

Phwfat. The gun fired through empty threshold, hitting the hallway wall. Her arm recoiled.

The footsteps halted.

"No!" Carla cried.

Leslie spun around as the man and Carla collided. Carla swung madly with both fists, the man trying to pin her arms, two desperate silhouettes in a fight to the death.

Sirens in the distance.

Where was the armed man in the hall? Leslie leapt to her right, toward the wall past the dresser. Pivoted, crouched down and aimed the gun at the doorway.

One second passed. Two. Carla and her attacker continued to fight. In the struggle they'd turned around, his back now to the hallway.

The armed man leapt into the room.

Leslie fired. His body jerked like a marionette. She fired again.

He crumpled to the floor.

Carla's attacker swiveled and dove toward the downed man.

"Jilke, stop!" Carla stumbled toward him.

Jilke. Had she killed Thornby?

Sirens drew closer. Leslie's arms wavered, all energy draining away. Her gun tipped toward the floor.

Jilke rose up, Thornby's weapon in his hands.

EIGHTY-TWO

All the sensations hit Carla at once—the *whow, whow* of police cars; the throbbing from her ankle, neck, and countless bruises on her body; the acrid smell of gunfire and bitter taste of panic. The dark shape of Thornby's small gun now in Jilke's hand some five feet away—pointed at Leslie.

Carla heard, felt, smelled, tasted, saw it all. Knew she and Leslie were going to die. But only one thought echoed in her head.

Rebecca.

Adrenaline surged through her body. With the cry of a raging mother, she sprang from the floor and toward Jilke—the man she hated with every sinew of her being. Jilke swiveled toward her.

Bright light flooded through the room's curtains, hit Jilke in the face. He squinted, tilted down his head.

Carla grabbed his right arm and twisted.

"Ugh!" Jilke fired the gun, the bullet zinging into carpet. Carla twisted harder, and his fingers loosened. The weapon dropped.

"Get back, Carla, get back!" Leslie reared up on her knees, her face white in all the light, gun aimed at Jilke.

Carla pivoted and leapt away.

The sounds tumbled over each other. Leslie firing, running footfalls outside, shouts—"Police!"—heavy banging on the front door.

Jilke rebounded and fell to his knees, then went down like a sinking ship, half on top of Thornby. Groans sputtered from his mouth.

Carla screamed.

Something in her let loose, something primal and full of fury. She fell upon Jilke in the glaring light like a maniac, kicking, pummeling, seething curses. She erupted in sobs, she hit and smacked and pulled hair. She would bash the man's head in, pull out his limbs. Kill him for all he'd done to her and Rebecca, the lies he'd told and evil he'd wreaked on behalf of Bryson Hanley, then and now. If only Bryson were here to kill too; she would do it, yes, she would—for Rebecca. Somehow then, as Carla thrashed and wailed, Jilke *became* Bryson, and her punches doubled, and her cries turned raw. The man beneath her groaned at her blows, and she hit harder, harder, shoulders aching and world blurring. She hit Bryson for betraying her trust at such a young age, for using her up and spitting her out, for stealing her daughter and leaving her to mourn. For his lies and manipulation and despicable, deadly *charm*.

Somewhere in the back of Carla's brain she registered the sound of feet running in the kitchen, shouts, the squeak of police gear. Leslie yelling, "Carla, stop!" But she pummeled on, choked, crying—until police rushed in, and strong arms pulled her away, somebody calling her name through a crimson haze, and more shouts and more feet running and voices over radios. And some other voice from the floor—a guttural whisper from Thornby—wasn't he dead?—saying a name over and over—"Timmy, Timmy, Tim—"

No. Rebecca, Rebecca, Rebecca . . .

Gentle arms encircled her, the sound of Leslie's voice in her ear, soothing, soothing.

Carla's world faded to black.

PART FOUR

Reparation

EIGHTY-THREE

Carla slumped on the sofa, distracted eyes half watching TV. Her ankle hurt a little, although it was much, much better. But a twisted ankle was the least of her worries. The shades of her blue house were all drawn, flimsy barriers against the crowd of reporters staking out her property. Stupid stalkers. Just sitting in her own house, minding her own business, she could hear them out there.

"Don't you just *love* the media?" Leslie grimaced. She sat in an armchair, blonde hair in a ponytail, wearing no makeup. Not like Leslie. Showed how tired she was.

"Oh, yeah."

This was the first time since last Thursday they'd had a chance to see each other in private. Leslie had called to declare she was coming over even if she had to run the gauntlet of a *thousand* reporters. Hadn't been quite that bad. Nine hundred and ninety-nine, maybe. Carla had peered through the corner of a window as Leslie got out of her car. The idiots dissolved into mass hysteria at her sighting. Leslie didn't let it stop her. Head held high, eyes straight ahead, and arms pumping, she stormed through the yelling mouths and thrust microphones. When she reached the porch Carla threw open the door. In an instant, bodies turned, all attention switching to her. Demanding voices swelled over each other like toxic waves.

"Miss Radling, how do you feel about Hanley's pulling out of the presidential race?"

"Have you talked to your daughter?"

"Has Scott Cambry contacted you?"

"Do you believe Hanley's statement that he knew nothing about the switched infants?"

"When will you—"

Leslie scurried inside. Carla slammed and bolted the door.

That was an hour ago. They'd eaten sandwiches, made coffee. Now they watched the news, flipping channel after cable channel. A nation in an uproar, talking heads expounding, law enforcement experts pontificating. Hanley's political career was over, all agreed. But could he be charged with anything criminal?

Carla was so tired of it. She knew Leslie was too. If only they could have their lives back. Leslie faced the sobering knowledge that she had killed a man. Tony Derrat, a.k.a. David Thornby, had died of gunshot wounds in the stomach on the way to the hospital. Clearly, Leslie shot him in self-defense. Still, she had taken a man's *life*. A man with a wife who believed he worked for the CIA. And a son. Timmy—the name on Derrat's lips as he lay dying. The little boy who reportedly adored his father and wanted to grow up to be just like him.

The things parents did to their children.

Brandon, the car salesman, had also faced some fallout. So much for trying to be a good citizen. He was having a hard time forgiving himself, knowing he had led Jilke and Derrat to the house. Leslie had told Carla she saw Brandon when she and S-Man drove to Spokane Chrysler to retrieve Carla's Toyota. Brandon apologized over and over, nearly in tears. Leslie gave him Carla's message—one Leslie also believed: he'd tried to help them. None of this was his fault.

Brandon was also being questioned by detectives and hounded by the media—reporters wanted anybody and everybody connected to the case. Brandon got them all back though, Leslie had told Carla with a chuckle. Every reporter who bugged him was hit up to buy a car. Brandon's business must be booming.

As for Carla, her life had been changed forever. Who knew when she could even act like a regular person again. Right now she couldn't work. Obviously couldn't so much as walk out her front door. Forget doing something as normal as grocery shopping, going to Java Joint for coffee. She was no longer Carla Radling, realtor. She would forever be the woman who brought down the nation's Golden Boy, the shoo-in forty-fourth president of the United States.

Not that she didn't deserve to see her life ruined—and more.

Carla hit FOX News and stopped flipping channels. Milt Waking—Leslie's favorite reporter—stood on a sidewalk in Terrin, Washington, the Hanleys' house behind him. "Of all the people on your doorstep," Leslie muttered, "why couldn't he be one of them? I'd have stopped and talked to *him*. Heck, I'd have invited him in for a party."

Carla tried to smile. "You told me you were going to start going out with Ted Dawson."

"Yeah." Leslie rubbed her forehead. "I am. But Milt Waking is *so* hot."

"Uh-huh. He's also an obnoxious reporter."

Besides, it was about time Leslie and Ted did start dating. S-Man had fallen head over heels for her months ago, everybody knew that. Leslie said they'd even set a date to go out to dinner last Friday. Of course, it had to be cancelled in all the chaos.

Leslie laughed. "Yeah, I know. One of *those*." She pushed a strand of hair from her eyes. "Ted came over last night. First time he had the chance; I've been at my parents' house every other night. Paige was at home too, when Ted came. I thought it might be awkward—I mean, I've never seen him outside of Java Joint.

Well, except for last March." She stared at the floor, as if reliving that horrible time. "Anyway, it was really good. Ted's so ... calm. He just sat and talked to us. After awhile Paige went into her bedroom so we could talk alone. Ted just has this way of grounding me. Of making me remember what's important and what's not. I realized when he left that I couldn't think of anyone else who would make me feel that way." She threw Carla a wry smile. "Who'd a thought, huh."

"Yeah. Just goes to show you never know."

They fell silent. Leslie fiddled with her ponytail. Carla reached for a pillow and hugged it to her chest. Thoughts of the hard days ahead crowded her mind.

She and Leslie had been questioned by police and detectives, then grilled some more. Detectives had taken her diary as evidence. All those handwritten pages of grief and pain, her fierce protection of sixteen years—snatched from her fingers, just like that. Carla had wanted no part of the investigation, but of course she had no choice. She would have kept the whole thing quiet. Let Bryson Hanley off completely, even watch him win the presidency. She was willing to never meet her own daughter, never let Rebecca look her in the eye and know Carla Radling was her mother. It would have been best, for Rebecca's sake. Better by far to protect the young girl's world, let her keep and cherish the only parents she had ever known.

But that was a fairy tale.

Carla closed her eyes. And this wasn't over yet. Not by a long shot. So much still to deal with, so many lies to undo. Her own lie, the worst of all.

Milt Waking's voice pulled at Carla. "... Sources close to the case say that Paul Jilke, recovering from the gunshot wound in his side, continues to insist that the late Dr. Hughes, a longtime mentor and confidant of Bryson Hanley, took it upon himself to switch the infant girls. Only later did the doctor confess to

Jilke the terrible deed he had done. Neither Bryson nor Catherine Hanley had any idea what had occurred, Jilke said. Bryson Hanley is not speaking to reporters. A spokesperson for his office asked that the media refrain from seeking him out, as he needs to tend to his wife, who reportedly collapsed under the strain, and is now hospitalized at an undisclosed location ..."

A sick feeling rolled over Carla. Mother to mother, she could only imagine Catherine Hanley's shock. To hear about her husband's affair with the mother of the baby she'd once tried to adopt, and then that the daughter she'd raised wasn't really her own, but that same, adoptive child. How could the woman ever recover?

And did Catherine Hanley even *want* her husband's tending? The man who had deceived her in such horrible ways. Who had manipulated her as well as Carla regarding the adoption that almost took place.

Carla plucked the remote off the couch cushion, punched the power button. The television picture clicked to black.

She and Leslie exchanged worn looks.

Carla licked her lips. "He's going to get away with it, isn't he."

Leslie sighed. "Afraid so. Think about it. The doctor died years ago. Now Tanya's dead. The story she told us—who's to prove it now? Jilke will just insist it was all a lie to bring down Hanley. He'll never, ever give his man up. 'Protect the guy at the top'—that's the motto of someone in his position. He'll take all the heat, including for knowing about the switch. He's already up for Tanya's murder, not to mention chasing after us."

Carla covered her face with both hands.

"At least Hanley lost his career, Carla." Leslie's voice was gentle. "And people know everything else he did to you. The detectives have your diary to prove that. Politics was his life."

People know everything else he did. Not completely. Not even Leslie knew everything in that diary. The world had heard the general story, not the details. But they would come out in the trial, every terrible one of them. Carla and Leslie would have to testify against Jilke. Carla would no doubt be on the stand for hours, maybe two days. She would have to answer for all of her choices in the past. She, the main prosecution witness—target of a defense attorney whose job it would be to tear her apart. Not that her choices as a teenager would exculpate Paul Jilke. But any attention on her, the lies she'd told, just might stir enough salacious talk to distract the jury. Isn't that the way the court system worked?

Justice would not be served, either, for the state trooper who had worked for Tony Derrat. Without Tony to testify, how could Carla prove anything? The trooper had stopped her, run her information, and let her go.

Another heartless person out there, free to cover up his lies. As well as anyone else who had helped Tony look for her.

Carla could only be glad the detectives kept her diary under lock and key, refusing to reveal a word of its contents. She could trust them. They didn't want to hurt the case they had just begun to build.

And Carla didn't want to hurt her daughter.

She lifted her fingers from her face. "I know Bryson Hanley lived for politics. But after all he's done, is that enough to lose? I don't know. I can't decide how I feel. Part of me is glad he'll get away with stealing my baby. Rebecca—Brittany—will never know *how* bad he is. She'll grow up. One day forgive him for his affairs. She'll never have to forgive him for taking her from her real mother. She's free to still love the parents who raised her—both of them."

"But she wants to meet you."

"Yeah. Imagine that."

"And you'll never tell her."

Carla's eyes burned. "She's lost enough, Leslie."

The tears Carla had fought for so many years came easily now—too easily. Especially when she thought of Rebecca, pictured the girl in her own room miles away, crying facedown on her bed as Carla used to do. Carla thought she had gone through such trauma as a teenager. But imagine hearing how the father you and the whole country so revered betrayed your mother. Imagine then hearing that the loving, attentive woman who raised you—*isn't* your real mother.

Carla and Rebecca—*Brittany*, her name was Brittany—had spoken on the phone yesterday for the first time. An awkward call of hesitant words, long pauses, spiraling emotions unsaid and partially yet unknown. Carla had been warned through one of Catherine Hanley's friends that the call was coming. When the phone rang at the designated time, she'd almost not picked up. Her hand hovered over the receiver, breath muddying her throat.

"Hi. Um, Carla Radling?"

"Yes, Brittany. It's me." *Your mother.*

"Oh. Hi. I just ... wanted to introduce myself."

Carla's eyes squeezed shut. *Oh, Rebecca, I* know *you already. And yet I don't.*

"I'm glad you called. But I'm also sorry. So very sorry. This must be so hard on you."

"It's a kick in the gut, that's for sure ..."

Carla almost smiled. Did she hear herself in her daughter?

That initial call, of course, was not the time to make her own confession. The one that could teeter Brittany's world over the brink. Time remained for that, but not for long. Despite Jilke's "confession" that he'd tried to kill two women to protect Bryson Hanley and his family from learning what Dr. Hughes had done, and despite Brittany's knowledge that the Hanleys' blended blood types could not create her own, formal testing still needed to take place. Blood would be drawn from Carla, and

Catherine and Bryson Hanley, then DNA tests run. The definite truth would then be proved, once and for all, to a shocked and disbelieving nation.

They were about to be shocked once more.

Carla knew she would travel to meet Brittany Hanley in person before those test results were ready. She had to. For no test, no doctor, not even the inevitably stunned parents who had raised Brittany could be the ones to tell her the unexpected results. The one last, terrible secret of her birth.

Bryson Hanley was not her father.

EIGHTY-FOUR

Tomorrow is the day.

Seventeen years ago on this day I was a week shy of four months pregnant. (Not three months, as I'd led Bryson and Dr. Hughes to believe.) Even then I could have turned back from my lie. Could have told Bryson I *wasn't* a virgin when we were first together and in fact, had missed my period just a week after our first time at the cabin.

All those entries in my diary when I agonized over what I was doing. Why didn't I change my mind? To cover myself with lies, deceive Scott in such terrible ways—just because I was afraid to lose Bryson. Looking back, even then I knew he wasn't worth it. I knew, but I didn't want to *see*.

Finally, after all these years, the day is almost here. Tomorrow I will meet my daughter for the first time. I wish I could know it will be a wonderful reunion. But, of course, my choices spoiled that long ago. As it is, tomorrow I must tell her the truth. The type-A blood she so desperately sought isn't me. I'm another common O. The type A belongs to her father, Scott Cambry.

I'm afraid she will hate me. Even though now, when we talk on the phone, she sounds so anxious to see me in person. But how can she not hate me when I tell her this? She's had enough lies. Even though she doesn't know her father stole her from me, there are still plenty of lies left on his plate. His deceit and affair all those years ago—an affair with someone practically her own age. How sickening for a teenage daughter to imagine! The manipulative way he tried to get his wife to adopt the baby he thought was his own. Yes, she should hate her father. And she does sometimes—when she's not loving him.

Sounds like someone else I once knew.

My daughter has emotions that will take years to straighten out. I can only pray she will forgive me for the terrible part I've played in all this—and let me help.

And yes, I do mean *pray.* Leslie said it well on that most frightening day of my life. "You can stumble around in a dark room or you can turn on the light." I'm still in that terrifying room. Some days I'd just as soon not get out of bed. But at least I've asked God to light my way.

Hey, with my choices, I figure He can only improve things.

Leslie found the "perfect" Bible verse for me. Psalm 18:36. "You [that is, God] broaden the path beneath me, so my ankles do not turn."

Ha-ha. But I think she's only half kidding.

I have so much to tell Brittany-Rebecca. I hope one day she'll listen. Of course, I shouldn't have to *tell* her at all. She should look at my life and her known father's life—and see the truth. See the tragedies that selfish choices can wreak, the lives they can hurt. See that we don't live just for ourselves, but what we do can affect so many people. But like most humans (why did God make us so stubborn?), she won't see this. Why didn't I see it in my own mother? Why did I fall into the same mistake she did—and at almost the very same age?

If only I could drill all of this into Brittany-Rebecca's head. Pour it right in and cover up the hole so it won't fall out. Ensure she'll never make a foolish decision.

Don't want much, do I.

So what can I do but come clean and ask her forgiveness. That may take awhile for her to grant. I'm not sure I've even forgiven myself. Although Leslie says I'd better, since God has. But it's so hard to grasp God's forgiveness when I think of all the horrible problems my lies have caused. Everything that has happened is my fault. *All* of it. If I hadn't lied, I could have raised my own daughter. Probably married Scott. Rebecca would never have been stolen from me. Sometimes the sheer weight of these thoughts drives me to my knees.

When I tell her all this, Brittany-Rebecca will ask me about her biological father. *Who* is he? I know a teenager's curiosity. I will tell her the simple facts. He lives in Central Washington and has built his own construction business. He's divorced, with two children who live with their mother – a son, nine, and a daughter, six.

What news that will be, to hear she has two half-siblings.

She will ask, "Does he know he's my father?"

Poor, poor Scott. No one deserves to be as jerked around as he has been. Through the breaking news of Bryson Hanley a month ago, he learned the baby I carried *did* live – but that she wasn't his. I tried to call him a week after the story broke, but he wouldn't talk to me. For two weeks I left messages until finally he picked up the phone. Another shock for him – a total about-face. I *hadn't* lied to him; I'd lied to Bryson. Rebecca *is* his daughter.

"Yes," I will tell Brittany-Rebecca. "He knows. And he wants so very, very much to meet you when you're ready."

Whether he'll ever want to see me again is another thing.

But as with my daughter, I can't force his forgiveness. I can only choose to live my life from now on in a way that would make them *want* to forgive.

God – please help me do that.

Seventeen years ago I kept a diary. A dark journal of lies and deceit, of a frightened teenager's hopeless, selfish decisions. Today I start a new one.

This one will be different. I promise that—for my sake, and my daughter's. This one, Rebecca, will be a mother's diary of love for you. Of truthful, honest choices. And ultimately, so help me, God ... of light and hope.

ACKNOWLEDGMENTS

My thanks once again to Tony Lamanna, school resource officer in Priest Lake, Idaho, who helped me with all issues related to law enforcement. Tony, you're the best.

In each of the Kanner Lake books I have blended fiction and reality. And so my gratitude also to the following:

Thanks to all those fans of the series who have written posts for the Java Joint characters on Scenes and Beans. You can read the real blog at the same address given in this story: www.kannerlake.blogspot.com.

Hats off, also, to aspiring novelist Stuart Stockton, who has graciously allowed me to feature his science fiction manuscript, *Starfire*, in all the Kanner Lake books. May the world be able to read *Starfire* in published form soon. Stuart is also the writer of all the Scenes and Beans posts for S-Man.

Finally, many, many thanks to Jay Lee and his family, owners of Spokane Chrysler, for allowing me to use their fine business in this story, and to Shawn Bird, the dealership's manager. And special gratitude to Spokane Chrysler's star salesman, Brandon, for his willingness to become a part of the action.

Be sure to read book four in the Kanner Lake series, *Amber Morn*.

ONE

Any man going on this mission wasn't coming back.

Cluttered kitchen, cluttered head. Kent Wicksell could hardly think straight. It wasn't supposed to start like this. Dread anticipation pumped through his veins as he faced off with his son. Vigilante Brad, gunning to take on the world. At twenty-nine, he thought he knew more than anybody.

Kent's voice seethed. "For the *fifteenth* time—you're staying home. We ain't leaving your mother alone."

They'd been arguing for the past ten minutes. Brad stood his ground, face like granite. His cool blue eyes stabbed Kent. "I *ain't* staying here." His voice remained low and steady. Brad was always a man in control. "I watched over T.J. since he was born, and I ain't stopping now."

Kent surged forward two steps, finger punching the air. "I'm telling you no! I *won't* let you—"

Mary caught his arm. "Stop, Kent! Let him go."

He turned to her, jaw loosening. She stared back, a terrible, grim determination pressing her lips. Kent's knees went weak.

No, no, no.

Where had that look on her face come from? Just last night they'd agreed—*again*—that Brad could never be a part of this. "You'd let him *go*?" Accusation heated Kent's face. "You'd trade one son for another?"

She held his gaze until her chin trembled. "It's for T.J.," she whispered. And she started to cry.

Kent should have known. He and his brother, Mitch, had been making plans for weeks. Brad had listened, silent, approving. Had even gone on their scouting missions with them. They'd been on Main Street in Kanner Lake three times, watching traffic, watching people. Noting the police station just two blocks up from Java Joint coffee shop. Last Saturday the three of them sauntered into the café and ordered coffee and pastries. They sat at a table, eyes roaming, taking in the big front windows, the layout and size of the place. Kent and Mitch took turns walking down the back hall in search of the bathroom. They'd catalogued the rooms off the hall—a small office, a storage area. The rear door with no glass, a lock and deadbolt.

But Brad going with them—never. He could not bear to think of Mary facing this day alone.

Pacing the kitchen, desperation clawing his heart, Kent argued and argued. But the clock ticked, and they *had* to leave. He and Mitch slid into their lightweight jackets with multiple large pockets. Brad snatched up one of his own and stalked out the front door. Straight to the truck he strode and climbed inside. He slid over to the middle.

Kent watched him through a dirty window in the living room. Mitch went on outside.

Mary's sobs filtered from the kitchen. Kent turned back to hold her. They stood there, hearts beating against each other's chests. He pulled back, looked into her worn face. She'd aged years in the last seven months, wrinkles deepened, crow's feet at her dulled eyes. She raised her gaze to his and nodded firmly. "Go, Kent. Do what you have to do."

He flexed his jaw and stared deep into her soul. "It'll work, Mary, I promise. And it won't take long—a few hours maybe. It'll work."

She managed a weak smile.

Kent broke away and strode to the front door. He would not look back.

On the porch, he and Mitch exchanged a look. Mitch seemed doubly nervous, as if he hadn't been anxious enough before. Not even away from the house yet, and things were already turning on them.

Brad sat in the truck, staring straight ahead, arms crossed. Immovable.

Kent got behind the wheel and started arguing all over again. Brad wouldn't budge. Mitch stood on the sidewalk, fidgeting. "Come *on,* Kent, we're behind schedule. We got to *go.*"

Kent kept talking. Brad refused to get out.

"*Forget* this, he's in." Mitch climbed into the seat and slammed the door, sealing Brad's place in the middle. "He's a third, Kent. It'll be easier with three."

Betrayed.

A curse spat from Kent. He leaned forward and glared at his younger brother. Mitch had always let him call the shots. Now listen to the man, attacking Kent's leadership—and in front of Brad. "Easy enough for you to throw his life away, since he ain't *your* son."

Mitch returned a sizzling stare. "If I didn't care about your boys, I wouldn't be in this truck right now."

The words hit home. Kent's anger melted back into fear for Brad. He looked at his firstborn. "Listen to me. Stay here."

Brad kept a stubborn focus through the windshield. "I told you I'm going. You need me."

Kent pressed back in his seat. Wild thoughts flew around in his head. Like maybe they should call the whole thing off. Go back and try talking to the lawyers again.

Yeah, right. The talking hadn't worked. And it never would.

"Dad, you got to help me!" T.J., crying like a baby.

"It'll work, Mary. I promise ..."

Kent took a long, labored breath—and started the engine.

His mouth twisted. Those people in Java Joint. They would *pay* for this.

As they drove away he pictured Mary's face. What she'd just sacrificed for T.J. If Kent thought about that too hard right now, he'd go crazy.

He pressed the accelerator, on the watch for cops. They had to make up for lost time.

His mind turned to logistics. What should Brad do during the attack? He and Mitch had broken down their tasks into parts, planned every move. Each second counted. Now it all had to be refigured.

Kent mulled it over. It was true, what Mitch said. Three men would make it easier. Now he and Mitch could hold the hostages at bay while Brad performed the busy work. Safer that way. Brad's fingers could prove just a little too trigger-happy in those first few minutes. Kent didn't want to loose any more hostages than necessary at the beginning. Hostages were bargaining chips.

With everything clear in his mind, Kent told the other two the revised plans. They agreed without argument. That was something for Brad.

Kent was back in charge.

They drove on in simmering silence. Every mile turned up the heat.

Kanner Lake approached. Mitch jiggled his leg against the floor. Kent wanted to lean over and slap it still. Adrenaline and fear slammed around in his veins too, but he'd just as soon deny it. Seeing that nervous leg broke him out in sweat.

"There ya go." Mitch bounced a fist against his window as they passed the city limits sign. "And after all that, only ten minutes late."

The truck's digital clock read 7:55.

Soon they passed Main Street—their target. Kent glanced up the road as they drove by. Quiet, as expected. A bunch of cars parked around Java Joint, on the right side and near the top of the second block. Java Joint—the café known across the country, thanks to its Scenes and Beans blog. Kent's lip curled. Java Joint would never see another a day like this one.

At Lakeshore, Kent turned left. Almost to ground zero. Brad's folded arms tightened and Mitch's leg bounced higher. On their right at the top of Kanner Lake rose the new hotel under construction, the one that had sparked such debate among residents the previous year. In three months, Kent had heard, it was supposed to be done. At the moment the site was quiet.

Good.

Two streets up, Kent turned left again on Second Street and pulled over to the curb. Cut the engine.

Tension ran like electricity through the cab. They all inhaled at the same time. Mitch and Brad looked to Kent.

He gave a firm nod. "Let's do it."

Mitch reached into the glove box for the guns.

Brink of Death

Brandilyn Collins

The noises, faint, fleeting, whispered into her consciousness like wraiths in the night.

Twelve-year-old Erin Willit opened her eyes to darkness lit only by the dim green night-light near her closet door and the faint glow of a street lamp through her front window. She felt her forehead wrinkle, the fingers of one hand curl as she tried to discern what had awakened her.

Something was not right . . .

Annie Kingston moves to Grove Landing for safety and quiet —and comes face-to-face with evil.

When neighbor Lisa Willet is killed by an intruder in her home, sheriff's detectives are left with little evidence. Lisa's daughter, Erin, saw the killer, but she's too traumatized to give a description. The detectives grow desperate.

Because of her background in art, Annie is asked to question Erin and draw a composite. But Annie knows little about forensic art or the sensitive interview process. A nonbeliever, she finds herself begging God for help. What if her lack of experience leads Erin astray? The detectives could end up searching for a face that doesn't exist.

Leaving the real killer free to stalk the neighborhood . . .

Softcover: 0-310-25103-6

Pick up a copy today at your favorite bookstore!

Dead of Night

Brandilyn Collins

All words fell away. I pushed myself off the path, noticing for the first time the signs of earlier passage—the matted earth, broken twigs. And I knew. My mouth turned cottony.

I licked my lips, took three halting steps. My maddening, visual brain churned out pictures of colorless faces on a cold slab—Debbie Lille, victim number one; Wanda Deminger, number three . . . He'd been here. Dragged this one right where I now stumbled. I'd entered a crime scene, and I could not bear to see what lay at the end. . . .

This is a story about evil.
This is a story about God's power.

A string of murders terrorizes citizens in the Redding, California, area. The serial killer is cunning, stealthy. Masked by day, unmasked by night. Forensic artist Annie Kingston discovers the sixth body practically in her own backyard. Is the location a taunt aimed at her?

One by one, Annie must draw the unknown victims for identification. Dread mounts. Who will be taken next? Under a crushing oppression, Annie and other Christians are driven to pray for God's intervention as they've never prayed before.

With page-turning intensity, *Dead of Night* dares to pry open the mind of evil. Twisted actions can wreak havoc on earth, but the source of wickedness lies beyond this world. Annie learns where the real battle takes place—and that a Christian's authority through prayer is the ultimate, unyielding weapon.

Softcover: 0-310-25105-2

Pick up a copy today at your favorite bookstore!

Web of Lies

Brandilyn Collins

She was washing dishes when her world began to blur.

Chelsea Adams hitched in a breath, her skin pebbling. She knew the dreaded sign all too well. God was pushing a vision into her consciousness.

Black dots crowded her sight. She dropped a plate, heard it crack against the porcelain sink. Her fingers fumbled for the faucet. The hiss of water ceased.

God, I don't want this. Please!

After witnessing a shooting at a convenience store, forensic artist Annie Kingston must draw a composite of the suspect. But before she can begin, she hears that Chelsea Adams wants to meet with her—now. Chelsea Adams—the woman who made national headlines with her visions of murder. And this vision is by far the most chilling.

Chelsea and Annie soon find themselves snared in a terrifying battle against time, greed, and a deadly opponent. If they tell the police, will their story be believed? With the web of lies thickening, and lives ultimately at stake, who will know enough to stop the evil?

Eyes of Elisha

Brandilyn Collins

The murder was ugly.
The killer was sure no one saw him.
Someone did.

In a horrifying vision, Chelsea Adams has relived the victim's last moments. But who will believe her? Certainly not the police, who must rely on hard evidence. Nor her husband, who barely tolerates Chelsea's newfound Christian faith. Besides, he's about to hire the man who Chelsea is certain is the killer to be a vice president in his company.

Torn between what she knows and the burden of proof, Chelsea must follow God's leading and trust him for protection. Meanwhile, the murderer is at liberty. And he's not about to take Chelsea's involvement lying down.

Softcover: 0-310-23968-0

Dread Champion

Brandilyn Collins

Chelsea Adams has visions. But they have no place in a courtroom.

As a juror for a murder trial, Chelsea must rely only on the evidence. And this circumstantial evidence is strong—Darren Welk killed his wife.

Or did he?

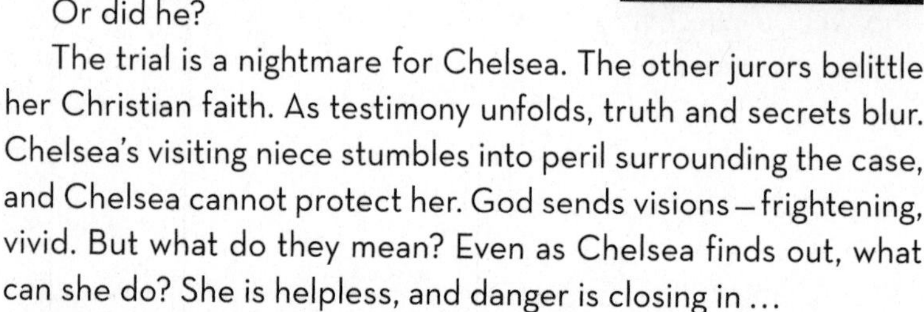

The trial is a nightmare for Chelsea. The other jurors belittle her Christian faith. As testimony unfolds, truth and secrets blur. Chelsea's visiting niece stumbles into peril surrounding the case, and Chelsea cannot protect her. God sends visions—frightening, vivid. But what do they mean? Even as Chelsea finds out, what can she do? She is helpless, and danger is closing in ...

Masterfully crafted, *Dread Champion* is a novel in which appearances can deceive and the unknown can transform the meaning of known facts. One man's guilt or innocence is just a single link in a chain of hidden evil ... and God uses the unlikeliest of people to accomplish His purposes.

Softcover: 0-310-23827-7

Pick up a copy today at your favorite bookstore!

Color the Sidewalk for Me

Brandilyn Collins

As a chalk-fingered child, I had worn my craving for Mama's love on my sleeve. But as I grew, that craving became cloaked in excuses and denial until slowly it sank beneath my skin to lie unheeded but vital, like the sinews of my framework. By the time I was a teenager, I thought the gap between Mama and me could not be wider.

And then Danny came along. . . .

A splendidly colored sidewalk. Six-year-old Celia presented the gift to her mother with pride—and received only anger in return. Why couldn't Mama love her? Years later, when once-in-a-lifetime love found Celia, her mother opposed it. The crushing losses that followed drove Celia, guilt-ridden and grieving, from her Bradleyville home.

Now thirty-five, she must return to nurse her father after a stroke. But the deepest need for healing lies in the rift between mother and daughter. God can perform such a miracle. But first Celia and Mama must let go of the past—before it destroys them both.

Softcover: 0-310-24242-8

Pick up a copy today at your favorite bookstore!

Capture the Wind for Me

Brandilyn Collins

One thing I have learned. The bonfires of change start with the merest spark. Sometimes we see that flicker. Sometimes we blink in surprise at the flame only after it has marched hot legs upward to fully ignite. Either way, flicker or flame, we'd better do some serious praying. When God's on the move in our lives, He tends to burn up things we'd just as soon keep.

After her mama's death, sixteen-year-old Jackie Delham is left to run the household for her daddy and two younger siblings. When Katherine King breezes into town and tries to steal her daddy's heart, Jackie knows she must put a stop to it. Katherine can't be trusted. Besides, one romance in the family is enough, and Jackie is about to fall headlong into her own.

As love whirls through both generations, the Delhams are buffeted by hope, elation, and loss. Jackie is devastated to learn of old secrets in her parents' relationship. Will those past mistakes cost Jackie her own love? And how will her family ever survive if Katherine jilts her daddy and leaves them in mourning once more?

Softcover: 0-310-24243-6

Pick up a copy today at your favorite bookstore!

Three ways to keep up on your favorite Zondervan books and authors

Sign up for our *Fiction E-Newsletter*. Every month you'll receive sample excerpts from our books, sneak peeks at upcoming books, and chances to win free books autographed by the author.

You can also sign up for our *Breakfast Club*. Every morning in your email, you'll receive a five-minute snippet from a fiction or nonfiction book. A new book will be featured each week, and by the end of the week you will have sampled two to three chapters of the book.

Zondervan *Author Tracker* is the best way to be notified whenever your favorite Zondervan authors write new books, go on tour, or want to tell you about what's happening in their lives.

Visit *www.zondervan.com* and sign up today!

ZONDERVAN.com/
AUTHORTRACKER
follow your favorite authors